DUDLEY PUBLIC LIBRARIES

THE MIXTURE AS BEFORE

THE MIXTURE AS BEFORE

Rosie Harris

This first world edition published 2015
in Great Britain and the USA by
SEVERN HOUSE PUBLISHERS LTD of
19 Cedar Road, Sutton, Surrey, England, SM2 5DA.
Trade paperback edition first published
in Great Britain and the USA 2016 by
SEVERN HOUSE PUBLISHERS LTD.

British Library Cataloguing in Publication Data

Harris, Rosie, 1925- author.
  The Mixture as Before.
  1. Widows–Fiction. 2. May–December romances–Fiction.
  I. Title
  823.9'14-dc23

ISBN-13: 978-0-7278-8529-6 (cased)
ISBN-13: 978-1-84751-632-9 (trade paper)
ISBN-13: 978-1-78010-692-2 (e-book)

All Severn House titles are printed on acid-free paper.

Severn House Publishers support the Forest Stewardship Council™ [FSC™],
the leading international forest certification organisation. All our titles that
are printed on FSC certified paper carry the FSC logo.

FSC MIX
Paper from
responsible sources
www.fsc.org FSC® C013056

Typeset by Palimpsest Book Production Ltd.,
Falkirk, Stirlingshire, Scotland.
Printed and bound in Great Britain by
TJ International, Padstow, Cornwall.

For Noah Frank Ockery
and Elliott Stephen Ockery

Acknowledgements

With many thanks to Kate Lyall Grant and her colleagues at Severn House, and to my agent Caroline Sheldon.

One

Dressed in black, they swirled around Margaret Wright like a cluster of grim crows as they emerged from the chapel at the Slough Crematorium.

Sitting in one of the front pews, she hadn't realized how many friends and acquaintances had joined the family gathering. She looked around with a sense of alarm, recognizing faces she hadn't seen for years, marvelling that they had bothered to come. She felt disorientated; her thoughts were elsewhere as she tried to acknowledge the murmur of condolences.

Relieved that the formalities were over she took a deep breath, savouring the pungent smell of wet flowers, damp grass and sodden soil. Why did it always seem to rain at funerals?

It had been a fine drizzle when they'd left Cookham, misting the windscreen and making the wipers squeal like trapped mice.

By the time they left the parish church it had become a steady downpour. Umbrellas had popped up like black mushrooms as the cortège wound its way like a crippled centipede down the gravel path. Then, as they drove along the Bath Road in convoy en route for Slough Crematorium the heavens had opened. It had been more like a tropical downpour than an April shower.

Now though, the rain had stopped and a thin, watery sun made the grass steam. A haze of luminous grey, like smoke seeping from the crematorium furnaces, hung over everything.

The thought that if it had been a traditional burial the grave would have been awash and they might even have had to postpone the burial sent a shudder through Margaret Wright's slim, black-coated frame.

She glanced at the tiny gold watch on her wrist, a present from Reginald on their twenty-fifth wedding anniversary fifteen years ago, and wondered how much longer it would be before people began to leave. She chewed on her lower lip. She wished she could go home, right now, make a pot of tea, sit down and quietly collect her thoughts.

And think about the future . . . her future.

'We'll be leaving any minute now, Mum,' whispered her daughter, taking her arm proprietorially. 'You're bearing up wonderfully well. Don't give way now.'

Margaret shook her arm free. 'Don't fuss, Alison!'

The hurt look on Alison's face made Margaret feel guilty. How could she expect Alison, or anyone else for that matter, to understand how she felt at this moment?

Everyone thought she was being brave because she was dry-eyed and composed, while most of them were sombre-faced and struggling to control their feelings. It wasn't stoicism on her part, but an overwhelming sense of relief.

She wondered what they would have thought if she had openly admitted that she wasn't heartbroken or feeling a sense of loss and that she hadn't cried even when the doctor had pronounced Reginald dead; or at any time since.

In fact, it was as if a load had been lifted from her shoulders and she was at last freed from the overpowering restraint that had blighted her days ever since Reginald's enforced retirement almost ten years ago.

She would miss Reginald, of course. After all, they had been married for over forty years and since his retirement they had not been out of each other's sight for more than five minutes. She was prepared for that; it didn't distress her in any way. In fact she felt exhilarated by the sense of freedom it gave her. It was as if she'd been in limbo for the past five years and now she was returning to the living world completely unencumbered.

Alison had been dabbing at her eyes ever since they'd come into the crematorium. Even Charles and Steven were emotional. As for the grandchildren, they all looked utterly bemused. She felt it had been wrong to bring them. Amanda had always been able to cry to order and she'd taken her cue from her parents and sobbed rhythmically throughout the service.

Margaret sighed. They were the ones behaving conventionally, reacting in the way expected of them. She was the philistine. You're supposed to feel grief, not relief, at your husband's funeral, she scolded herself silently.

She glanced covertly at Alison and felt a sense of unease as she saw the way she was struggling unsuccessfully to hold back her tears.

She edged away from her daughter, pretending to look at the flowers. It was a good thing Reginald wasn't still with them or he would have been sneezing his head off, she thought as she stared down at the assortment of wreaths and sprays banked up in regimented formation on the grass outside the chapel. Flowers always gave him hay fever, or so he complained whenever she'd had any in the house. Yet, they never seemed to affect him if they were on the table when they attended an official function, or on the rare occasions when they visited other people's homes.

'Come along, Mother, everyone is waiting for us to depart. We have to leave first, you know.'

Margaret looked up startled as her eldest son spoke. Tall, like his father, Charles had the same straight dark hair and dark eyes beneath firm dark brows, the same robust good looks. Strange, she thought, today even his voice seemed to have the same authoritative tone as Reginald's.

To her, Charles was still the shock-headed toddler, the studious schoolboy, the anxious teenager, so eager to join his father's firm. Now he was head of the family!

He was taking his responsibilities so seriously his father would have been proud of him, she thought wryly as he took hold of her elbow and propelled her firmly through the hovering black-hatted friends and relations.

'Yes, of course!' Conscious that her black handbag was banging against his side she quickly transferred it to her other arm.

'You'll be in our car going home,' he told her as he saw her looking round for the sleek black limousine she had arrived in.

'Oh, I see!' She didn't really but she felt it was not the moment to cross-question him as to why he had sent the other car away.

Her two granddaughters were already in the maroon Jaguar. She had been shocked by the way they were dressed. They were both wearing black pleated skirts and long-sleeved white blouses. Their white panama hats were trimmed with black bands and they wore black shoes and knee-high white socks. In her opinion, at sixteen and fourteen they looked childish dressed like that on such an occasion. In her opinion their outfits were more suitable for a school concert than a funeral.

'Are you going to sit in the back with us, Gran?' they chorused.

'Grandma will ride in front . . . it's only proper,' fussed their mother. She, too, was dressed in black and white. Her black linen suit had a scoop neck white silk blouse under it and she was wearing ultra-sheer black stockings, high-heeled black court shoes and a large-brimmed black straw hat.

'You always say it makes you feel carsick if you travel in the back . . .'

'Quiet, Charles!' Helen's carefully pencilled eyebrows drew together in a warning frown.

'It's all right, Helen, I would sooner ride in the back with the girls,' insisted Margaret.

She sat in the middle of the maroon leather seat. Her youngest granddaughter, Amanda, nestled in beside her, her feet pressed against the back of the front passenger seat. Petra climbed in on the other side.

Sandwiched between them, Margaret kissed first one and then the other on their satin-soft cheeks as they waited for Helen to belt herself into the front seat.

As they pulled away, Amanda clung to Margaret's arm as tightly as if it was a lifeline. Her thin little body shaking with gulping sobs.

'Shush,' murmured Margaret. 'There's nothing to cry about.'

'It's because Grandad has died and has gone forever and ever. We're going to . . . to miss him an awful lot,' explained Petra.

'Miss him! You hardly ever saw him . . . except on pocket money day!' snapped Helen.

Amanda looked questioningly at her grandmother, her mouth quivering. 'Will . . . will we still get pocket money? Now that Grandad's dead, I mean.'

'Amanda!' Helen's voice registered both shock and annoyance.

'Of course you will,' Margaret assured her. 'In fact, I think I might be able to manage a rise all round . . .'

'Don't encourage her! This is neither the time nor place,' hissed Helen, turning round to scowl at her eldest daughter and then at Margaret.

Margaret tried not to smile, because she knew Charles was watching her in the driving mirror. His face had gone dark with anger, just as Reginald's had used to do if she treated something he considered to be a serious topic in a frivolous manner.

Taking Amanda's hand, Margaret gave it a comforting squeeze. 'Here.' She opened her handbag and took out a lace-edged handkerchief and handed it to the child. 'Use this to dry your tears.'

Amanda scrubbed her eyes dry and gave her grandmother a lopsided grin as she screwed up the square of linen and handed it back.

'Would you like a peppermint?' Margaret fished a packet of Polo Mints out of her black handbag and fumbled to open them.

'Here, I'll do it for you.' Petra took the packet and deftly peeled back the silver foil. She took two, opened the wrapper back further and offered it to her grandmother and then to Amanda.

'Do you want one, Daddy?'

'No! This is no time to be eating sweets.'

'Put them away and behave yourselves,' ordered Helen. 'And for goodness sake sit still, Amanda. Your feet are digging right into the small of my back,' she added irritably.

As Petra handed the packet of peppermints back to her, Margaret slipped them inside her handbag. She was sure that indirectly the rebuke had been meant for her.

In the oppressive silence that followed, Margaret's thoughts focused on the ordeal that lay ahead. She had hated to come away and leave complete strangers in her home, but Helen had insisted that she should call in a firm of caterers to organize the reception at Willow House that was to follow the service at the crematorium.

'Surely there's enough of us in the family to arrange a buffet spread. Alison and Sandra will help and . . .'

'Most certainly not!' Charles was adamant. 'Father would have hated such a disorganized arrangement.'

'But he's not going to be there!'

The withering look Charles had given her had made her cringe. He'd had the ability to do that ever since he was a small child, to make her feel she had said something so utterly crass that it was beyond the pale.

'Surely, you can see that if people are invited to the family home to pay their last respects to him, it is only fitting that the catering is properly organized.'

His tone implied that the statement was his considered opinion, and therefore didn't need an answer, so she didn't bother to argue. She'd long ago learned not to fight battles she had no chance of winning.

What did it matter, she asked herself. It would all be over in a few hours and then she could close the door on the past. The old order would be broken. After that, there would be no one to dictate what she could and could not do.

She'd told herself the same thing a hundred and one times over the past week as she'd listened to Charles, Alison and Steven, aided or frustrated by interventions from Alison's husband Mark and Steven's wife, Sandra, argue, bicker and wrangle over the funeral arrangements.

Not once had they thought to ask what she wanted. It was as if she was invisible. They probably thought she was too overcome by grief to be able to organize things, she told herself, giving them the benefit of the doubt.

She'd seen more of them and they'd seen more of each other in the week preceding the funeral than they had for years, reflected Margaret. Although they all lived within a radius of five miles, and practically passed each other's door to visit her, they rarely called in on each other. A family gathering at Christmas, or the barbecue she liked to have on her birthday in July, was the extent of the family get-togethers since they'd married and left home.

Over the past week, however, they had seemed to be vying with each other to prove their closeness. Each in his or her own way anxious to be the one to shoulder the most responsibility.

It was all so hypocritical that she wondered if it came from a sense of guilt. Apart from Christmas and on his birthday they had all tended to avoid Reginald.

Not that she blamed any of them. He wasn't the easiest of men to get on with and he had grown increasingly difficult to live with over recent years, especially since he'd had his heart attack.

It was as if once he was past middle age he'd experienced some sort of metamorphosis. Unlike the chrysalis that turned into a gorgeous butterfly, he had done the reverse.

The nineteen years difference in their ages had become frighteningly important. Margaret kept remembering her mother had warned her that it was foolish for a girl of only nineteen to marry a man of thirty-eight.

'By the time you're forty-five he'll be a cranky, grey-haired old devil, ready for retirement. You mark my words!'

She'd ridiculed the idea that a man as handsome and pulsating with vitality as Reginald had been in those days could ever grow old and cranky, but of course her mother had been proved right.

Only Charles, identical to Reginald in so many respects, had ever really managed to see eye-to-eye with him. And that, she suspected, was because it had always been Charles's ambition to take over the family firm and in order to do that it had been necessary for him to work in harmony with his father.

The minute Reginald had decided to take retirement and had given Charles a free hand, he had wasted no time in instigating a whole new way of running things.

At first it had been new carpets, modern desks and massive pots of green plants in the office. Then he'd installed a fax machine and introduced mobile phones. Next he had updated their computer system to deal with accounts records, enabling him to use advanced techniques as well as word processing for mailing shots.

At the time, Alison had even gone as far as to say that it was the shock of so much modernization that had brought on her father's heart attack. That was complete nonsense of course, as Mark, Alison's husband who was a doctor, had pointed out.

'Your dad's been planning his retirement for almost ten years. If he was going to have a heart attack over the changes Charles had made then it would have occurred a long time ago.'

'It could be delayed shock. He's been brooding about it and . . .'

Charles had silenced Alison with one of his withering glances. He considered most of his sister's remarks to be muzzy and badly expressed and in the same mould as his mother's.

Steven, who was always ready for an argument, especially with his eldest brother, had taken up the cudgels on Alison's behalf.

'Alison could have a point. The old man has always been a bit of a traditionalist. He's always hated change of any kind. Remember how it took years to persuade him to install central heating at home. It wasn't until Mum wasn't feeling too well and she asked him to clean out the grates after they'd had a coal fire that he realized how much work was entailed.'

Margaret hadn't listened to the rest of the argument. She'd

gone out into the kitchen to brew some tea. Sandra, Steven's wife, had followed her, hesitantly trying to apologize for her husband's insensitivity.

'There's no need to worry about it,' Margaret assured her. 'Those two never did see eye to eye. Steven likes to get his own back whenever he can for the way Charles used to bully him when they were little.'

'Thank heaven we have a boy and girl, not two boys,' sighed Sandra.

'Are you saying that Matthew never tries to bully Hannah?'

'I don't think he does!' Sandra looked startled and her grey eyes widened. 'He always tries to protect her . . . in fact, she's more likely to boss him about than the other way round.'

'That's the great advantage of only having one,' said Alison who'd followed them into the kitchen and was busying herself laying out cups and saucers on a tray.

'Don't you find that Christopher is awfully lonely at times?'

'Heaven's no! He has plenty of friends and leads a very busy social life, I can tell you.'

'But he has no one to share experiences with—'

'Nonsense! He is always having friends to stay or he is invited to sleepovers at their homes. When they are at our place then if they start bickering or quarrelling with each other then they go home. It's a perfect arrangement, I can assure you.'

'You would have liked to have had a daughter, surely.'

'No way!' Margaret heard the hard note creep into Alison's voice. 'Another like me! Perish the thought.'

Margaret had smiled non-committally. Why did Sandra have to open up old wounds? Of course Alison wasn't going to admit to wanting a daughter, or even another son. Not now. Sandra knew all about Mark and Alison losing their second baby, so why raise such a sensitive issue?

Alison was right though, in some ways. It was more convenient having only one child. There was a lot of nonsense talked about children needing brothers and sisters, of them being company for each other, of them benefiting from being part of a family unit.

Experience had shown Margaret that it wasn't true.

From a very early age all three of hers had been self-orientated. She was sure that in a family environment they were probably more selfish and more possessive than an only child would be. Leave a toy or any other precious possession lying around and it became general property.

Even more to the point, an only child didn't have to suffer the indignity of wearing hand-me-downs. Everything was new and bought specifically for them. And once they'd developed a sense of dress and learned how to manipulate their parents, then usually it was exactly what they wanted.

Sandwiched between Charles and Steven, Alison's great advantage had been that, because she was a girl, most of Charles's hand-me-downs had been kept for Steven.

Possibly that was why Charles had gone through life with such a superiority complex, mused Margaret as she studied the back of his head. Nothing fazed him. He was always in control of his feelings and of every situation. Being so laid back and so confident was probably why he was so competent when it came to business matters.

Since Charles was always so relaxed about everything, calm when everyone else was panicking, decisive when all the others were uncertain what to do next, she found herself wondering why it was that Helen was so often agitated and snappy.

She studied her daughter-in-law's profile. An angular face with high cheekbones that she attempted to soften by wearing her copper-coloured hair swept forward on to her cheeks. There were stress lines around her green eyes and at the corners of her mouth.

She'd been as slim as a ruler and sweetly pretty when Charles had first brought her home. Petra took after her. She was thin and had her mother's reddish brown hair. Even at sixteen she was already dreaming of the day when she would be old enough to be a model with the single-mindedness that had made her father so successful in his business career.

Amanda was the exact opposite. Although she was only fourteen, she was already highly-strung, dramatically reacting to every situation around her. Ever since she'd been a tiny tot she had mastered the art of crying almost to order. Her crocodile tears vanished the moment she managed to get her own way.

Margaret sighed. She was a devious, scheming little girl who seemed to be quite capable of manipulating the world to do her bidding.

As they drew up outside Willow House, Margaret switched

her thoughts back to the trauma ahead of her. She wondered how many of those who had been at the crematorium intended to come back to Willow House. There must have been about twenty close friends, and as many, or possibly more, business acquaintances. In addition, there were numerous relatives that they only saw at funerals, weddings and christenings.

The thought of the noise and turmoil that sixty or more people would cause sent a shudder through her. How long were they all going to stay, she wondered. Two hours, three hours? Surely they'd leave once all the food and drink had gone. It wasn't a party, damn it!

She longed to be completely alone. She needed solitude. She wanted to sit down in her favourite armchair with a cup of tea and analyse her thoughts. Her mind was so confused that she couldn't think straight.

Although she hadn't shed a tear, nor had any feelings of grief, she was experiencing a sense of loneliness. It was as if she was poised on the edge of a great void.

Two

Looking round the crowded room, she listened to the buzz of unfamiliar voices. Margaret wondered what Reginald would have thought if he'd known that his send-off would have resulted in such a gregarious gathering.

Everyone seemed to be having a splendid time, she mused as laughter boomed out on the other side of the room. It was more like a party than a funeral wake.

The food was good, much better than she and the family could have put on and she was glad she'd listened to Charles and hired outside caterers. It left her free to circulate without worrying about whether glasses needed to be topped up or plates of food handed round.

She'd dreaded the thought of all these people coming back to Willow House, invading her home, but now they were here she was actually enjoying it. So many faces that she hadn't seen for years.

The never-ending sea of faces of those who had come to show their last respects to Reginald became a kaleidoscope of jumbled memories as they slowly came over to greet her. People who seemed to be as pleased to see her as she was to meet up with them again, murmuring their kind wishes and condolences for her loss. Yet they all seemed so old.

Reginald's younger brother, Silas, and his wife, Monica, were both grey-haired and very portly. Their son, Edward was already balding although not yet in his forties. His slightly younger brother, Peter, was a tubby, heavily jowled man who looked like a farmer, but was in fact a skilled computer analyst.

As Reginald's sister, Hilda, a thin, shrewish woman and her equally scrawny husband Jack kissed her goodbye, Margaret wondered if they were on a perpetual diet. If so, it wasn't one shared by their daughter Gillian, who was the size of a house and wobbly with it.

Her own sister Vivienne seemed to be glad to get away. Older than her by ten years, she was almost in her seventies and crippled with arthritis that distorted her body into an ungainly shape. Her lined face bore the ravages of the pain she endured.

Their mother had suffered with the same disease. In old age, her hands had been so gnarled she could barely hold a teacup. She would sit with them wrapped in a scarf, or hidden inside the sleeves of her cardigan, as if ashamed of their disfigurement.

Joseph Chapman, their brother, took after their father. Stocky and immensely strong, he'd always led an outdoor life. Even as a young boy he had taken an interest in gardening and had spent his weekends and school holidays mowing lawns and weeding gardens for their neighbours.

He'd worked on the greens at a nearby golf course after he'd left school, becoming head groundsman when he was twenty.

After he married, he and his wife, Hetty, had decided to start their own market garden. They'd acquired a stony field on the outskirts of Cookham. The soil was poor, so they'd erected a glasshouse and concentrated on raising bedding plants. It was successful, so they'd expanded and begun to specialize in indoor flowering plants until greenhouses and glasshouses covered the entire field.

Margaret had fond memories of her frequent visits, before Reginald retired, to the long misty glasshouses filled with heady smells and packed with colourful, exotic blooms. Occasionally, unable to resist the temptation, she would bring home one of their eye-catching plants and smuggle it into the small front bedroom which was designated as her sewing room.

It was the one place in the house Reginald rarely went in, yet he had an unerring instinct to do so if she had a flowering plant in there. The bout of hay fever that followed made her feel so guilty that if the plant wasn't hardy enough to put out into the garden, she would return it to Joseph's nursery.

Hetty always made it quite plain that she thought it was a ridiculous state of affairs. 'Tell him to keep out of the room. He doesn't have to go in there, now does he?'

'He can't help getting hay fever.'

'Nor can you help getting a cough from those stinking cigars he's always smoking,' Hetty would state firmly.

It was an irrefutable argument, but Hetty didn't have to live with Reginald, she did.

Hetty wasn't alone in her belief that Margaret should stand up for her rights. Her friends Thelma Winter, Brenda Williams and Jan Porter were all of the same opinion.

If one half of the things Thelma told the three of them, in the days when they'd met regularly for coffee, were true, Thelma led her husband a dog's life. She did exactly what she wanted to do; everything revolved around the schedule she imposed.

At the time, Margaret had thought it amusing. Later, after Reginald's heart attack and the cosy routine she had established was completely disrupted, she'd felt envious. By then, he'd taken over her life and was running it in much the same way as he had his office. Economies were the order of the day.

The first thing to go had been her car.

'There's no longer any need to run two cars,' he'd stated. 'If we go out it will be together, so we may as well dispose of your Ford.'

Her one-careful-lady-driver-only Escort had been snapped up, sold to the first person that had come to look at it. True she had only used it as a run-around; popping into town to the shops, collecting groceries from the supermarket or going to visit her friends, but she missed it greatly. She felt trapped.

It mightn't have been so bad if they had taken it in turns to drive his car when they went out. Reginald never even asked if she wanted to but automatically took the driver's seat as though he had a god-given right to do so. Furthermore, whether they were going shopping or somewhere for a walk, he was always the one who decided on the destination and the route they would take.

Even if she suggested somewhere in particular, it made no difference. It was almost as if the car was programmed in advance to do what he wanted. After a time she'd given up caring. She'd consoled herself with the thought that one shopping centre was much the same as another. If she didn't like the location he'd chosen for their walk then she could always imagine herself somewhere else.

Sometimes she felt it was like living in limbo, or watching the antics of the world from the other side of a plate glass window.

Occasionally there were paralysing moments of insight when she feared she had lost the ability to enjoy life. She teetered on a tiptoe of anxiety. She was too apprehensive to risk doing or saying anything that might disturb the uneasy peace that existed between them.

Thelma, Brenda and Jan lost patience with her when with monotonous regularity she declined their invitations to play bowls, go swimming or on a shopping spree, join them for away-day's or even to meet them for coffee.

'I'm afraid I can't leave Reginald on his own, not now he's retired.'

'He's left you on your own all day, even at weekends, for years and years.'

'That was quite different. Reginald was always at work then.'

'You need a life of your own,' they protested. 'It isn't even as if you both share a hobby or even have the same interests.'

They were right, of course. Until he'd retired and had a mild heart attack, Reginald had had a very active social life. He'd always had a great many business meetings and some of these had necessitated him having to be away from home overnight. He had played golf on Saturdays and Sundays, as well as most evenings during the summer, and afterwards he would participate in a drinking session in the clubhouse.

Although his heart attack had been a fairly mild one, he was told that golf was too strenuous and drink strictly limited. Out of sheer boredom he had stuck to her side like a limpet and insisted on accompanying her everywhere she went.

When he'd first retired he'd volunteered to help around the house. The novelty of pushing the vacuum cleaner around or dusting the furniture quickly waned, but not before he'd made so many changes that he'd altered the entire atmosphere of their home.

He had found having to move ornaments and framed photographs in order to dust was far too time-consuming, so these had all been banished to the attic. Next all the rugs disappeared together with all the unnecessary bric-a-brac; trivia that she'd collected over the years and put on display because it brought back memories.

The clean sweep left easy-to-clean, uncluttered surfaces but, in her eyes, it had expunged all the personal touches that turned a mere house into a home.

She knew that she should have insisted on putting them back but when she had propped up a snapshot of Steven's little girl, Hannah, on the mantelpiece and half an hour later found it had been taken down and put in a drawer, she'd simply given in. Reginald was right of course, bare surfaces were so much easier to dust.

Having made his point over what he termed irritating clutter, Reginald had then turned his attention to cooking. At first he had simply hovered over her in the kitchen. When he began telling her better ways to chop onions, mix up custard powder and add seasoning, she'd lost her cool.

'You do it, if you know so much better than me,' she'd exploded, biting back her tears of frustration.

'There's no need to be like that,' he told her huffily. 'That's the trouble with doing everything your own way all these years; you're stuck in a rut.'

'That's probably because in the past I've been left to get on with things,' she'd retorted with an unexpected show of spirit.

'Well, I'm trying to rectify that and to bring efficiency into the kitchen at the same time,' he'd snapped grimly.

'Don't bother. I like doing things my way.'

'I've noticed that,' he flared. 'You can't stand the slightest criticism, can you?'

They hadn't spoken to each other for the rest of the morning.

She took refuge in gardening, venting her anger by plunging the trowel savagely into the soil as she cleared the weeds from a border.

When she went back indoors to prepare lunch he had already started cooking it. She resigned herself to the new pattern that had been established. He used double the pots and pans necessary and always left the washing up and clearing away for her to do, but peace reigned.

It was inevitable that he became involved in the shopping. Since she no longer had her own car, she relied on him to take her to the supermarket. The first time this had happened she had felt as though she was caught up in some TV farce and had half expected that at any moment Jeremy Beadle would pop up from behind one of the gondolas followed by an entire camera crew.

Reginald had scoured the shelves like a starving marauder, picking up anything that caught his fancy and tossing it haphazardly into the trolley. Some of the more unsuitable items she'd managed to sneak back on to the shelves again, albeit in the wrong places, while he was foraging for new delights.

Even so, when they reached the checkout the bill was three times what she normally spent. All the way home he had ranted on about the need to pull their horns in now that he was retired.

On their next visit he'd gone armed with a calculator to make sure they didn't overspend. He insisted on selecting the cheapest brands, refusing to listen when she said he wouldn't like them or that they weren't good value.

For the rest of the month he'd abstained from cooking, letting her take the blame when meal after meal failed to reach the usual high standard because the ingredients were second rate.

'You push the trolley and I'll find the things we need,' she'd suggested on their next supermarket trip.

That hadn't worked. He'd grown impatient and irritable. He'd left her to stack from the trolley on to the counter, wandering off as though he was no longer with her. She'd breathed a sigh of relief. At least it would mean that she would be able to make sure that the onions weren't packed next to the butter.

He'd reappeared, however, by the time it was her turn to pass through the checkout. He'd insisted on doing the packing, squashing bread and cream cakes beneath cans of beans, and putting soap powder into the same carrier bag as the fish.

'Stop fussing! It all tastes the same, anyway,' he'd snapped when he'd caught her trying to redress some of the damage by surreptitiously moving the carton of potpourri away from the cheese.

'I shouldn't bring him along next time,' advised the middle-aged woman on the checkout, sympathetically. 'Mine's the same. Brought up in the days when you wrote out a list and handed it to your grocer in the morning and you collected it later in the day, or else it was delivered to your door. He's too old to train, that's the trouble.'

Margaret had to admit that the woman was right, even though it made Reginald sound like a wayward dog.

After that, the shopping had become a chore rather than an enjoyable pursuit to be looked forward to. She'd gone to the supermarket less and less. Instead she had picked up items like bread, butter, bacon and eggs from a small local shop when they had to walk down to the village each morning for the milk and daily paper after Reginald had sacked both the milkman and the newspaper boy as one of his many economy measures.

'No point in paying to have them delivered when I can collect them each morning,' he stated.

'But you hate going into the local shop since you had that argument with the manager about the way he stacked his shelves.'

'You can walk down with me and I'll wait outside for you. Do you good to get out each day. You don't take nearly enough exercise.'

'I used to go swimming and play bowls . . .'

'Swimming. At your age! Have you thought what you look like in a swimming costume? Parading sagging flesh in front of the rest of the world is obscene. No woman over thirty should be allowed anywhere near a swimming pool. Walking is a far better exercise . . . and one we can do together. I intend for us both to enjoy my retirement.'

Thelma, Brenda and Jan had been furious when she'd told them she was giving up swimming, especially when she told them the reason.

'Your figure is as trim as it was when you were thirty. And I wouldn't mind betting you are exactly the same weight as you were then,' argued Thelma.

'What else is Reginald going to stop you doing?' Brenda asked heatedly.

'You can't let him disrupt your life like this. It isn't good for either of you,' protested Jan.

'That's right. You need to get away from each other sometimes, if only to recharge your batteries and to have something fresh to talk about.'

Margaret knew they were right, but she also knew she was powerless when it came to explaining or reasoning such matters with Reginald. He hadn't been a managing director for the past thirty years without learning how to win an argument. *He* might have retired but his brain hadn't . . . nor his tongue.

The change of lifestyle, though, had quickly taken its toll on Reginald. Frustration made him bitter and moody; boredom made him disgruntled. Having once had his finger on the pulse of business affairs he resented hearing things second-hand and began to avoid ex-colleagues and even old friends.

The change had wrought havoc with her lifestyle, too. Unable to handle the situation, Margaret had simply withdrawn into her shell, letting the many changes flow over her head, whereas Reginald had fought them savagely. He resented not being able to play golf, it irked him that he had to watch his diet, cut out cigars and cigarettes and ration his intake of wines and whisky.

In the past he had been indifferent about the garden. Margaret had always tended the flower beds herself and a man had come in one day a week to cut the grass, trim the hedges and help with any heavy work. It had been a very amicable arrangement. Bert had always been willing to help, not only with any digging that she wanted done, but also with any other jobs she couldn't do herself.

With Reginald at home, all this changed. He became super-critical, constantly making derogatory remarks about the appearance of the garden whenever Bert was within earshot. Bert tolerated the situation for a few months, then announced he wouldn't be coming again.

After three different odd-job men had flatly refused to put up with Reginald's interference, Margaret had found a female gardener. Young, sturdy and a chain-smoker, she worked at top speed. She not only made a neat job of mowing the lawns and trimming the hedges, but she was quite happy to help out generally.

Reginald found her infuriating and followed her round, alternatively offering advice and criticizing what she was doing and the way she was doing it. She simply shrugged off his disparaging remarks.

'I do it for the money not for praise,' she said with a laugh when Margaret tried to apologize. 'As long as you are satisfied then that is all that matters. See you next week.'

Margaret envied her insouciance. Perhaps if I had reacted in the same way I mightn't have lost contact with so many of my friends, she reflected.

Three

Margaret Wright tried to keep her attention focused on what was happening as she stood alongside her daughter and her two sons in the hallway of Willow House saying goodbye to people as they left.

'Who says you can't turn the clock back?' murmured Jan, as she kissed Margaret goodbye. 'You *will* be joining us for coffee next week?'

'Well . . .' Out of habit, Margaret was about to demur then remembered there was no longer any need for her to do so. 'I'll phone you,' she promised. The possibility haunted her after Jan, looking regal in black, her blonde hair sleeked back into a French pleat, had left the gathering.

Why not? Why shrink from doing something she had always enjoyed and had missed so much? It would help to get her back into the mainstream of life once again, she told herself. And if she could quell the feeling of guilt that waved like a banner every time she thought about it, then it could be fun.

Brenda also expressed the hope that they would all be able to meet up for coffee just like they'd done in the old days. And so, too, did Thelma.

Margaret felt a warm glow at the show of loyalty from her

three oldest friends. Reginald had always been so offhand with them whenever she had invited them to Willow House that she had felt embarrassed. She had been almost relieved when gradually they had stopped phoning or dropping in to see her. Even Thelma, a seasoned local councillor with an argumentative streak almost as strong as Reginald's, had found his manner so abrasive that she had eventually thrown in the towel.

A coffee morning would be an excellent way to dip a toe into the water again, she resolved. Would she enjoy it, though, or would she find the trivia and gossip as inconsequential as Reginald had claimed it to be?

There was only one way to find out, she decided. She'd accept the challenge and she'd join them the next time they planned to meet up.

It was seven o'clock before the last of the mourners departed and another hour before the rest of the family finally left.

'Are you sure that you don't want to come and stay with us, just for tonight?' persisted Helen.

'I think you should,' urged Charles. 'I don't think you are in any state to be left here on your own.'

'I'm all right. Really.'

'Daddy, Gran doesn't want to come to our house, she wants to be on her own.'

'Petra! Go and wait in the car. You don't know what you are talking about,' admonished Helen severely.

'But I do.' Petra's voice rose. 'Stop treating me like a baby. I know a lot more than you think and I know that Gran wants to be on her own because she's said so, only you don't listen.'

Margaret sighed. 'Petra's quite right. I do want to be on my own.'

'Not the first night, surely! You're going to be on your own for the rest of your life, remember.'

Charles frowned. 'We would feel much easier if you stayed with us . . . for tonight, at least.'

Margaret tried not to smile. That's what all this argument was about. Peace of mind for Charles and Helen. If she slept at their house there would be no need for him to waste time worrying about her.

Give in to him this time and it would be the start of a snowball that wouldn't stop rolling. It would be daily phone calls to check she was all right, lunch and tea on Sundays, going on jaunts with them, even joining them when they went away on their annual holidays.

Before she knew what was happening, he'd be persuading her that the house and garden were too much for her to maintain and suggest they should build a one-bedroom granny flat on to the side of their house so that they could keep an eye on her.

'I shall be fine, I promise you.'

She walked to the door and opened it, waiting for them to leave. Halfway down the garden path Helen hesitated, then turned round and came back.

She took Margaret's hand in hers. 'Look,' her voice was wheedling as if she was addressing an intractable child, 'if you should change your mind you have only to pick up the phone and one of us will come and collect you.'

'I won't change my mind.'

Helen's green eyes hardened. 'You might! Reaction may set in later when we've all gone. You've scarcely shed a tear you know,' she said reprovingly.

Margaret closed the front door before the car had even pulled away. She stood with her back pressed against it, listening to the silence. She felt a deep sense of peace and yet, at the same time, she had a feeling of tremendous anticipation. Like a four-year-old on Christmas morning, or setting out on the first stage of a long holiday to some unknown destination.

She wanted to dance; to twist and twirl and waltz around with complete abandonment. Instead she walked through every room in the house, from top to bottom, like an animal establishing its territory.

The air of gentle decay was depressing. She was dismayed by how shabby and dreary everything looked. It was only to be expected. Over the past few years, ever since Reginald had retired, they'd done no decorating at all. He'd said he couldn't stand the fuss and upheaval involved, and that the smell of paint would bring on his hay fever. She hadn't insisted. It was easier to leave things as they were and keep the peace.

Now, though, it saddened her to see how neglected it all looked. The entire house called out for loving care – lots of it. It needed decorating and refurbishing from top to bottom, she decided, as she took stock.

The pile on the carpets was threadbare – not only in the hallway but in most of the other areas where it got a lot of use. There were shiny patches on the upholstery, scuff marks where people had rested their feet on the stretchers of the chairs and stains on the dining table where Reginald had placed down hot dishes without a protective mat underneath them.

In the hall and living room, the wallpapers had faded and the once pristine-white ceilings were now a murky grey. The oak kitchen units that had been her pride and joy fifteen years ago looked dated. Most of the work surfaces were chipped and stained with use, the glaze on the tile surrounds dulled by constant cleaning. The bathroom, too, was drab and dingy, and old-fashioned.

In her mind's eye, Margaret viewed the interior of her house as a prospective buyer might see it and envisaged all the things that needed to be done to bring it up to date. It would be a mammoth task, she told herself. Quite a daunting prospect in fact.

Still, she thought, there was one consolation – there would be no arguments. There would be no one to try and dissuade her by telling her that this or that was all right for another year or two. Nor would she have to choose the conservative sort of colour schemes Reginald preferred.

She felt suffused with pleasure. Everything would be to her taste, no conferring with anyone. She could have the sunny yellow kitchen she'd always hankered after; she could bring down all the ornaments and pictures that were stored away in the attic and replace them throughout the house.

She'd be able to indulge her every whim, give rein to her preferences, not only for colour and choice of fabrics for curtains and bedspreads, but even the sort of furniture she chose for each room.

She couldn't wait to get started. She'd begin in the main bedroom . . . her bedroom, she decided. It had wonderful proportions and a big bay window looking out over the garden. It should have felt spacious, yet it always felt claustrophobic. She was sure it was because of the heavy dark furniture; two massive wardrobes, a matching dressing table, a chest of drawers and bedside cabinets all in dark mahogany. There had once been a matching dark mahogany headboard but, after years of complaining, she had finally managed to persuade Reginald to change it for a padded velvet one. However, even that had been dark brown, so it had done nothing at all to relieve the sombre tone of the room.

Now she could have walls in lilac or pink, stark white, light blue or primrose yellow. The options were endless. She felt as excited as a child with a new paint box. She would change the entire appearance of the room.

Years ago she had suggested that they should have fitted wardrobes in French grey with mirror doors and gilt trims and a rose-pink deep pile carpet.

'That sounds more like a French boudoir than a serviceable bedroom,' Reginald had pronounced, dismissively.

'It's so dark as it is . . .'

After a long argument he'd agreed to have it redecorated with white ceiling and cream walls.

With so little wall space left on view it hadn't made a great deal of difference. Now she could get rid of all the old-fashioned furniture and make it as light and airy as she chose. It was an exhilarating thought.

Reginald would turn in his grave if he knew she was spending money in such a frivolous manner, she thought guiltily. Still, why not? She tried to assuage her conscience by telling herself that it was pointless hoarding it to leave to Alison, Charles and Steven. They all had good jobs and already had lovely homes. They all had their own cars and they were always buying new clothes and going off skiing or else on some exotic holiday, so why should she have any compunction about spending money in whatever way she chose?

It wasn't as though she was squandering it. Beautifying Willow House was an investment. They'd be the ones to benefit when they eventually came to sell it. Even so she felt guilty about how much it was bound to cost to do all the things she was planning to do.

Perhaps she ought to discuss it with someone first. Not with Charles. On principle he would veto the idea. Alison, too, would probably try to talk her out of it and say it was far better to spend the money on clothes. Steven? No, he wouldn't be much help. He'd simply give her a bear hug and tell her to please herself. Or advise spending the money on a holiday. To him, a holiday was the answer to every problem.

The only ones in the family who might understand what she was trying to do were Joseph and Hetty. They both had an artistic streak and a strongly developed sense of colour so they would appreciate why she felt it was so important to give Willow House a facelift. Was it fair though, Margaret wondered, to burden them with her problem? There was so much more to it than merely picking the right colours; coordinating textures and styles could be quite tricky. And what about quality? Ought she to have Axminster, Wilton or one of the man-made fibres for the carpeting? She had no idea how they compared for wear or value for money.

It was the same with curtaining. How did you know how much material you needed if you wanted pinch pleats for example, or gathered or with drapes? Everything was metric now and she still hadn't really got the hang of that.

It was such an enormous undertaking that perhaps she ought to get professional help. It needed someone with expertise to do the actual physical work; not just a slap-it-on-the-wall handyman, but a skilled decorator.

She really needed advice from someone who would listen to her ideas and fantasies, and interpret them. He'd need to be an expert who would also know where to find the right tradesmen to carry out the various stages of the work that would have to be done. She didn't know how you found someone like that, except in the Yellow Pages.

Perhaps Thelma, or Jan, or Brenda could recommend someone. She must remember to ask them when they met for coffee, she mused as she undressed and climbed into bed. She stretched out and lay spreadeagled, luxuriating in the vastness of the king-size bed. Feeling blissfully content, she reached out and switched off the light and felt herself floating towards sleep.

Four

The sudden darkness seemed to activate a switch within her head. Her thoughts began to race, the events of the day rotating crazily like the barrel of a fruit machine. Then they became horrifyingly jumbled as though she was caught in the throes of some monstrous nightmare.

Unable to bear it, she switched on the light, pulled on her dressing gown and went downstairs. She wandered around the house feeling lost and lonely, listening to the eerie sounds from the water pipes, and the creaks and groans from the floorboards as they shrank and settled as the temperature dropped.

When the children had been small, such sounds had scared them. They'd thought the house was haunted. Sometimes when they were watching television and the lounge door suddenly clicked open, it had been difficult to convince them that it was a draught or build-up of air pressure and not some unseen hand.

Now, alone in the house those sounds were making her feel edgy, and she felt she must satisfy herself that all the windows and the outside doors were firmly bolted before she went back to bed.

As she made her tour, the house seemed vast. Five bedrooms, three rooms downstairs as well as the kitchen and utility room. It did seem rather a crazy idea to go on living there on her own. Even before Reginald had died she had thought it was much too big for them but now, on her own, it was ludicrous.

Yet she didn't want to leave Willow House. Her roots were here, it was where she'd raised her children. For that reason alone it was special and at the moment she felt that it was the only stable thing in her life.

She went into the kitchen, made herself a coffee and took it back up to bed with her. Propped up against the pillows she sipped it and contemplated her life. She felt so vulnerable that, for the first time in her life, she wished she could pray. She went to church for weddings and funerals like everyone else, but she wasn't a believer. She understood now, though, how people could derive comfort from prayers and she envied them.

It must be very reassuring to be able to turn to an all-powerful, all-wise presence when you were lonely or beset by problems; to be able to pour out your innermost thoughts and feelings to an invisible presence who wouldn't condemn or censure you, either by look or word.

Instead of bottling up your fears, guilt or desires you made them known to this unseen deity. It was a kind of psychotherapy, an act of self-indulgence that exonerated your mind and your conscience. The relief must be enormous. And once you'd voiced your peccadilloes and faced up to your imperfections, it was more than likely that you could see a solution to what was troubling you.

Did praying to an unseen God also help to combat loneliness, Margaret wondered. Was that why people flocked to church on Sundays, because it was a meeting place for those who felt lonely and bereft?

It might be the answer for some people, but she was sure it wasn't right for her. She wasn't the type who joined clubs. Anyway, she wasn't looking for new friends – family and friends surrounded her, so it was her own fault if she was alone. Heaven knows she'd had enough invites.

She smiled to herself, remembering Helen's parting remark. She wondered what Helen's reaction would be if she rang her right now, at half past two in the morning and said she had changed her mind and wanted to stay at their house, and would one of them drive over and collect her.

She'd better settle down and try to sleep or she really would be talking to herself, she thought wryly, as she drained her cup and put it down on the bedside table.

Before she switched off the light, she turned on the radio. She'd always longed to lie in bed and listen to music, but had never been able to do so for fear of disturbing Reginald. His bedtime routine never varied. He always read for ten minutes precisely and then put out his bedside light and expected her to do the same. After so many years it became a habit.

She found the music soothing. She snuggled down beneath the duvet and it lulled her into a floating dreamlike state. Her body felt so feather-light that she ran the tips of her fingers over her arms and breasts just to reassure herself that she was still there.

In response her body trembled, shivers meandered across her shoulders. With quick little butterfly touches Margaret stroked herself again. Her breath became ragged. She closed her eyes and gave herself up to the sensations that swept through her. Her mind went blank. It was as if an unseen force, over which she had no control, had taken possession of her pulsating body. The tension mounted until, suddenly, she felt a cascading release.

The lilting strains of a string orchestra drifted from the radio.

She knew she ought to turn it off, but she felt so utterly drained that she couldn't make the effort to do so.

It didn't matter anyway. There was no one to grumble about the noise and she quite liked the idea of waking up in the morning to the sound of music.

Five

Charles Wright folded up his *Times* newspaper and pushed his chair back from the breakfast table with the smooth, confident gesture of a man with a purpose in life.

He straightened his light blue silk tie, flicked crumbs from the front of the well-cut jacket of his navy pinstripe suit and ran a neatly manicured hand over his receding dark hair.

'Five minutes,' he announced to no one in particular.

'I'm ready.' Petra uncurled her skinny, black-clad legs from around the rungs of her chair and stood up, smoothing down her pleated skirt and slipping her arms into the royal blue blazer draped on the back of her chair.

'Good! How about you, Amanda?'

Amanda sniffled loudly. 'I want my hair in a plait.'

'Come here.' Helen put down her cup, swivelled round in her chair, pulled Amanda towards her and deftly began to plait the mousy brown hair.

'Can we phone Grandma before we go to school?'

Helen looked across at Charles.

Charles glanced at his watch, impatiently. 'Not now! We're late as it is.'

'We really ought to phone to see if she is all right,' pleaded Petra.

'Of course she's all right. You only saw her yesterday.'

'Oh Mummy, can we phone Grandma?' Amanda wailed.

'I'll phone her later on . . . not now in case she's having a lie-in,' Helen promised.

'Good! That's settled.' Charles gave his wife an approving look. She was wearing a crisp white blouse tucked into a blue denim skirt and looked as efficient as a hospital matron and her tone was as authoritative.

'You won't forget, Mum, will you?' Petra persisted anxiously.

'Of course not. I might even take you both over to see her after you come out of school.'

'Splendid!' Charles smiled his approval. 'See if you can persuade her to come and stay with us for a few days,' he added as he kissed his wife's cheek.

Conscience cleared, Charles strode out into the hall and picked up his briefcase and his umbrella. 'Come along then, girls, or you'll be late for school and I have a very busy day ahead, so don't waste time.'

Flanked by Petra on one side and Amanda on the other, Charles Wright hurried out to where his maroon Jaguar was parked on the gravel driveway in front of the house.

'Are you going over to see your mother this morning?' asked Mark Shepherd as he bent to kiss his wife goodbye before setting out for the surgery.

'Probably. I thought of going over there some time today to help her sort out Dad's belongings. The sooner she gets rid of them the better.'

Mark frowned. 'Don't rush her too much. She needs a period of mourning, you know. It's an essential part of the mental healing process, remember.'

'I thought she was doing very well. She wasn't at all weepy yesterday.'

'That's exactly what I mean. She should have been in tears. Especially at the crematorium.'

'Well, it wasn't exactly a shock . . . Dad dying, I mean. She's been expecting it for years, ever since he had that heart attack, hasn't she.'

'Death is always a tremendous shock for those close to the person who has died,' responded Mark in clipped professional tones.

'You're assuming that my mother is one of your normal medical cases. She's not.'

'They'd been married for over forty years, for heaven's sake, so it was bound to come as a shock!'

'You won't have to remind her of that,' Alison snapped. 'In fact, if you want my opinion I think she's feeling relieved that Dad's dead.'

Mark shook his head in disbelief. 'You really are a heartless bitch at times,' he told her disparagingly.

'No, I'm not. I'm just stating the truth. Would you have liked to live with him?'

'That's not the point, is it?'

'Well, come on; be honest.' Alison's grey eyes were challenging.

Before Mark could answer, Christopher breezed into the room. He was dressed ready for school in black trousers and maroon blazer, a black haversack style satchel over one shoulder. He looked from his father to his mother impatiently.

'Which one of you is taking me to school this morning?'

'Your mother will . . .'

'Your father . . .'

They spoke simultaneously.

'I'm not dressed yet,' protested Alison, clutching her blue quilted dressing gown more tightly round her.

'I'll come with you then, Dad. Are you ready yet? I hate being late.'

'Coming.'

Mark paused in the doorway to look back at his wife. 'Take it easy with your mother, Alison. Don't . . . don't bully her.'

Joseph and Hetty Chapman walked into the farmhouse-style kitchen of their house together. It was ten o'clock, time for their morning break. They had both been hard at work since seven o'clock that morning and were looking forward to the chance to sit down and enjoy a cup of coffee and some digestive biscuits and compare notes.

For Hetty it was the best part of the day. She loved the crisp freshness of the early morning especially when the sun rose in a dazzling blaze in the east, glinting across the span of glasshouses that made up their market garden complex.

The air was as fresh and invigorating as a glass of spring water. It was the time of day she felt full of enthusiasm for their enterprise and bursting with new ideas.

She liked to be able to tour the glasshouses before any of the staff arrived, to take stock of what was for sale and note down any changes or improvements in their display or layout that she felt needed to be made.

Joseph carried out much the same routine, only for him it was more practical; new bedding, pricking out seedlings, potting up and irrigation work.

Then, when she and Joseph met up for coffee, they would air their opinions about what they had seen and make decisions. They'd discuss the marketing strategy for the day, what work needed to be carried out and deal with any staff problems that may have arisen.

They worked as a team; they always had. It was the secret, not only of their business success, but also of the long-lasting camaraderie between them. They even dressed alike: blue denim jeans, Arran sweaters, peaked denim caps and green Wellingtons. Often, because they were the same height and of similar build, it was difficult to tell them apart when they were working.

Their mid-morning break was also the time of day when they aired any personal problems that might have arisen. Today they both shared the same thoughts, their concern over Joseph's sister, Margaret Wright.

'I must say, our Margaret stood up to things very well yesterday,' murmured Joseph, dunking a digestive biscuit into his coffee.

'Mm! She looked to me as though she was in a daze,' Hetty commented.

'Well, stands to sense she is. Not been easy for her since Reginald retired now has it,' Joseph defended.

'I'd say that it completely changed her lifestyle,' Hetty mused, shaking her grey head from side to side.

'She used to be so independent at one time, nipping about here, there and everywhere in her car.'

'Reginald getting rid of her car put a stop to all that.'

'That's true. It certainly put an end to her popping over to see us.'

'A shame, really; she got so much pleasure out of looking round the nursery, didn't she?'

'Well, she'll be able to fill her house with plants and flowers now he's gone,' Joseph sighed noisily. 'Him and his hay fever; I reckon a lot of that was put on, you know.'

'Of course it was. He was showing his authority.'

'I never understood why she put up with it.'

'She wanted a quiet life, that's why. You know how domineering he could be when he was roused.'

'Mm! Arrogant old bugger.' Joseph's weather-beaten face creased into a grin. 'You don't know how lucky you are having an easy-going chap like me for a husband, do you?'

They smiled in unison, happy and at ease with each other knowing they felt the same on this matter as they did on most topics.

Joseph emptied his mug and put it down on the table. 'Do you think I ought to pop over some time today and see if she's all right?' he asked anxiously.

'I'll go after lunch, if you like. You've got the soil analyst coming this afternoon.'

'So I have. I'd forgotten about him for a minute. You go then. Why don't you take a pot plant along with you? That would cheer her up no end.'

'I thought I'd go over and see my sister-in-law today, what do you think?'

Jack Smart stopped with his hand on the doorknob and looked at his wife in surprise. 'You only saw her yesterday.'

Hilda Smart patted her tightly curled grey hair, nervously. 'I know but I didn't get a chance to really talk to her.'

He looked puzzled. 'What on earth do you want to talk to her about?'

'Well, things . . . you know . . . Reginald's things.'

'Do you mean his clothes and such like?'

'That's right. She's bound to throw them all out.' Her mouth set in a disapproving line.

'They wouldn't fit me! Reginald was twice my size and he had a great paunch on him.'

'I wasn't thinking of his clothes,' persisted Hilda, 'but you do take the same size in shoes.'

'I don't want any of his belongings!' Jack rejected the idea firmly, shaking his grey head to emphasize the point.

'What about his golf clubs?'

'I wouldn't mind those if no one else wants them. Always bought the best did Reginald.'

'I'll ask her about them then.'

'I suppose Margaret will be getting rid of them. That's if she hasn't done so already,' he added thoughtfully. 'Reginald hasn't played golf since he had his heart attack.'

'I'll find out, shall I?'

'It might be an idea but not today. Makes us look like vultures so soon after the funeral.'

'If we leave it then someone else will probably jump in and have them.'

'That's a chance we'll have to take. I don't want to upset Margaret just for the sake of a set of old golf clubs.'

'I don't think it would upset her. She didn't look very upset at the funeral, or afterwards. Smiling and chatting with people as if it was a birthday party, certainly not a wake.'

'Well, it wasn't a wake as you call it. Your family's not Irish nor are they Roman Catholic. It was just a gathering of Reginald's friends. A farewell.'

'Call it what you like, Margaret certainly seemed to be enjoying herself,' Hilda retorted sharply. 'Even our Gillian commented on it when we came home.'

Jack shrugged his scrawny shoulders and fastened his raincoat. 'I'm going to be late. See you tonight.'

'If I'm back from seeing Margaret by the time you get home.'

'You mean you are going there today?'

'That's what I said, wasn't it?'

'I thought it was your Women's Institute meeting this afternoon?'

'It is but it won't hurt to give it a miss for once. You've got to get your priorities right, haven't you?'

Dr Gerry Cook made a note on the pad on his desk to phone Margaret Wright the moment his surgery was over.

He'd known the Wrights and their family both socially and as their doctor for over twenty years and he was more than a little bemused by Margaret's manner at the funeral.

Come to think of it, he told himself, she had been a little strange when Reginald had collapsed the previous Saturday afternoon.

Of course Reginald had known ever since his heart attack that he had a heart condition and presumably Margaret had prepared herself for something like this happening. Even so, she had been remarkably self-controlled when she'd called him out. No trace of distress or panic at all.

He had expected her to show signs of grief at the funeral service, certainly so at the crematorium. Very few close relatives could hold back their tears when the coffin containing the body of their loved one was being carried down the aisle. Those final moments before the coffin rolled away out of sight were the most traumatic of all, yet she had remained dry-eyed and calm even then.

He'd been called away before the end of the gathering at Willow House but, from what he had seen even then surrounded by family and old friends, she had seemed to be in complete control of her emotions.

He hoped it didn't mean there was going to be trouble in the future. Holding back grief, trying to brave it out, so often resulted in a breakdown later on. He'd give her a ring as soon as he'd finished surgery and, if necessary, call in and see her when he went on his rounds.

Six

Steven Wright shrugged himself into the jacket of his smart grey suit. 'Will you drop in and see Mother some time today or shall I?' he asked, jingling his car keys impatiently.

Sandra looked up from the newspaper she was reading, a piece of toast poised halfway to her mouth. 'She's your mother,' she protested.

'I know that but I have a heavy day. I have to be in Warwick by ten for an area meeting and I'm not sure what time I will be able to get home.'

'You can speak to her on your car phone as you're travelling, can't you?'

His mouth tightened. 'Yes, OK. I'll try to do that if you think you are going to be too busy to see her.'

Sandra pursed her thin lips. 'I might manage to get around to see her after I've picked Matthew up from school.'

'Yes, yes, yes,' shouted Matthew. 'Let's do that, Mum. I like going to see Gran. She gives me coke and choccy bickies.'

'Bickies, bickies, choccy bickies.' His sister Hannah, younger than him by eighteen months, banged noisily on the tray of her high chair.

'Quiet, Hannah!' Sandra pressed a hand to her forehead.

'Well, are you going to see Mother or not?'

'Oh all right, I'll do it.' Sandra slammed the newspaper down on to the breakfast table angrily. 'I don't suppose I have any choice, do I!'

'Just say one way or the other, that's all I'm asking.'

'I've said I'll go and see her when I pick Matthew up. What more do you want me to say?'

'Fine.' He bent and kissed her on the cheek. 'See you tonight. Don't wait for me for dinner, I might be late.'

'You always are!' She waited until he reached the door. 'Steven!'

'Yes?'

'It might still be a good idea for you to ring your mother . . . in case I don't manage to get there today.'

'Mummy! You said we were going to see Granny today.' Matthew's face crumpled.

'Do stop whingeing.'

'But you did, you did, you did.' His voice rose shrilly. 'You told Daddy we were going to see her after school.'

'And so we are.'

'So why ask me to phone her?' demanded Steven angrily.

Sandra began to collect up the dirty breakfast dishes and stack them in a pile.

'She is your mother so you should be the one to get in touch with her.'

'And I will. It's just that I know I am going to be pushed for time today. Anyway, I'm sure she'd love to see Matthew and Hannah. It would help to take her mind off things.'

'I think you worry more about her than you do about me,' Sandra told him peevishly.

'Don't be silly. I don't like to think of her on her own at a time like this, that's all.'

'Then go and see her yourself.'

'I will, tonight. I'd take the day off if it was possible but this meeting has been set up and it is too important to cancel.'

'Lovely funeral they gave your Reginald yesterday. I was dreaming about it all night,' said Monica Wright with a sigh as she washed up the breakfast dishes.

'Certainly a lot of folks there,' agreed Silas. Picking up the tea towel, he began drying the dishes as she stacked them on the draining board.

'Nice to see so many of the family all together like that.' Monica's plump face softened into a warm smile. 'Some of those youngsters had grown so much I hardly recognized them.'

'Yes, it was more like a family gathering than a funeral.'

'Nice though! I would like to think that's what folks would do when I go. Have a happy get-together. Good food, plenty of drink and a good old chinwag. There's no sense in being miserable about it, now is there?'

'Can't bring you back, can they?' agreed Silas. 'Our Reginald had a pretty good innings. Two years older than me.'

'And he's been ill with his heart for such a long time, poor man.'

'It proves one thing; it's worry that brings on heart attacks and not what size you are,' commented Silas, patting his protruding stomach.

'You ought to get a bit of weight off you though,' said Monica, frowning. 'We both could do with losing a couple of stone. Our Peter could as well. He weighed fourteen stone the last time I got him to stand on the scales.'

'What about Edward?'

'He's not quite so hefty. He's thirteen stone and a bit, mind you, but then he's a couple of inches taller than Peter.'

'Furthermore he takes a lot of exercise. Peter never does a damn thing except sit and watch the television. Couch potato that one.'

'I think I'll put us all on a bit of a diet,' Monica said thoughtfully.

'Lay off those ideas. Good food never hurt anyone. When did one of us last have a cold?'

'I'm not talking about colds, I'm thinking about heart attacks. They probably run in your family. I think I'll go over and ask Margaret's advice.'

'On how to kill me off?'

'No, on how to make sure you don't kill yourself off by overeating.'

'Margaret won't want to be bothered with all that nonsense at a time like this. Only drag up what's happened. Have a bit of feeling, woman.'

'She didn't look all that upset to me. Probably found it a relief to know he'd gone. Crabby old devil, your Reginald, and you know it.'

'That was because he didn't get enough food to eat. Feed me the same as she fed him and I'd be crabby.'

'What do you mean?'

'That diet she had him on. No fats, no alcohol, not much meat, no puddings, cakes or biscuits, and just one egg a week.'

'It doesn't mean he went hungry,' protested Monica. 'They probably had lots of fish, salads and fruit.'

'No substance in rabbit food! Our Peter will have something to say if you start serving up those sorts of meals.'

'He can always move out if he doesn't like what I put in front of him.'

'You'd miss him if he did. Look how upset you were when Edward moved into a place of his own a couple of years ago.'

'I didn't mind him moving into a place of his own, it was the woman he moved in with that I objected to!'

Silas chewed his lower lip in silence. He hadn't liked Edward going off to live with a black woman any more than Monica had. Still, they seemed to be happy enough together and Edward was no oil-painting, even Monica admitted that. He was not yet fifty, he was already bald and had run to fat, so perhaps he'd been the lucky one to find someone who'd have him.

The trouble with Monica was that she made too comfortable a nest for her chicks, Silas reflected, as he looked affectionately at his plump little wife. That was why neither Peter nor Edward had been in any hurry to leave home and fend for themselves.

Now she was paying the price. Here they were, both in their late sixties, and not even one grandchild, whereas at Reginald's funeral there had been five second-generation youngsters.

If anything happens to me, Silas thought morosely, Monica will be a very lonely old woman.

He ran a hand through his thinning grey hair; he didn't want to think about that. Reginald popping off like he had didn't mean a thing. He was good for another ten years; perhaps even longer and by then Peter could be married and might have two or three children.

'When we go shopping we could nip round and see if Margaret is all right,' suggested Monica breaking into his thoughts. 'She might be feeling a bit down in the dumps being all on her own.'

Jan Porter slipped from between oyster-coloured satin sheets, slipped her arms into a coffee-coloured satin negligee, her feet into fluffy toning mules and padded into her en-suite bathroom. Ten minutes later, revived by a shower, she was back in the bedroom ready to plan her day's activities.

She walked over to the window and pulled aside the turquoise damask curtains. The bright sunlight of a glorious April morning flooded the room. She gazed across the manicured communal lawn in front of the block of flats to the glittering River Thames beyond, feeling it was great to be alive. Crossing the room to the built-in fitted wardrobes, she dropped her negligee and stared at the reflection of her statuesque nude body speculatively.

'Not bad for almost sixty, not bad at all,' she murmured, approvingly, as she ran her long tapering fingers over her firm breasts and hips. Even her legs were still as shapely as they had been when she was in her teens.

She swept her shoulder length blonde hair up on top of her head, twisting this way and that to study her profile, wondering for the hundredth time whether or not to have her hair cut short. It was so fine that, unless she had it permanently waved, it needed a short style to keep it looking good. She hated perms. With her type of hair they invariably ended up looking frizzy.

Thelma wore her hair cut short and dyed black; sculpted to her head at the back and taken from a side parting in front. And because she had such strong features it looked far too mannish in Jan's opinion. Then, she reflected, Thelma liked the sleek tailored look; it showed in her choice of clothes.

Brenda's hair was naturally curly and frothed, like a mottled halo, around her plump face from which her blue eyes peeped alertly. She was a round dumpling of a woman with more money than style when it came to clothes. Her choice was always the exact opposite to Thelma's.

It was probably because of their individuality that they had remained friends for so long, Jan reflected, as she selected a white pants suit and a brilliant red blouse.

It would be great having Margaret back with them again. The four of them had been almost inseparable until a few years ago when Margaret had dropped out after Reginald's heart attack had led to his retirement. She'd missed her a lot.

Perhaps they could all meet this morning for coffee, she mused as she put the finishing touches to her face. The idea delighted her. Impulsively she reached for the phone. She'd ring round right away before any of the others went out or made plans for the rest of the day.

The sooner the old order was restored the better, she told herself as she began dialling Margaret's number.

Seven

'Right! You want me to be there at ten thirty? Yes, Jan you're so right, it will be quite like old times!'

Margaret Wright felt a thrill of anticipation as she replaced the receiver. Just like old times, she wondered. Could you turn the clock back all those years? Could you pick up the broken threads and tie a knot in them as you did when you were sewing? Or did you have to weave them in carefully so that the ends didn't show, like strands of wool when you were knitting?

It wasn't always successful when you did that, she mused thoughtfully. Mostly it was better to start a new ball of wool at the beginning of a new row, so that the ends could be merged into the seam and then they didn't show at all.

She'd like to think that now with Reginald's funeral over she had just come to the end of a row and was about to start a fresh one and that she was joining on a completely new ball of wool.

Not one in the same colour, either. This one would be in a vibrant, glowing shade so that it would lift her spirits, and bring joy to her heart.

She thought back to previous coffee mornings; the bright, inconsequential chatter, the exchange of news, their individual accounts of what had been happening to them since they'd last met. Before they parted they usually planned an outing or shopping trip of some kind, and she wondered if they still did.

In those days, the four of them rarely made any major moves without talking it over together first, whether it was purchasing an item for their home, buying a new dress or a hat, or even deciding on what colour to redecorate a room.

It had been this more than anything else, Margaret reflected, that Reginald had found so infuriating.

'Why do you have to take them into your confidence and ask them what they think? It's none of their business,' he would rant whenever she passed on an opinion voiced by one of them.

'Surely it's always a good idea to hear what other people think?'

'Depends who it is you are listening to. If you are being given advice by someone of professional standing then, yes, of course it is worth listening to, but pronouncements from a bunch of giggling women, no! Especially those three! They all strive to say the opposite of each other simply in order to be different.'

That was an exaggeration, of course, but Margaret had to admit he did have a point. Jan, Brenda and Thelma were individualists, and determined to remain so. That, to her mind, was what made them such good company. They would comment, even criticize, but they didn't try to reform each other.

Jan was all for luxury and elegance. With the generous settlement she received after her divorce from an oil magnate she could afford to indulge her expensive tastes. She spent lavishly on clothes as well as on her home. She liked to be in the height of fashion but she refused to follow current trends unless they met her personal criteria and suited her.

Margaret had always been impressed by the way Jan stamped her individual personality on all her possessions, and surroundings, with brilliant touches of colour or dramatic design.

Brenda's taste was so completely opposite that Margaret sometimes wondered how the two of them had ever struck up a friendship.

Brenda liked the cottagey look. She'd been a widow for so long that no masculine traces remained in her cosy little bungalow. There were lots of frills, mountains of cushions, countless bowls and vases of flowers, a plethora of ornaments and photographs of her grandchildren covering every available surface.

Thelma's home, on the other hand, was practical and highly serviceable. Even her antiques were the robust kind; solid Georgian pieces that could be polished energetically without risk of damage.

Margaret wandered into her own sitting room and looked around. The place was badly in need of redecorating. What had once been a silver-striped wallpaper was now dingy, and had faded into an indistinct grey. The ceiling had lost its pristine whiteness and the once gleaming paintwork had yellowed with age.

She looked down at the multi-patterned green and beige carpet, and noticed that it was threadbare in places. Fortunately, the canvas backing was so close in tone to the beige background that it didn't show unless you looked closely.

She studied the rest of the room. One or two pieces of antique furniture, like the writing bureau and matching bookcase, were worth keeping. The beige velvet three-piece suite had lost its looks long ago and most certainly needed replacing. The cushions were lumpy and misshapen, and shiny with wear. She hated the ultra-modern TV with its enormous screen that Reginald had chosen because he had liked a big picture.

In fact, she thought, as she looked around her critically, the room was a hotchpotch. A terrible miscellany of individual items which had not been put together with any care or attention.

Thelma had a mix of old and modern in her living room but they blended harmoniously. Brenda's room was so bright and cosy with its chintzy curtains, and red carpet, that you didn't even question whether the bookcases, cabinets full of Goss china, and little tables covered by lace cloths that were almost hidden beneath pots of flowers, and framed photographs of her grandchildren, were old or new.

Margaret walked out and shut the door firmly behind her. She intended changing the look of the entire house but the sitting room, she determined, would be the first room to get 'the treatment'.

There was so much to be done that it was quite daunting.

She'd like to have a completely new bathroom; have her bedroom fitted out with built-in wardrobes; install an up-to-the-minute kitchen with a dishwasher, a new washing machine with a tumble-dryer, a new fridge-freezer and a cooker with a built-in extractor hood. She sighed, the list was endless.

She'd start with the sitting room, she decided, as she got ready. The bedroom could wait until later. She'd talk to Jan and the others about it. They'd have plenty of ideas. Jan had probably had her place done over two or three times since she was last there.

It was only a ten-minute drive to Jan's flat in Maidenhead, but she wanted to give herself plenty of time.

Using Reginald's set of keys she opened up the garage. Reginald's pride and joy, his immaculate silver grey BMW sat there in solid glory. She had never driven it so it was with a feeling of nervous trepidation she unlocked the door and slid behind the wheel.

The dashboard looked so complicated that for a moment Margaret felt like a pilot in the cockpit of a plane for the very first time. Taking a deep breath, she slipped the key into the ignition and switched on. The engine whined. She tried again. It whined and died. She felt a moment of panic. The battery must be flat. What did she do now?

She sat for a moment, studying the controls. Then relief flooded over her. She hadn't used the choke. But surely that was automatic? It was only in an older car like the Escort she'd had that the choke was operated manually.

She switched the ignition on once more. This time the engine fired. She pumped the accelerator, revved up too quickly, or too violently, and the engine spluttered and died. Now she'd flooded the damn thing!

It was almost as if Reginald was hovering in the background trying to stop her taking his car. Biting down on her lower lip she counted very slowly to ten. Then she tried again.

This time she used the accelerator very gently and felt a sense of achievement as she managed to maintain the revs. Cautiously, she put the BMW into reverse and backed out on to the driveway.

She knew she ought to stop and shut the garage doors but she was afraid to take her foot off the accelerator in case the engine died again. Leaving them wide open she carefully backed down the driveway and on to the road.

The BMW was twice the size of her Escort and Margaret felt as if she was driving a bus. She felt a sense of panic as she reached the main road and realized that she didn't even know where the indicators were. All the controls were in different places to where she was used to.

She'd known where the reverse gear was simply because when she'd sat in the front passenger seat beside Reginald he had always caught her leg with the back of his hand when he was using reverse. She had no idea where the rest of the controls were, though. As soon as she got back from Jan's place she would read up the handbook, she told herself. She daren't take it out at night until she knew how to work the light switches.

She felt herself breaking out into a cold sweat as she went over the level crossing at the end of Lower Road in Cookham. Even though the lights weren't on red and everyone else was driving over it, she was scared stiff that a train would appear out of nowhere and sweep her away down the track.

There wasn't much traffic across the Moor but as soon as she entered Cookham High Street she was caught up in congestion. With cars parked all the way down on the left-hand side there really wasn't room for two cars to pass and the amount of traffic coming the other way was quite horrendous.

Margaret froze as a high-sided lorry tried to squeeze past her, its offside wheels mounting the pavement on the left as it went by her.

And the speed they were all moving at! Didn't any of them realize that there was a thirty m.p.h. limit?

She shivered; thank heaven it wasn't much further to Jan's place. At the end of the High Street a right-hand turn would take her along by the river, past Boulter's Lock and she'd be there.

It sounded simple enough but, because she had positioned herself in the centre of the road, and forgotten to indicate, she found herself cutting right across the front of the car travelling behind her that was also turning right.

The driver blasted his horn in exasperation and, in panic, Margaret slammed on her brakes. There was a squeal of tyres from the car behind her and as its bumpers jammed into those of the BMW the impact jarred her forward on to the steering wheel.

She wasn't hurt, but she was very frightened.

Aware that she was causing a hold-up and that it was a busy road junction, Margaret drove slowly to the next side road and then pulled in.

She was trembling so much that she couldn't think what to do next. Shaking, she sat there with the engine running waiting expectantly for an irate driver to hammer on her window.

Instead, the car that had bumped her and which was still behind her pulled out and sped away down the road towards Maidenhead in a cloud of dust. As it roared past her the driver raised his fist in a threatening gesture but with a broad grin on his cheeky young face.

Astonished, yet at the same time relieved, she looked back at the road junction. Traffic was flowing smoothly; no one was taking any interest in the incident.

Nervously she pulled out into the road and drove on. It was less than a mile to the block of luxury flats where Jan lived so she decided to wait until she got there to check if there was any damage to the BMW.

She parked in one of the lined-off sections labelled 'Visitors' and switched off the engine. She was still trembling when she walked round to the back of the car to inspect for possible damage.

Apart from the merest smudge of red paint on the heavy black bumper there wasn't a mark to be seen. She couldn't believe it!

Although she'd had a seat belt on, the impact had been hard enough to throw her forward on to the steering wheel. It hadn't hurt much at the time but now her ribs were quite painful. She was sure they were bruised.

She did a double check on the BMW, bending down to see if the exhaust pipe was all right, if the number plate and rear lights were damaged and breathed a sigh of relief to find they were all unscathed.

Everything seemed to be in perfect order. Fate had been kind to her. She could imagine Charles's reaction if she had damaged Reginald's car the very first time she took it out. He would probably have told her she shouldn't have been driving it.

He was right, of course. It was far too big for her. She'd have to sell it, and buy something smaller. Not an Escort but something a bit more upmarket. She'd always fancied having a Mercedes coupe. She'd never mentioned it to anyone because she knew only too well what Reginald's reaction would have been.

Still, she reminded herself, he wasn't here now to stop her or to make cutting, sarcastic remarks. She could buy whatever sort of car she fancied. And she would!

In fact, she decided that would be the very first thing she would do. She'd get rid of Reginald's BMW, and buy something she was happy with; a car she would enjoy driving.

It would be her first step towards independence. She wouldn't consult Charles, or Steven, or even Alison. She'd do it all by herself.

'Yes, your days are numbered,' she muttered aloud as she locked the doors of the BMW and dropped the keys inside her handbag.

She hadn't felt so excited, or confident, for ages. Not for years, in fact, she thought happily as she crossed the gravel drive to the entrance to the block of flats.

Eight

Utterly bemused by all the chatter, her senses dazzled by the splendour of the decor and furnishings, Margaret drove away from Jan Porter's penthouse in a state of euphoria.

Instead of returning to her own house in Cookham she turned right along the river road to the A4 and then right again towards the centre of Maidenhead. On her left was a large garage with an array of pumps lining the forecourt and an enormous glass-sided showroom full of gleaming expensive cars, most of them so new that they didn't even carry a registration number.

She pulled in, parked, locked up her car and went into the showroom.

There's no harm in browsing and seeing what is on offer, she told herself.

Some of the price tags horrified her. Still, she mused, the BMW had an extremely low mileage so she ought to get a very good trade-in price for it.

She tried to avoid the slick young salesman wearing a light grey three-piece suit, pink shirt and garish pink and blue tie. His rubber-soled black shoes made no sound at all as he glided to her side.

Even before he spoke she knew he was studying her critically. Probably wondering if a woman on her own is a serious buyer or not, she thought wryly.

He coughed discreetly. 'Good morning. Can I help you in any way?'

She shook her head firmly. 'No thank you, At the moment I'm only looking.'

'Feel free. They're all unlocked if you want to sit in any of them.'

He wandered away. She watched him out of the corner of her eye. He appeared to be admiring his reflection in the plate glass windows, but she knew he was still watching her. She was sure that he was ready to pounce if she showed the slightest interest.

He's only doing his job, she told herself. Come on, be decisive and show some confidence. Lead him on. Kid him into thinking you're going to buy one. Let him get into his spiel. You don't have to commit yourself to anything. As long as you don't sign anything you can always walk away.

She thought back to the last time she had been there, when Reginald had ordered the BMW. He had been so high-handed with the salesman that she'd felt embarrassed. He'd been abrupt to the point of rudeness and practically told the man that he didn't know his job. When the salesman told him that there was a six-week wait for the model he wanted he'd demanded to see the manager.

It had worked, of course. The manager knew Reginald personally. They'd belonged to the same golf club, and so he had bent over backwards to placate Reginald. He'd assured him that he would deal with the matter personally and ensure immediate delivery. It had still taken six weeks and when it had arrived the colour hadn't been the one Reginald had specified.

Margaret sensed that the salesman was about to pounce again so she turned away quickly and focused her attention on the car nearest to her. Her breath caught in her throat, it was the car of her dreams; a Mercedes coupe!

She stood transfixed. She had always loved the elegant lines of the Mercedes coupe but this one was a dream. It was a pale metallic green; a delicate shade that reminded her of the newly uncurled leaves in spring on the willow tree that grew in her garden.

'Why don't you sit in it so that you get the feel of it?' urged the salesman in persuasive tones.

The serpent tempting Eve, thought Margaret. Like Eve, she obeyed.

Ensnared in the car's luxurious interior, instinctively her hands gripped the wheel. She was overcome by desire. This was the car for her. She'd never wanted anything as much as this in her whole life.

'Would you like to take it out on the road for a test drive, madam?'

Margaret shook her head. She didn't need to do that because she knew it would drive perfectly.

'It's automatic. Have you driven an automatic car before?' He looked out on to the forecourt as he spoke, trying to decide which of the several cars parked there might be hers.

'You will soon get used to it. You will find it is far easier than driving with a manual gearbox. Much less tiring when you are in traffic.'

Margaret nodded without speaking. She was acutely aware that he was assuming she was going to buy it. Could she? Dare she?

'It really is your sort of car,' he murmured, quietly.

He sounded so serious that she looked up at him, startled. As their gaze locked and she saw genuine interest in the dark eyes fixed on her, she was aware of him as a person, not a mere robot programmed in the mode of salesman.

She relaxed. 'It is a car I've always dreamed of owning,' she admitted.

He nodded understandingly. 'What do you have at the moment?'

She indicated towards the forecourt. 'The silver grey BMW out there.'

'Really?' His interest heightened and thin lips formed into a silent whistle.

'It was bought from here so what sort of trade-in price would you give me if I should decide to replace it with this one, I mean?'

'Well—' he looked thoughtful, letting out his breath in a long, sibilant hiss, and puffing out his cheeks slightly – 'I'd have to check the BMW over before I could say.'

'Here.' She held out the car keys. 'Why don't you do that and let me know.'

'Right!' His dark eyes brightened. He was the robot salesman once again with pound signs of his commission dangling like carrots in front of his eyes.

While he was gone, Margaret sat in the Mercedes again. Her hands wandered tentatively over the dashboard, moving the controls, testing out the lights. She had never felt so comfortable in any car as she did in this one. She felt so much in control that she wanted to drive it out of the showroom there and then. And why not?

While the salesman was checking out the trade-in allowance he could make on the BMW she did some quick calculations.

Before he'd retired, Reginald had made her a generous allowance to cover the cost of running her own car, buying clothes, taking days out, and paying all her other personal needs. She'd expected him to cut it back after he'd sold her car, but he had gone on transferring the same amount into her bank account as previously even though she had mentioned that she didn't really need as much.

In the years that followed she had bought very few new clothes, and since whenever she went out anywhere it was always with Reginald, he had always paid, so she'd spent very little of her allowance. So, from time to time she'd transferred most of it from her current account into a high interest savings account.

It had earned a good return and become a sizeable nest egg. She hoped it was going to be enough to pay the difference between the trade-in allowance on the BMW and the cost of the Mercedes.

To her great relief, it was. Even so she hesitated, not sure whether she ought to take such a step without consulting Charles first of all.

The salesman, fearing he was about to lose the deal, grudgingly lowered the price by a further two hundred pounds. Unable to resist such a bargain, Margaret agreed to buy the Mercedes.

Oozing success, he guided her to the office at the far end of the showroom to complete the paperwork.

I must be meant to have that car, she thought excitedly as she settled herself in the chair he pulled out for her and faced him across the polished desktop.

'You do own the BMW?'

'Of course!' She fished around in her shoulder bag and brought out the relevant documents, and laid them on the table. Normally she never carried papers of that sort with her yet some instinct had dictated that she should pick them up before she'd left the house.

Eagerly he reached out for the documents.

He frowned as he studied them. 'The BMW is registered in your husband's name . . .'

'I know that!'

'Then we will need his signature.'

'That's impossible!'

The dark eyes challenged Margaret. 'You mean he doesn't want to sell?'

'He's dead. His funeral was last week!' Her laugh sounded a little hysterical.

'I see!' He ran a finger around his collar. 'Give me a moment . . .'

A feeling of despair began to creep through Margaret's veins. Nothing had changed. Even now Reginald was still managing to stop her getting her own way.

Her heart pounded and the colour rushed to her cheeks as the salesman returned accompanied by the manager. They recognized each other simultaneously.

'Mrs Wright.' His hand went out. 'I was so sorry to hear about Reginald's death last week. Very sad.' He held her hand in both his own in a gesture he intended to be comforting. 'Now, about his car.'

'I want to trade it in for a Mercedes coupe. The light green one that you have in your showroom.'

'Ah, I see. The BMW is too big for you, is it? They can be quite a handful. A man's car, really.'

'I've always wanted a Mercedes coupe.'

'Yes, yes. A lovely car.' He ran a hand over his thinning grey hair. 'Just one small point, though. The BMW is in your husband's name.'

'I know that . . . but its mine now.'

'Yes, well, we will have to sort the details out first. We have to establish ownership, that sort of thing. Mere formality,' he hurried on as she was about to speak. 'It should only take a few days.'

'A few days!' She bit down on her lower lip in exasperation. 'I wanted to complete the transaction now and drive home in my new car.'

She saw the two men exchange glances. She was making a mess of this. She sounded like a spoilt child not a confident adult.

'I don't think that is going to be possible. We do have to establish that the BMW has been left to you and that might take a little while. It probably means waiting until after the will has been dealt with and—'

'You mean probate? That could take months!'

'Perhaps I should ring your son Charles, Mrs Wright. We know each other quite well. He might be able to advise me on how to proceed.'

Margaret stiffened. 'It has nothing to do with him whatsoever.'

'Very well . . .' He hesitated. He was as reluctant as the salesman to see the deal collapse through what was, after all, a mere technicality.

In an attempt to placate Margaret he said, 'Look, what I could do is hold on to the BMW and if you paid the difference between the amount I think we can allow you on it and we could let you take the Mercedes and we'll sort out the details at our leisure.'

'Great! That sounds fine to me.'

'I would still require confirmation from Charles, or whoever is dealing with your husband's affairs, about the legal ownership of the BMW, Mrs Wright,' he added uneasily.

'Oh! Well, if you must contact him, you must, I suppose.' She shrugged resignedly.

'Good!' He rubbed his thin hands together. 'I'll go into that side of things then while you go ahead and arrange the changeover of insurance cover. When you've done that, and your cheque has been cleared, I'll be happy to complete the transaction.'

'Surely even that is going to take several days?'

'I'm afraid you're right.' He gave an ingratiating smile. 'Meanwhile,' he picked up a red SOLD sticker, and handed it to the salesman, 'we'll take great care of your Mercedes, and make quite sure no one else snaps it up.'

Margaret didn't answer.

Listening to him was like hearing a replay of Reginald's plati-
tudes when she became worked up about something. With a few
words he had managed to eradicate her feeling of happiness and
excitement.

Ask Charles, indeed! She knew what Charles would say. 'Of
course the BMW is too big for her. What she needs is a nice
little second-hand Metro, or bottom-of-the-range Ford. Nothing
too powerful. She never goes anywhere. Simply potters around
locally or to the shops.'

Well, that was where he was wrong. She wasn't going to content
herself with pottering around locally. Not any more. There was a
whole big world out there just waiting to be explored. She slammed
the BMW into gear, reversed out of the garage forecourt and
headed for the multi-storey car park in the centre of Maidenhead.

If she couldn't have a new car then she'd go ahead and have
a holiday. There were several travel agencies in the shopping
precinct; one of them must have something available that would
suit her needs. She didn't mind where it was just as long as she
could go right away.

'If you are travelling on your own then maybe it would probably be best if you took a package deal,' advised the travel clerk.

'You mean go with a party and have a guide taking care of us?'

'That's right.'

'Oh, no!' Margaret shook her head emphatically. 'I want to go
on holiday on my own, not with a crowd of people I've never
met before and don't know.'

'It's not very wise . . . not these days . . . not for an . . .' The
girl bit her lip, and pulled herself up quickly. 'We don't recommend women to travel on their own.'

'I see.' Margaret straightened up wearily. 'Perhaps I'd better
think it over then.'

Feeling utterly depressed, and disillusioned, Margaret made her
way to the nearest cafe. Over a cup of black coffee she pondered
the situation. Possibly the girl was right. With her limited knowledge of foreign languages it might be difficult to make herself
understood if she travelled to a country where they didn't speak
English. Even so, she ought to be able to manage Malta or
Gibraltar, or even Cyprus.

Steven and Sandra had gone there for their honeymoon and

they'd said that most Cypriots spoke English, in the main holiday resorts, at any rate.

That's where she'd go; Cyprus!

Revived by the coffee, her spirits once more soaring, Margaret once again went to make a booking. She deliberately chose a different travel agency. She didn't want to meet up with the same well-meaning girl in case she came up with some other warning.

This time she was in luck. The clerk said they could book her in for Cyprus right away at a top-class hotel in Limassol. The flight would be from Gatwick the next day.

Margaret's heart thudded in excited anticipation as he began to fill in the necessary paperwork.

'Could I see your passport?'

'Passport?' Margaret stared at the blonde in her tailored navy and white uniform.

'You haven't brought it with you? Well, if you'd like to let me have some other form of identification, so that we can verify your cheque . . .'

'I will need my passport though . . . when I get to the airport, I mean?'

'Of course you will. Does that present some sort of a problem?'

Margaret looked vague. 'I'm not sure.'

'You do have a passport?'

'Yes, yes . . . of course.'

As she spoke, Margaret tried desperately to think where it might be. Reginald had always insisted on looking after all those sorts of important documents; birth certificates, wedding certificate, deeds for the house, income tax forms and every other kind of form that came into the house. Her passport would probably be with those, and they were locked away in the bureau in his study. She didn't even have a key. He probably kept one at the office, and the other on his key ring and Charles had taken possession of that.

It had been lucky for her that there had been a spare set of car keys hanging in the hall otherwise she wouldn't have been able to use the BMW, she mused.

'Your passport is up to date?' The girl's voice was edged with impatience.

Margaret shrugged helplessly. 'I . . . I don't really know. It's quite some time since I used it.'

She felt uneasy and all hot and bothered. She ran her hand over her forehead pushing back the strands of hair that had fallen over her face.

'I think I'd better find it and make sure it's in order before I book.'

The girl didn't answer, but her manner as she swept her papers together spoke volumes. Her voice was hostile as she snapped, 'Good morning,' and moved away to attend to someone else.

Tears of defeat misting her eyes, Margaret made her way back to the car park, and began looking for the BMW. She was sure she had been on Ground Floor A, but although she walked down every aisle she couldn't see it.

I can't have lost it. It's bigger that most other cars and such a distinctive colour I should be able to spot it, she told herself. I must be on the wrong floor.

The lift wasn't working so she walked up the concrete steps to the next floor. This time she stood at the end of each row and let her eyes do the work of searching for her. The BMW wasn't there.

There were five levels. She knew it hadn't been the top level because that was open to the sky. Starting at the level below that she worked her way down, checking each row methodically.

Her feet were aching and her nerves ragged, by the time she located it. The annoying thing was that it had been on Ground Floor A all the time. She couldn't understand how she had missed it the first time.

The ticket machine registered four hours. Four hours, and she had achieved nothing, nothing except frustration.

Nine

'Your mother phoned about ten minutes ago. Apparently she just missed you at the office,' Helen called out from the kitchen as her husband walked into the house.

Charles groaned. 'Did she say what she wanted?'

He dropped his monogrammed, black leather briefcase on to a

chair in the hall in a gesture of despair. He'd had a hard day, and
to be greeted by that piece of news the moment he came through
the front door was just too much. Helen could have waited until
he'd had a drink, he thought irritably.

'It was something to do with her passport. I couldn't quite
follow. She said you had the keys to your father's bureau, and so
she couldn't open it and she thinks that her passport is in there. She
asked me to make sure you rang her the minute you got in. You'd
better do it; she seemed to be in a bit of a state.'

'It can wait until I've had a drink, surely!'

'That's up to you, darling. If you're pouring one then I'll have
a gin and tonic. Could you bring it through into the kitchen?'

'Will do. I'll just get changed first, though.'

'Do I take it you didn't go round to see Mother, today?' Charles
asked ten minutes later, as he placed Helen's drink down on the
work surface.

He had changed out of his navy pinstripe suit into sludge-
coloured cords and a tan and navy sweater over a tan polo shirt.
He looked relaxed as he hoisted himself up on one of the tall
kitchen stools and sipped his whisky and soda.

Helen tasted her drink and pulled a face. 'More tonic than gin
in this, isn't there?' she commented sharply.

'Did you go and see Mother?' Charles repeated ignoring her
comment about the drink.

'Of course! I went round there just as you asked.'

'And?'

'She wasn't in.'

'What time was that?'

'Ten . . . half past . . . I don't know! What does it matter?
She was out.'

'Did you notice if she'd gone out in Dad's car?'

'I couldn't help but do so. The garage doors were wide open.
Anyone could have walked up the drive, and helped themselves
to the lawnmower, or any of the gardening tools in there. Your
father would have had a fit. You know how particular he always
was about the garage doors being kept locked.'

'Half past ten this morning. You're sure about that?'

'About then. Why?'

'Well, I had a phone call from Simon Wood, the manager of

Bridge Garage, just before lunch. Apparently, Mother was in their showroom trying to swap Dad's BMW for a Mercedes coupe.'

'She was doing what?' Helen's green eyes hardened like diamonds. 'You've got to stop her.'

'Don't worry. It's impossible for her to do it because the car was registered in Dad's name and—'

'It wasn't his to leave to her anyway, was it?' Helen interrupted.

'No, not really. For tax reasons it was a company car the same as mine is. Even though he'd retired he still had a holding in the firm so that meant he could keep his car and his membership of BUPA and so on. Simon Wood guessed this was the case because he'd dealt with the paperwork when Dad changed his car about a year before he retired.'

'Did he tell your Mother that?'

'Well, no. He rang me instead. He knew about Dad dying last week and . . . well . . . he didn't say so in as many words, but he thought Mother seemed a little odd. Distressed, you know. He assumed it was because of what had happened and told her he'd reserve the Mercedes she wanted to buy but there were certain details that had to be sorted out before he could release it. As soon as she left he phoned me.'

'Well, that wasn't what she was phoning you about.'

Charles took another mouthful of his drink and looked at his wife quizzically. 'How do you know?'

'I told you only, as usual, you weren't listening.'

'Told me what?'

'It's something to do with her passport. She said your father kept it locked up in his bureau and that she didn't have a key.'

'So what does she expect me to do about it . . . break the lock?'

'She seems to think you have his keys. He kept them at the office or something.'

'Not that I know of.' He picked up Helen's empty glass. 'Want another?'

'No. Not at the moment. Dinner will be ready in about ten minutes. I've put a bottle of Chablis in the fridge to have with it.'

'Good!' He drained his whisky and put the glass down on the draining board. 'I'd better go and phone Mother then before we start eating, or she'll be ringing up in the middle of our meal.'

Helen frowned. 'She'll probably insist that you go over and see her.'

'If she does she will have to wait until tomorrow.'

'I've been to Margaret's place twice today, and she's still not in,' grumbled Hilda Smart as she poured her husband a cup of tea.

'I wonder where she's been. Gadding off and enjoying herself, I suppose?' Jack said with a smile as he cut into the meat pie on the plate in front of him.

'She probably can't bear being in the house on her own,' he went on. 'It gets people like that, you know, after they've lost someone close to them. They can't stand the sound of silence. It seems to close in on them. Frightening thought, really.'

'I wouldn't know, I never get the chance to be on my own for more than half an hour,' Hilda replied tartly.

'Think yourself lucky, then. I bet that's why Margaret was out, because she couldn't cope with being in the house on her own.'

'Well, you may be right. The point is, though, I didn't get a chance to ask her about Reginald's golf clubs.'

'Don't worry about it. I'm sure she'll let me have them, if she's still got them when next I see her. Like I said, though, she's probably got rid of them by now.'

'Or had them stolen.'

'Stolen?' Jack spread his pie liberally with home-made chutney. 'What do you mean, whatever makes you say a thing like that?'

'If she's as careless with them as she is with the rest of her things then it's more than likely,' Hilda told him primly. 'Do you know, she'd gone out and left the garage doors wide open. All those expensive gardening tools hanging there and that new electric lawnmower that Reginald bought only last year, and—'

'Left the garage doors open? Are you saying she'd gone out in his BMW?'

'Well it wasn't in the garage and as I keep telling you, she wasn't there either.'

'I can't believe she'd do that! Reginald wouldn't even consider letting her drive it. He always said it was much too powerful for a woman to control.'

'Typical! He would say a thing like that.'

'He was probably right! He usually was about such matters.

She'll have an accident if she tries to drive it. It's much too high-powered for her to handle.'

'Well, it wasn't in the garage and as I said, the doors had been left wide open. Anyone could have walked in and taken whatever they'd wanted.'

Jack speared up the last bit of pie. 'She shouldn't be living there on her own, not at a time like this. She needs company, someone to keep an eye on her.'

'It's not your problem, so don't start thinking it is,' warned Hilda. 'She's got two sons as well as a daughter to take care of her.'

'True, but they've got families of their own to keep them busy.'

'So have you! And don't you start calling round there to see if there's any odd jobs she wants doing. She'll put on you. She'll have you climbing up ladders, or lifting things and the next thing you'll be laid up and I'll have all the trouble of looking after you.'

'Margaret wouldn't put on anybody. That's the trouble with her, she's too independent!'

'Huh!' Hilda exploded in anger. 'I've never noticed it.'

'It's a pity she doesn't go and stay with her sister, Vivienne,' Jack went on, ignoring his wife's look of incredulity. 'Or have Vivienne to live with her. They're both widows now so they'd be company for each other. Save money, too, having only one house to run between them.'

'You're talking through your hat, Jack Smart! Margaret can't stand her sister and Vivienne Peterson can't bear to be in the same room as Margaret for more than ten minutes, and well you know it.'

'What an utter load of twaddle!'

'Then why was Vivienne one of the first to leave after Reginald's funeral? Answer me that? You can't. Well I'll tell you. It's because she doesn't hit it off with Margaret, and never has done.'

'Rubbish, woman!'

'It's not rubbish. They're as different as chalk and cheese. You've only got to look at them to see that.'

Jack laughed. 'You mean that Vivienne's like a little grey mouse and Margaret's more of a bird of paradise.'

'I mean that Vivienne is crippled with arthritis. It would cramp Margaret's style if they were living together and she had her to look after.'

'Yes, I suppose Margaret deserves the chance to enjoy herself. She's certainly had a dull sort of life since Reginald had his heart attack,' reflected Jack.

'That's what happens when you marry a man who's nearly old enough to be your father. Married for money, didn't she? I can remember when our Reginald first brought her home. Made up to the nines and dressed to kill she was, with her stiletto heels and nipped-in waist. Made me feel like a real dumpling.'

'She's still as slim now as she was when I first met her,' mused Jack.

'Slim? I'd call it scrawny. Bit of fat helps to pad out your cheeks; and keeps the wrinkles at bay.'

'I never noticed that Margaret had any wrinkles.'

'How would you or anyone else know, for that matter? The amount of make-up she piles on camouflages what's underneath.'

'Make-up! Margaret? She doesn't bother with any of that sort of stuff!'

'Of course she does! You surely don't think for one moment that her skin would look that soft and creamy without any help, do you? Even the colour in her cheeks comes out of a pot!'

'She uses it very discreetly then. I'd not noticed.'

'You wouldn't,' his wife told him scornfully. 'You've always had a soft spot for her.'

'She's a lovely person. Quietly spoken, kind, always looks nice, never wears anything too outrageous . . .'

'She certainly hasn't done so since Reginald retired,' sneered Hilda. 'I was only thinking the other day how dowdy she looked. Probably see quite a change in her now,' she added with a prophetic gleam in her beady brown eyes.

'I forgot to tell you, I saw your Margaret today,' Hetty Chapman remarked as she placed the paperback she'd been reading face down on her bedside table, and switched off the reading lamp on her side of the bed.

'So you did manage to find time to pop round to see her then.' Joseph's arm went round his wife's plump body, drawing it closer to his own in the big double bed. 'How was she?'

'I didn't manage to speak to her. I saw her when I was delivering some plants to Bladon's. She was driving along Cookham High Street.'

'Driving?'

'Yes. She was in Reginald's BMW.'

'Are you sure about that? She always said he wouldn't let her drive it.'

Hetty chuckled. 'Well, he's not around any longer to stop her, is he!'

'Well, well, you do surprise me. Did Margaret see you?'

'No. At least, I shouldn't think so.' Hetty yawned loudly. 'She was concentrating on the traffic. You know how congested it always is in the High Street. I'll pop over and see her tomorrow if I can fit it in.'

For a long time after Joseph had settled down to sleep with a steady, rhythmic snore, Hetty lay awake thinking about her sister-in-law.

It had been Reginald's car alright. She had a good memory for number plates. Anyway, who could forget it? RW 1000. He'd had that registration for as long as she could remember. He always transferred it from one car to the next. She wasn't sure whether he did so because he felt that it made him appear important, or whether he did it so that no one knew when he bought a new one.

It was well after ten o'clock when Steven Wright parked his dark blue Rover outside his house, and let himself in with his latchkey. There was a thin sliver of light, and the sound of a TV sitcom, with its loud spurts of canned laughter, coming from the sitting room, but the rest of the house was in darkness.

He found Sandra curled up on the settee, her eyes glued to the screen, a vodka and tonic on the small table beside her, She was wearing a white towelling dressing gown over black silk pyjamas and as he bent to kiss her he caught a whiff of the heady smell of the exotic bath oil he'd given her at Christmas.

'Your meal's in the microwave and I'll have a coffee if you're making one,' she told him as she freed herself from his embrace.

On his way to the kitchen, Steven shed his jacket, and hung it over the newel post at the bottom of the stairs. He set the microwave to four minutes, checked the kettle had some water in it and switched it on. Then he found a tray, put a knife, fork and salt on it, spooned Nescafé into two mugs and placed them on a tray as well and then waited for the microwave to ping and the kettle to boil.

The kettle was first so he poured water over the granules and topped both mugs up with milk from the fridge. By the time he had done that his meal was warmed through so he piled the plate and mugs of coffee on to the tray and took the whole lot through to the sitting room.

Sandra was still watching television. The late news had already started. He handed her a mug of coffee and balancing the tray on his knees settled down in an armchair to watch.

'You're going to spill that coffee,' warned Sandra, flicking her straight blonde hair back from her face.

Silently he removed it from the tray and put it on the floor beside his chair.

Sandra sipped at her cup of coffee. 'Did you phone your mother?' she asked, looking across at him.

'No. I didn't get a chance. Did you go and see her?'

She shook her head. 'I didn't think there was much point.'

'Why not?' He looked across the room in surprise, a forkful of food halfway to his mouth.

'She wasn't in.'

'How do you know she wasn't if you didn't go to see her?'

'I was going to call and see her on the way home from collecting Matthew from school, since it's the kids she likes to see not me . . .'

'Well?' Steven used the remote control to kill the sound on the television.

'Don't switch off, I'm watching that,' Sandra wailed petulantly.

'The news?' Steven's eyebrows shot up. 'Come off it, you never watch the news. Not unless you think there might be something special on.'

'Do you mind!' She glowered at him furiously. 'Put it back on. I want to see the programme that's coming on next.'

'I'll switch it back on for that. Now, tell me what happened when you went to see Mum.'

'I've already told you, I didn't go round to see her. One of the women waiting at school said she'd seen her in Maidenhead, so there wasn't any point in me driving to Willow House.'

'I wonder what she was doing in Maidenhead?' mused Steven.

'Oh, I know what she was doing!' Sandra smiled smugly, waiting for Steven to stop eating and look up. When she had his complete attention she said, 'She was booking a holiday to Cyprus.'

'She was doing what?'

'You heard what I said. She was in the travel agents, booking a holiday to Cyprus.'

Steven stared at his wife utterly bemused. 'How do you know that?'

'This woman had called in to pick up some theatre tickets, and she overheard all that was being said. They booked her into a hotel in Limassol!'

'She's going to Cyprus on her own?'

Sandra shrugged. 'It looks like it. She was only booking one seat. Hardly the grieving widow.'

'Sandra!' Steven frowned with annoyance. He knew his wife didn't particularly like his mother, but there was no need to make snide comments like that, he thought angrily.

If her information was right, though, Sandra did have a point. It was rather soon for his mother to go gadding off on a holiday, especially on her own.

He looked at his watch, wondering whether or not to phone her. It was rather late. Perhaps he'd better leave it until first thing in the morning. If he was up in time he might even call round on his way to work.

Ten

Margaret Wright studied Charles covertly as he rose from his father's armchair, and walked over to the drinks cabinet. As, he helped himself to a whisky she stared fixedly at the back of his head. It was hard to believe that this giant of a man, whose straight dark hair was already showing a sprinkling of grey, was her beautiful first born. He'd been such a bonny baby. She'd been overjoyed when she had first cradled him in her arms.

Watching him now was like seeing a reincarnation of Reginald; Reginald as he had looked when they'd first been married.

The thought sent a shiver through her. He'd been her boss, and she'd been head over heels in love with him. Or thought she was; she'd often wondered since if it had been love or merely infatuation. He'd been so handsome, so self-assured, that she had been enraptured when he'd singled her out for special attention.

She tried hard to merit his approval and when he appointed her as his private secretary she was bursting with pride.

Determined to please, she'd checked and rechecked her work anxious to justify his faith in her ability, and prove herself to be an ultra-efficient secretary. She sometimes worried about whether he really noticed her as a person

She was absolutely obsessed by trying to please him. He filled her thoughts not only from the moment she opened her eyes in the morning until she closed them at night, but in her dreams as well.

His occasional words of praise, the card and single red rose on her birthday, the expensive perfume at Christmas had all delighted her.

He was wonderful, a boss in a million, she told all her friends.

Then came the 'working lunches'. These tête-à-tête meetings outside the office became the highlight of her working day.

The whirlwind courtship that followed left her breathless. The term 'swept off her feet' suddenly had tremendous meaning for her. The first time they kissed she felt as if a fire had spread through her. After that she had ached for him so much that she was utterly convinced she had fallen in love.

She had been seventeen, burning with innocent desire, and pent-up longing. He had been an experienced man in his mid-thirties and more than willing to quench those fires.

A strict moral upbringing, coupled with a fear of pregnancy, had made her reject Reginald's amorous advances at first. Being held at arm's length had made Reginald even more determined to have her and, when all else failed, he'd proposed marriage.

In seventh heaven, she'd ignored her father's objections because she was so young and her mother's warnings that Reginald would be impossible to live with because not only was he too good-looking and much too debonair but also far too worldly-wise.

Impulsively, on the eve of her nineteenth birthday she had said yes.

Reginald's business connections, together with the difference in their ages, ensured that their wedding a few months later made local headline news.

He was her first lover, her only lover, fulfilling every romantic fantasy she had ever known.

At first she hadn't realized how possessive and aggressive he was, or that he completely dominated her life.

Starry-eyed, she was swept along on a whirlwind of change. She had no idea she was pregnant until she blacked out one morning while out shopping.

Reginald's initial astonishment speedily turned into pride. Overnight he became a sober family man, taking his responsibilities so seriously that he changed completely. Almost at once he lost the dazzling flamboyance that had attracted her to him in the first place.

Three babies in quick succession had made her feel trapped and she found herself wondering whether Reginald wanted a wife or a breeding machine.

Absorbed by the children, indiscernibly their own relationship had cooled. One minute, or so it seemed to Margaret when she looked back, they had been turgid lovers, the next pragmatic parents.

Reginald had shown a strong preference for Charles. Perhaps it was because right from his birth Charles resembled him so closely.

There had been a natural affinity between the two of them. As a toddler, Charles had been his father's shadow. As a gangling schoolboy he'd hung on Reginald's every word, obedient to his wishes, eager to please him in any way he could.

It had been as natural as night following day that Charles should go to work for his father as soon as he left college. Pupil, disciple . . . he'd been both, echoing his father in words as well as mannerisms. Nepotism had triumphed over experience, and time and time again Charles had been promoted until eventually, at twenty-one, he became a director of the company.

In the years that followed, the workload had gradually shifted from Reginald to Charles so there was no problem when, after his heart attack, Reginald had decided to take retirement. Charles was already groomed to take over as managing director and had assumed the role without any hesitation.

Reginald's name still remained on the company letterheads. It looked more imposing that way. Also, as she since learned, it had meant that Reginald could continue to have the use of a company car, as well as membership of BUPA and various other perks.

Margaret knew she should be proud of Charles and she was, in a detached sort of way. There never had been much warmth between the two of them, not once he started school. Even as a small boy he had always been so laid back, so aloof, so self-contained, that she had felt superfluous.

As Charles reached adulthood she was intensely conscious that he didn't approve of her. Not that he ever voiced the slightest criticism, of course. That wasn't his way. He was far too well mannered to do such a thing. Yet she was sure he knew instinctively that he possessed the power to make her cringe inwardly without ever uttering a single word.

No one else seemed to notice but she was acutely conscious of his facial expressions, the lightning lift of his thick dark brows, the inscrutable look in his dark eyes as they raked her from head to toe, the controlled tone of his voice as he answered her questions.

She obviously irritated him and most of the time his mute annoyance when she expressed an opinion created an impenetrable wall between them.

Reginald had a very similar effect on her, only in his case he voiced his opinions aloud. When she had worked as his secretary, she had steeled herself to turn a deaf ear when he ridiculed anything she said. She accepted his sarcasm without comment or retaliation. Chauvinism had been part of his attraction.

At work he was so confident about his own ability. He believed that he was always right and that he always knew best. He was so self-assured that she accepted, without question, everything he said.

Later on, after they were married, she knew she ought to stand up to him. On the few occasions when she had attempted to do so he had destroyed her argument with a few blistering words that had left her feeling utterly crushed and deflated.

Realizing that she was no match for a man used to supremacy both over his staff and in the boardroom, she had avoided further confrontations. She had accepted that it wasn't worth the hassle to fight battles she knew she stood no chance of winning.

It had meant that he had made all the decisions; whether it was the colour scheme they should have when the house was redecorated, how the garden should be landscaped, or where they would go for their holidays each year.

While Reginald had been at work and she had been free to organize the day-to-day details of her own personal life, it hadn't mattered too much. It was after his enforced retirement, after he had sold her car and expected her to spend every minute of the day with him that her inner resentment had begun to flare up.

By then, of course, it had been too late to do very much about it. Reginald's heart condition had been like a protective shield. It would have been unthinkable to involve him in an argument. So her life had become more and more intolerable. The countless years of avoiding any hassle had established a pattern that she couldn't break even if she'd wanted to. Her ability to stand up for herself had been so undermined that she felt as helpless as an orphan taken into care.

She didn't altogether blame Reginald for organizing everything to his dictate. He'd probably never for one moment realized how resentful she felt. If she had attempted to tell him, especially after he had retired, she knew he would have raised his bushy grey eyebrows and given her a look that spoke volumes, and made her feel so inferior.

Now Charles was doing the same thing. Treating her as though her opinion was of no importance at all and assuming that she was not capable of managing her own life. Exactly as his father had done, he was dictating what she must do and expecting her to accept his advice unconditionally.

This time she didn't intend to give in. Leastways, not without taking a stand. It was a long time since she had stood up for herself, but now she was determined to do so. What was even more important was that she intended to win.

She'd refuse to let Charles supplant Reginald in her life. She'd visualize him as he had been some thirty or more years ago. A skinny little kid who was expected to do what she told him.

Margaret sighed. Even that wouldn't work. Even as a small boy he had been independent of her. He had never answered her back like Alison, or tried to wriggle out of doing things, like Steven. If she told him to tidy his room he would acquiesce quietly, and disappear upstairs. He didn't tidy the room but instead he kept out of her way long enough for her to forget that she had asked him to do it.

The two younger ones had played together, Charles had always remained aloof. As the eldest he always did everything first, always had the new bicycle, the new tennis racket. He never had to accept hand-me-downs of any kind. Perhaps that was why he had always had such a superior manner; perhaps such preferential treatment had made him assume that he was better than the others.

'Is it really necessary to talk about all this tonight? Surely it could have waited until tomorrow,' muttered Charles impatiently, irritated by her brooding silence.

'You were the one who decided you would come over this evening,' Margaret reminded him.

'Only because on the phone you seemed to be in such a state . . .'

'No, because you were in such a hurry to eat your dinner that you wouldn't listen to what I had to say!'

He looked taken aback. 'Nothing of the kind!' he defended. 'Anyway, it's now almost ten o'clock . . .'

'You and Helen never go to bed until after midnight.'

Charles sat up straighter in his chair. 'Come on then, let's discuss whatever it is that's bothering you. What's the problem?'

Eleven

'There are two things I want to do,' Margaret told Charles as he waited impatiently for her to start. 'I want to change the BMW for a different car and I want the key to your father's bureau so that I can check if my passport is in there.'

Charles ran a hand over his hair. 'Let's deal with the car first. You can't exchange it.'

'Why not?'

'Because it's not yours . . .'

'Nonsense!' She stared at him belligerently. 'Your father left all his personal effects to me.'

'He didn't own the BMW. It belongs to the firm. You are not even covered to drive it, so you shouldn't have taken it out today.'

The colour drained from Margaret's face. She bit down on her lower lip to keep it from trembling. So that was why Reginald had never let her drive it. All these years, and she'd never known that she wasn't insured to drive it.

'And the key to the bureau?'

'I can't help you there. As far as I know there are no keys of his in the office.'

'So how do I get into the bureau?'

Charles shrugged. 'Call in a locksmith, I suppose.'

'That will take days! Will you see if you can force the lock for me?'

'Don't be silly, Mother!' He laughed mockingly, his dark eyes fixed on her in sharp antagonism. 'That bureau is a very valuable antique; it would deface it if I forced the lock. In fact, it would probably lower its value by hundreds when you want to sell it.'

'But I don't want to sell it. I merely want to open it so that I can see if my passport is inside.'

He shook his head, searching for some way of deterring her. 'I take it you wanted the passport as proof of your identity at the garage?'

'No.'

'Then why do you need it in such a hurry?' He made no effort to conceal his irritation.

'What do you usually want a passport for?' she snapped back.

'To go abroad, but you're not going abroad, now are you?' The subtle inflection in his voice, as if he was talking to a child, angered her.

'Who says I'm not? I intend to take a holiday in Cyprus and—'

'On your own?' He looked shocked.

'And why not?'

'It's not safe for a woman of your age to be travelling alone, that's why not. Especially when you will be travelling to a foreign country where you don't understand the language. You could be mugged or even murdered.'

'Grow up, Charles!' She steeled herself to make her voice casual. 'I'm quite able to look after myself. I need a holiday. I haven't been abroad for over ten years. I fancy some sea and sun . . .'

'You can get those in this country,' he interrupted. 'What's wrong with Bournemouth? You and Father went there every June—'

'Which is precisely why I don't wish to go to Bournemouth on holiday.'

He looked dismayed. 'I'm sorry. That was insensitive of me . . . I didn't mean . . . memories, and all that . . .'

'Memories have nothing at all to do with it,' Margaret told him crisply. 'I don't want to go to Bournemouth ever again because I am fed up with the place. I want to take a holiday somewhere quite different. That's why I've decided to go to Cyprus.'

Charles became more conciliatory. 'I can see you feel the need to get right away but I really don't think it's a very good idea to go abroad on your own.'

Margaret hid a smile. Charles's tone had changed and so, too, had his approach. He hadn't been so courteous to her for years. Nevertheless, she intended to stand her ground.

'Stop being such a fuddy-duddy, Charles,' she chided. 'Come on, see if you can open up the bureau and let me have my passport.'

It took very little effort to prize open the lock. Everything inside was stacked in neat piles. Electric bills, gas bills, phone bills, and other household papers on the left. Reginald's personal bills for his golfing expenses, tailor and wine merchant on the other side. In the centre there were various documents, his bank statements and personal insurances. There was also the one thing that interested her, their two passports.

'Do you want me to take all these papers away, and go through them?' asked Charles.

'No, leave them. I'll do it at my leisure. There's probably nothing of any great importance in there, anyway. Except this of course.'

She clutched at her passport like a drowning man grabbing at a lifebelt. She'd go back to the travel agent's first thing in the morning. If that particular holiday had gone then she'd book another. She didn't care where it was. She simply wanted to get away, to taste her new-found freedom.

Charles held out his hand. 'Let me check it.'

'What for?' She clung on to it. She didn't want to let it out of her hold now that she had it.

He held up the other one that he had taken from the desk. 'This one is Dad's and it is out of date, so yours probably is as well.'

'Out of date?' She stared at him in disbelief. It couldn't be, it *mustn't* be. She felt tense as she opened it. The photograph came as a shock. Taken twenty years or more ago it showed her as an attractive dark-haired woman about the same age as Charles was now. Her fingers felt clumsy with the tension building up inside her as she turned the pages. She couldn't even read the date of expiry her hand was shaking so much.

Charles took the passport from her and read out the date stamped inside it.

'So has it expired?' She had to fight to keep her voice steady. 'I'm afraid so.'

Seeing the melancholy expression on her face, he placed an arm around her shoulder. 'Cheer up! It's not the end of the world. You can get it renewed.'

'That takes time . . .'

'So, what's the hurry? You have all the time in the world.' His tone was calm and conciliatory, as if speaking to a fractious child.

'My mind's made up.'

'You will be able to plan exactly the sort of holiday that suits you,' he went on ignoring her interruption. 'Saga have some splendid schemes . . .' He stopped, shocked into silence by her withering stare.

'Why don't you pack me off to an old people's home and have done with it,' she snapped bitterly, moving away from him, brushing the back of her hand across her eyes. She felt an over-powering sense of doom. It was as if the whole world had turned against her.

'Mother!' His slightly condescending tone carried scorn, embarrassment, irritation and impatience.

'First the car, and now this!'

He shrugged. 'That's the way things go. Look,' he went on in a lighter tone, 'Why don't you come and stay with us for a few days. Being here on your own is making you feel depressed—'

She cut across his words, 'No, thank you! I want to be on my own,' she stated fiercely. 'I'm not feeling in the least lonely,' she added before he could speak.

'Right!' He stood up, ran a hand over his hair and pulled his sweater down over his hips. 'If that's really how you want things to be left then I may as well go home. I did offer, remember.'

'I know, and I'm grateful for your suggestion, but it's not what I want to do. From now on, I intend to do what I want, not what other people think I ought to do,' she added, her voice rising.

Charles lips parted very slightly in a cold, aloof smile. He walked over to the door then stopped and looked back.

'You will remember about the car though, won't you? Our insurance doesn't cover you to drive it.'

Margaret struggled to keep her voice steady. 'Then you had better move it out of my garage.'

'I'll see to it. There's no hurry though, is there? It's not as if you were going to use the garage for anything.'

'I need it for my own car.'

'What are you talking about? You haven't got a car?' His voice rose on the last word, making his statement a half-question.

'I probably will have tomorrow.'

'I've already told you, you can't use the BMW in part exchange.'

'That's all right. I'll buy my own.' She sensed his astonishment but she avoided his eyes. The Mercedes she longed to own might be out of her price range, but she was sure that her little nest egg would be enough to purchase something else.

'You want to be careful about buying a second-hand car. Salesman are looking for—'

'Mugs like me. Women who don't know what's under the bonnet?'

'Well, you don't have a lot of experience in that field, do you?' He spoke in such a low, controlled voice that she had to strain to hear what he said.

'And do you? I've never seen you get your hands dirty repairing your car.'

'I have other talents.' He smiled smugly. 'All our cars are on a maintenance lease, anyway. If you leave it for a couple of weeks, I'll consult with the rest of the Board and see if its feasible for some arrangement to be made for the company to loan you a car . . .'

'No, thank you. I would hate to be under such an obligation. I'll buy my own car the moment I have a garage to put it in.'

Charles shrugged. 'As you wish. I'll arrange for the BMW to be collected. Will tomorrow be soon enough?'

He didn't kiss her goodbye. She didn't go to the door to see him off. She stood rock still by Reginald's desk holding her breath, waiting until she heard his car door slam and the engine throb into life.

She was still fuming over his high-handed manner and the injustice of things when she went upstairs to bed an hour later. She lay there in the darkness trying to reason out how she could shape the future to her own advantage. One thing was sure, she ruminated, she couldn't count on Charles being supportive. He was obviously going to make things as difficult as possible for her.

She wondered how the other two would react when they heard about her plans for the future. Alison would probably look glum, point out the error of her ways and then try and talk her out of making any changes.

She sighed. Alison was as bad as Charles when it came to knowing how other people should organize their lives. She'd been bossy even as a child. Nursing had made her worse because she'd been in a position to make people do as she told them.

Running her own life the way she wanted to was going to be hard work, Margaret decided. She smiled to herself in the darkness. She was quite looking forward to the challenge.

Twelve

The doorbell rang before Margaret was out of bed next morning. Throwing back the bedclothes she grabbed her pink and white quilted dressing gown from its hook behind the bedroom door, and slid her arms into it. Hastily she combed her hair back from her face, and secured it behind her ears with two ornamental combs that she had been wearing the day before, and which were still lying on the dressing table.

For the first time since Reginald had died, she hadn't slept well. The bed had seemed so vast that she had been unable to get comfortable. She couldn't understand it. She and Reginald had always kept to their own sides of the bed yet, even though she'd tucked the bedclothes in tight around her back, she'd felt cold. She'd woken several times with a sense of loss. It was as if something was missing.

The doorbell rang again. She looked at the clock and frowned. It was only half past eight. Who on earth was it at this hour of the morning?

Perhaps it was the postman with something that was too large to go through the letterbox. It might even be Charles, full of remorse and wanting to make amends for being so unhelpful last night.

She didn't think there was much possibility of that. It was much more likely to be the electricity meter reader, or even the gasman, she told herself as she slipped her bare feet into pink fluffy mules and padded down the stairs.

Tentatively she slipped on the safety chain before opening the door a mere couple of inches.

'Good morning! Would you like to see my identity card, madam?'

'Steven!' Her heart thudded with happiness as the dark shape from the other side of the glass panel was revealed. 'Hold on!'

Closing the door she slipped off the chain then opened it back wide and was immediately swept up in a bear hug that squeezed the breath out of her.

'How are you, Mum? Having a lie in? Have I disturbed you? Do you want to go and get dressed while I make some coffee?' The questions showered down on her like confetti.

'Oh, Steven, do put me down,' she gasped. 'Come into the kitchen and I'll make us both a pot of tea.'

'Only if I can have some chocolate biscuits!'

'You are an idiot!'

She lifted her hand and stroked his newly-shaven cheek, breathing in the smell of his aftershave as her fingers outlined the oval profile. He was so very handsome, she thought admiringly.

Such expressive grey eyes, such a beautifully shaped mouth and the most engaging smile she had ever known.

She stretched up and pushed back the springy dark hair that hung over his brow and kissed him. He responded by kissing her cheek.

'It is good to see you, Steven. You must come more often now!'

Tears misted her eyes as she remembered the constant bickering between him and his father. He was so much more overt than Charles, exuding an openness that was both beguiling and disarming, with a boyish grin which could melt the hardest hearts.

It was probably why he was such a successful salesman, and had been made area manager before he was twenty-five. He invariably got his own way but it was done with so much wit and humour that no one, with the exception of Reginald and Charles, ever bore him a grudge.

Even Alison adored him. In her eyes he was still her baby brother. The empathy between the two of them excluded everyone else. She took his side no matter whether he was right or wrong. Margaret suspected it was one of the reasons why Alison, and Steven's wife, Sandra, didn't get on all that well.

Margaret had always tried not to show a preference for any of her children. To her they were equally dear, but in different ways. Yet, with Steven she was conscious of warmth that was beyond description. She felt so very much at ease with him. His confident approach to problems always calmed her fears. If she was feeling despondent, his sophisticated wit would lift her spirits. His visits always left her feeling calmer and happier.

He had always seemed to know instinctively how trying she sometimes found life with his father. Steven's dark brows would lift imperceptibly whenever Reginald made some irritable or deprecating remark, and he would quickly start to talk about other things. Later, discreetly, he would follow her into the kitchen, or out into the garden, so that he could be alone with her.

'Everything all right?'

He wouldn't wait for her to reply but instead would enfold her in a bear hug that was far more reassuring than a thousand words could be.

From now on, she thought happily, there would be no need

for them to hide their affection for each other. She felt his hand under her chin, tilting her face so that he could look directly into her eyes.

'Cry if you want to,' he murmured gently. 'You should, you know. It helps to heal. You were very brave at the funeral, but there's no shame in having a good weep.'

'I don't want to cry,' she pulled back with a tremulous smile.

'Are you sure? It looks to me as if there's tears in your eyes.'

'If there are then they're tears of happiness because you're here.'

'That's alright then.' He grinned, understandingly. 'Now, what are you up to? I hear you've been out and about making plans for a holiday.'

'Who told you that?'

'Ah, I have my spies.' He tapped the side of his nose with one finger. 'Well, is it true, or is it true?'

'I did try to book a holiday yesterday,' she admitted. 'I wanted to go to Cyprus.'

'That sounds extremely enterprising. When are you off, then?'

Margaret shrugged. 'I've no idea.'

'Problems?'

'You could say that. My passport was locked away in your father's bureau and . . .'

'Do you know where the key is?'

'I thought it might be at the office . . .'

'That's easily solved. Phone Charles and tell him to bring it over.'

'I've done that. Charles came over last night. He didn't think that there were any keys at the office. I managed to persuade him to force the lock on the bureau. We found my passport, but it's out of date.'

'That's no problem. It's easy enough to get it renewed. They shouldn't be too busy at this time of the year. You can get the necessary form from the post office. If you have any difficulty in filling it in give me a bell and I'll pop over tonight, and sort it out for you.'

Her face lit up. 'Right! I'll do that. I suppose I'll have to get a new photo taken.' She giggled. 'The one in it is twenty years old. I'd get arrested on suspicion of using a false passport.'

'Mm.' He frowned. 'You'll probably have to go to Maidenhead

to do that. I'm not sure if there's a booth at the railway station, but I am sure there are plenty of places where you can get one taken.'

'I'll be going by train so I'll check if there is. If not, perhaps the travel agent can tell me where I can get a passport photograph done.'

'Why go by train? Why not take the BMW?'

Margaret shook her head. 'I daren't. I'm in Charles's bad books because I was driving it yesterday.'

'Why on earth should he object?'

'It belongs to the firm.'

Steven's eyebrows shot up. 'Really? I never knew that.'

'No, nor did I,' she admitted. 'Not until I tried to swap it for a Mercedes coupe yesterday.'

'You did what!' His roar of laughter made her chuckle.

'Charles was furious. I went to that garage by Maidenhead Bridge and just when I thought I'd done a deal they realized it wasn't registered in my name. The manager phoned Charles, and that was the end of that.'

'Mum, you really are the limit!' He hugged her impulsively. 'Come on, make that pot of tea. We'll take it through into the sitting room.'

'You see to it, darling. I had better slip up and put some clothes on, it *is* getting late . . .'

'Go on then, but don't take too long. I do have to go to work, you know.'

Margaret didn't stop to shower, merely freshened her face, combed her hair, and slipped into the first thing she found in her wardrobe; brown slacks, and a beige sweater.

She was putting on some lipstick when she heard the doorbell ring.

She called out to Steven. 'I'll answer that, I'm just coming down.'

He was there before she reached the top of the stairs. As she heard his exclamation of pleasure, she guessed it was Alison.

'How are you, Mum?'

'Fine! Come on in, you're just in time for a cup of tea . . .'

'And chocolate biscuits,' Steven called from the kitchen. 'Go in and sit down and I'll bring the tray through.'

'Are you quite sure you're alright, Mum?' Alison looked at her mother searchingly. Margaret bristled. 'I've already told you that I'm fine. Did you expect to find that I had disintegrated overnight?' she snapped.

'You're certainly looking better than I've seen you for a long time. But are you alright . . . in yourself, I mean.'

'Never better.'

'I expected to find you in floods of tears, or at any rate depressed,' persisted Alison.

'Well, I'm not.'

'I can see that. Aren't you feeling lonely . . . lost . . . you know . . .?'

Margaret suppressed a smile. 'I'm far too busy planning all the things I've dreamed of doing for years but have never been able to do!'

'You've done your hair differently.'

'Suits her, doesn't it,' chipped in Steven. 'I never did like it pulled back into a pleat. Much too severe. You always used to wear it loose around your face like that.'

'That was years ago, when we were children.' Alison frowned. 'And it was much shorter, in tight curls if I remember.'

'Have you both finished? The reason my hair is like this is because I haven't had time to do it properly as yet. Steven arrived before I was up, and—'

'So you didn't sleep well,' Alison interrupted.

'I slept like a top once I managed to get off. I couldn't get warm,' Margaret admitted reluctantly, caught out by her daughter's probing gaze.

'That's only to be expected, Mum.' Alison's face softened with compassion. 'It's bound to feel different when you're sleeping on your own after sharing a bed for all those years. Perhaps you should change your bed. Get a smaller one.'

'Don't worry, I will. I intend to change everything in the bedroom completely, so a new bed is on the cards.'

Alison looked anxious. 'Now don't go rushing into things, Mum. Don't make changes you'll regret when . . . when things get back to normal.'

'Back to normal! Don't talk rubbish, how can things ever get back to normal,' argued Steven, heatedly.

'Well, I know that. Mum understands what I mean. Once she's stopped grieving . . .'

'I'm not grieving! Do try and understand. All I feel is a sense of relief.'

'Mother!' Alison's grey eyes were suddenly hostile. Her mouth tightened into a prim line that accentuated her high cheekbones and made her face look longer than it was.

'You know what Mum means,' intervened Steven. 'She's had a pretty hard time of it looking after Dad.'

'He couldn't help being ill.'

'No, but he didn't have to make her life a misery as well,' interrupted Steven.

Margaret clamped her hands over her ears. 'Stop it you two. I hate to hear you bickering. Anyway, you're both right in what you say. Your father did give me a hard time. For the past few years, ever since his heart attack, he has been a sick man, but there was nothing he could do about that. The point is that I've had no life of my own at all since he retired. Now I intend to change all that.'

'Mother, you are under stress. Give it time and this feeling will pass and you'll settle down again and—'

'Then I'd better act quickly before it does pass.'

'Good for you, Mum.' Steven rose to his feet and placed his empty cup and saucer down on the table. 'I must be off, I've a living to earn,' he told her, kissing her on the cheek.

'Thank you for popping in.'

'Give me a bell if you want any help with filling in that form for your passport, or if you see a car you like and want me to run an eye over it before you buy it.'

'Thank you, darling. I'll keep in touch.'

'Make sure you don't go shooting off to foreign parts without letting me know, either,' he warned. 'Bye then, I'll see myself out.'

'Car? Foreign holiday?' Alison bridled. 'What on earth is Steven on about?'

'Apparently your father's BMW was a company car and Charles tells me I am not insured to drive it so I'm getting a car of my own,' explained Margaret tersely.

'At your age?'

'What does that mean? I'm fifty-nine. My hair might be going grey but I'm sound in wind and limb and I can still see and hear, so I'm not ready for my grave just yet.'

'Mum, I didn't mean that.' Alison's voice was full of contrition, and her face blotched uncomfortably.

'I'm also planning to take a holiday. Abroad. On my own,' Margaret went on relentlessly.

'You won't enjoy it. You don't speak any foreign language and the hassle of getting through customs, flying, sorting yourself out at the hotel at the other end and all the rest of it, will be too much for you.'

'Alison!'

'I'm right, Mum. You'd be much better off going to Bournemouth. What about that nice hotel that's right on the sea front where you and Dad went each year. The staff there know you and they'd look after you and none of us would have to worry . . .'

'So that's what all this sudden concern is about? You don't want to have to worry about me. Well, let me assure you there's not the slightest reason why you should. I am quite able to fend for myself.'

'Mum, you haven't been outside the village unless Dad was with you for the past five years. You haven't even been up to London, and that's only twenty-five miles away. Things have changed, Mum. The pace of life has increased. It's a jungle out there. You'll be conned silly.'

'Stop treating me as if I were a child.'

'Stop behaving like one, then. Take a look at yourself; dressed in slacks and a sweater and your hair hanging down your back like a teenager. You haven't even gone into mourning!'

They regarded each other like sparring partners. Alison's grey eyes were dark with a mixture of concern and anger.

Margaret forced herself to remain calm. She had no intention of being browbeaten into sitting back and taking things easy for the rest of her days. Alison might think she was too old for change, but she intended to prove differently, not by arguing but with action.

'Yes, Alison, I intend to change my entire lifestyle,' she went on in a firm voice that brooked no argument. 'If I have to wait for my new car and my holiday then I'll get on with the other thing I have in mind.'

Alison frowned. 'What is that?'

'I intend to redecorate this house from top to bottom. Change it completely. I shall start with our bedroom. Everything out and replaced by all new furniture; absolutely everything new.'

'Mum, you can't possibly do that! Dad will turn in his grave.'

'Spin more likely when I've finished making changes,' Margaret pronounced.

'You've never done any decorating in your life before,' Alison pointed out. 'It's hard work, you know.'

'I don't intend wielding a paint brush or hanging wallpaper or anything like that,' Margaret assured her. 'I intend to call in professional help.'

'That will cost the earth! What's more, they will still need some sort of guidance on what changes you intend to make.'

'Oh, I'll give them precise instructions. I know exactly what I want done.'

'Be careful, Mum. Very modern surroundings may clash with your furniture.'

'I'm getting rid of all the heavy old pieces that have been here ever since the day we married. I intend not only to redecorate but to refurnish and to have new carpets and curtains as well.'

'That's a mammoth task; you'll never be able to do it on your own.'

'I don't intend to even try. I shall hire an interior designer.'

Alison shook her head and looked nonplussed. 'I really don't know what to say. Do be careful though; there are some sharks about, you know.'

'You mean they may try to take advantage of me because I am so old?'

'No, no, of course I didn't mean that but there are so many people claiming to be professionals . . .' Alison's voice trailed away as though she wasn't at all sure what she was talking about.

'Don't worry, there are some very knowledgeable interior designers; some who have excellent reputations, like the chap Jan hired when she decided to refurbish her flat and he certainly did a first-class job.'

Thirteen

'I called in at Willow House to see my mother today, Mark.'

'You did! Good! How was she?'

'I'm not sure.'

Mark looked at his wife sharply. Her voice registered such deep bewilderment that he felt professional concern.

'Delayed shock?'

'I . . . I don't think so.'

He noted the uncertainty was still there. She sounded baffled rather than upset.

'What seemed to be amiss?' He tried to keep his voice casual although mentally he was rapidly diagnosing cause and effect. By his estimation, Margaret had behaved far too rationally at the funeral. There had been no tears and hardly any sign of emotion at all. It had been the same day Reginald had died, he recalled. She had neither broken down and cried, nor showed any other sign of distress.

It had surprised him. They'd been married a long time. Of course, Reginald had been a lot older than Margaret, and since his heart attack a few years back their lifestyle had changed dramatically.

At the time he'd been surprised that Reginald had been prepared not only to take early retirement but also to give up his golf and his political interests and prepared to take things so easy.

He might have been happy enough to relax in his armchair with his newspaper or a book, watch television and have a couple of weeks at Bournemouth once a year, but what about Margaret? Had she resented not being able to maintain the social life she'd grown accustomed to, with visits to the theatre and various other nights out that helped to put the zest into everyday living?

She was a good-looking woman and still had a lot of life to live, reflected Mark.

He recalled their first meeting. He'd been twenty so she must have been about forty, a slender, blue-eyed blonde with a warm, friendly smile that had set him at ease immediately.

Alison had the same facial bone structure as her mother but that was where the resemblance ended. Alison's eyes were grey, she was shorter and more buxom and her hair was dark brown.

Alison's younger brother took after their mother in looks and disposition, but Alison was more like her father in temperament. She was argumentative and had his pragmatic approach to life.

After they had lost their second child in a cot death her personality had changed completely. She had become moody and despondent. He knew she blamed him for what had happened because he had been looking after Christopher and the baby, so that she could have a night out. Nothing would convince her that it could have happened anyway, even if she had been at home.

As soon as Christopher started school he had suggested she might like to return to work on a part-time basis. She had always enjoyed nursing, and he hoped that a few hours outside the home each day might alleviate her recurring bouts of depression, which had become worse after her father's heart attack.

He had been concerned at how distressed Alison had been when her father died. He had been dreading the funeral in case she broke down. She assured him she wouldn't. She intended to put on a brave face on things for her mother's sake. Mark wasn't at all sure that such fortitude was necessary. Margaret's apparent lack of grief had puzzled him.

'She was so remarkably controlled at the funeral, it's only natural that she should be mourning now,' he murmured gently as Alison remained silent.

'Mourning! She's not mourning,' Alison said caustically, her mouth tightening into a thin hard line. 'Quite the opposite, in fact.'

'What do you mean?'

'Well, you know all about the car incident and the idea of going away on a package holiday, well, that's nothing compared with her latest caper.'

'Go on.'

'She's going to have the entire house redecorated from top to bottom, starting with the bedroom that she shared with Dad. She's getting rid of all that beautiful walnut furniture, and replacing it with modern built-in wardrobes. Its enough to make Dad turn in his grave!'

'Perhaps it's her way of mourning,' he said helplessly.

'Or of making a fresh start! Next thing we know she'll be getting married again.'

'I suppose that's possible. She's not all that old, you know.'

'What are you talking about?' Alison's grey eyes flashed angrily. 'Dad was in his late seventies!'

'Yes, I know that, but he was almost twenty years older than your mother.'

Alison stared at him angrily. 'That's still no reason for desecrating his memory.'

'Don't be ridiculous. Redecorating their bedroom isn't violating anything. Making a complete break with the past might be her way of dealing with her grief . . .'

'Grief? What the hell are you on about? You're not listening to a word I'm saying. She hasn't shed a tear or shown the slightest remorse. I'm beginning to think she's actually glad he's dead.'

Mark shrugged non-committally. 'She might well be relieved. The last few years have been pretty gruelling for her. It can't have been easy for a woman of her age to live under such enforced restrictions. He can't have been an easy man to nurse.'

'You would take her part. She's always been able to twist you round her little finger,' Alison snapped, contemptuously. 'She's only had to turn those blue eyes of hers on you to sweet talk you into doing anything she wants.'

Mark reddened. 'Don't talk rubbish.'

'It's true.' Alison's voice broke and suddenly she was in floods of tears.

'Oh, come on. Don't take on so.' Mark gathered her into his arms, rocking her as if she was a small child, stroking her dark hair, in a desperate attempt to calm her.

She raised her face to his, her eyes drowned in tears. 'Nobody seems to care,' she gulped. 'Charles is too busy playing managing director in the office, Steven is too wrapped up in his own career to notice what's happening, and Mum is trying to wipe out all memory of Dad just as fast as she can.'

'No, no. It's not like that at all,' protested Mark. 'They all care but they're so busy getting on with their own lives it doesn't show. Don't judge your mother too harshly. Ever since your father had his heart attack five years ago she's known he could die at any time. She's already done her grieving. It's natural that she feels a sense of relief. She probably thinks it's high time she got on with her own life.'

Mark ignored the pained look Alison gave him. It was the truth as he saw it and the sooner Alison accepted the fact that her mother was entitled to lead her own life the better.

Anyway, it was early days. When the euphoria of being free from the responsibility of having to nurse a sick husband had passed, Margaret still might succumb to a feeling of desolation or despair.

Contrary to what Alison thought, he didn't regard anything Margaret had done so far as sinister. The fact that she wanted to change the car, or was planning a holiday, or that she intended reorganizing and redecorating her home was merely a positive expression that she intended on putting her life into gear again.

He knew it was useless trying to convince Alison of this. She was determined to interpret her mother's actions as deliberate attempts to obliterate all traces of her father.

It was quite extraordinary, Mark reflected, how differently Alison and her two brothers were taking their father's death.

Alison had phoned them both during the course of the evening to tell them about her mother's plans for Willow House. Charles had been furious, especially when he heard that she intended to call in Jason Parker to advise her and oversee the proposed transformation.

'The man's a complete charlatan who takes advantage of vulnerable women,' he'd exploded angrily.

'I knew it!' Alison had been overjoyed by his reaction, and triumphantly relayed Charles's opinion to Mark. He had demanded further explanation.

'Tell Mark he latches on to wealthy widows and rich, pampered wives, and charges them an exorbitant fee for his services. Then he inveigles them into introducing him to their friends.'

'Ask him if the man's work is any good?'

'I don't need to. Mum said he did Jan's place up and it was absolutely magnificent.'

'If Jan Porter introduced him to Mother then it will probably cost the earth,' commented Charles. 'He probably thinks Mum's loaded.'

'As long as your mother is getting pleasure from it, does the money side matter?' protested Mark.

'Of course it does,' Alison snapped.

Charles agreed with her. 'It most certainly does matter. Father left his money in trust. She's spending our inheritance. Having a holiday is one thing, and I can even go along with her buying a car but squandering capital on unnecessary changes is something else. There's very little wrong with the house. A spot of decorating may be necessary to freshen the place up but to completely refurbish the main bedroom is something else. And once that's completed, heaven alone knows what else this Jason Parker will talk her into having done.'

Charles and Alison had analysed the matter for a further twenty minutes, Charles expressing objections in the strongest possible terms until even Alison had felt compelled to take her mother's side.

As soon as Charles hung up, Alison dialled Steven's number. His opinion that if their mother felt the need of change, whether it was in the home, or in the pattern of her life, then he was in full agreement, swung Alison back on to the defensive.

'Don't you care that she's trying to obliterate all the memories we have?' she yelled down the phone.

Steven laughed derisively. 'Stop being so theatrical,' he teased. 'Why is there this sudden change of heart from you, anyway? When Dad was alive you were the one who was always criticizing him and complaining about his moods.'

'I didn't mean it unkindly.'

'No, you were being honest because you could see that the more Mum did for him the more difficult he became.'

'He was a sick man.'

'Yes, and he was determined to make Mum and the rest of us suffer along with him!'

'That's cruel!'

'It's the truth and you know it. You were always his pet, Alison. He had a soft spot for you. Ever since you were a toddler you could get away with things neither Charles nor I dare attempt. Yet, despite this, you left home and married Mark the moment you were legally old enough to do so, didn't you?'

'That had nothing to do with Dad.'

'Who are you kidding?'

'Well, you left home too.'

'I know, and I admit that I did it because I was fed up of having him breathing down my neck all the time and checking up on where I'd been, or who I'd been with.'

'I really don't know what all this has to do with what Mum is doing,' Alison told him huffily.

'Everything. I'm trying to make you realize that there is nothing sinister about her behaviour. She's simply enjoying her freedom and doing exactly what she wants to do, so stop criticizing her.'

Alison tried another tack. 'Charles is worried.'

'Is he?' Steven sounded disinterested.

'He says she's squandering our inheritance.'

'What the hell does he mean by that?'

'Dad left his money in trust for her lifetime and then it comes to us, doesn't it?'

Steven's guffaw of laughter made Alison stiffen.

'Trust Charles to be thinking about the pennies. What the devil is he worrying about?'

'Like I said, our future inheritance.'

'Look, let's get things straight. Charles inveigled Dad into letting him take over the business years ago and he's probably making a bomb out of it. Sitting on top of a gold mine, I'd say.'

'You can never have too much money,' retorted Alison, balefully. She sensed Steven was laughing at her and she felt piqued.

'I've got all I need at the moment and so have you,' remonstrated Steven firmly. 'If you want more, work for it.'

'I do!' Alison said sharply. 'And nursing is hard graft, I can tell you. It's not like modelling where all you have to do is sit around and look glamorous.'

'Tell Sandra that. She'll soon put you right. Posing for four or five hours at a stretch under overhead lights can be pretty gruelling.'

'She's got a good memory, has she? Must be at least five years since she faced the cameras.'

'I can see she hasn't been keeping you up to date.'

'You don't mean she's gone back to work? Who's looking after

Matthew and Hannah? They're still only babies. They shouldn't be farmed out—'

'Hold it!' Steven cut short her tirade. 'You can see now what I mean about being able to do what you want without people checking up on you or interfering.'

'I'm not interfering.'

He chuckled. 'You would, though, if you were given half a chance.'

'I'm just concerned about them. They're so young to be left with—'

'With Sandra's mother? I'm sure she takes good care of them. She returns them in perfect order,' he added mockingly.

'Well, I didn't know she was leaving them with her mother, did I?'

'So easy to jump to the wrong conclusions, isn't it, Alison? I rather think that's what you're doing with Mother. You're condemning her for making changes without stopping to think why she might be making them.'

'Anyway,' he added as she made no reply and the silence became protracted, 'if you don't believe me, then why don't you ask her outright.'

'She wouldn't tell me the truth.'

'I think you're wrong there. She's never been one to hide her reasons for doing anything.'

'Come off it, Steven! For years now she hasn't voiced an idea, or expressed an opinion,' retorted Alison sourly.

'Not to you, perhaps because she knows you would have gone straight back to Dad and told him what she'd said. She has to me, though.'

'Only to you?' she asked, mockingly. 'Well, you always were her favourite.'

'No, she loved each of us equally but I was the only one who bothered to listen and—'

Alison slammed down the receiver at her end, abruptly cutting short their call.

Angry and frustrated she turned her anger on Mark, blaming him for suggesting she should ring Charles and Steven in the first place.

It had been the same ever since she could remember, Charles

had always been cold and supercilious, Steven teasing and self-opinionated.

She stormed off to bed feeling bitter and upset, her throat tight. She was sure that she wouldn't be able to sleep because her head was pounding. The only person who had ever understood her, she thought in frustrated rage, had been her father, and now he was dead. No one else, not her mother nor either of her brothers, seemed to be in the least bit concerned.

Fourteen

Frowning, Jan Porter replaced the receiver. She felt both mystified and annoyed. It was the third time she had phoned Jason Parker at his studio only to be told by one of his staff that he was not available. Again she had left a message for him to return her call and at the same time pointed out in no uncertain terms that she had left the same message twice before and he had not done so.

It was her sixtieth birthday in three weeks' time, on the nineteenth of May and it was imperative that Jason contacted her immediately. She had invited twenty of her friends to a dinner party and she was relying on him to design the room setting and table presentation. She had no ideas whatsoever and she was relying on him to come up with something spectacular.

She walked across her elegant sitting room, opened the patio doors and stepped out on to the white iron balcony.

It was a beautiful spring morning. She looked down at the Thames as it flowed by on the other side of the roadway, iridescently streaked like molten metal in the glinting sunlight. Ducks and moorhens squabbled and dodged each other, stately white swans moved in graceful circles, skilfully avoiding the leisure craft and pleasure boats that chugged and chuffed up and down the river.

Jan sat down on one of the white wrought-iron chairs. It was an idyllic scene and from the balcony quite peaceful. She was far enough away not to be disturbed by the pounding of the engines as the boats queued up to go through Boulter's Lock, or the raucous squawks of wildlife.

Occasionally there were excited outbursts from children as they were led over the humpbacked bridge into the gardens on the other side of the river, or into the pleasure park a little further down the road in the opposite direction.

If Jason didn't contact her in plenty of time to devise a spectacular setting for her dinner party then perhaps she'd do something completely different this year, she mused. After all, sixty was a milestone and she intended to mark it in style.

It didn't bear thinking about.

Once you'd turned sixty you began to slow down. Bones became stiff, joints ached and rheumatism and all the other age-related problems started.

Even your appearance began to go downhill. Wrinkles, bags under the eyes, indigestion, sagging muscles, flaccid skin, middle-aged spread; they all became firmly established when you reached sixty.

You started to have trouble with your teeth and your eyesight, and your hearing began to fail. Worst of all was the risk of a heart attack. Look at Margaret's husband, she thought gloomily. He'd been in his sixties when he'd had his heart attack. True, it had been his late sixties but they did say women were prone to attacks earlier than men.

The thought that she might have to cut back on her many activities, or even give up golf, badminton and the other sports she indulged in from time to time, sent a shudder through Jan. Sixty, she decided was certainly a major milestone. One you either met head on, or shied away from.

She jumped up from her chair, and went back inside. She'd meet it head on, of course. She hadn't been born under the sign of a Taurus for nothing. She prided herself on the fact that she never retreated from any problem. She preferred to act and not only overcome obstacles but turn them to her advantage. Which was what she had done when her marriage had gone sour.

She hadn't wasted time or energy trying to make the best of things or affecting reconciliation as Alan had begged her to do. Instead she had sued him for divorce on grounds of adultery. She'd hired the sharpest solicitor she could find, and he'd made quite sure the alimony she received would keep her in luxury for the rest of her life.

Her bout of introspection brought home to her how difficult things must be at this moment for Margaret. Perhaps she ought to pop over to Cookham, and pay her a visit; a quick coffee, and a chat.

She changed her velvet mules for casual white slip-ons that looked right with her navy linen trousers, and a white silk open-necked blouse.

Her face was already immaculately made up but she added a touch of deep blue eye shadow and sprayed perfume on to her wrists and the base of her throat. Picking up her white shoulder bag, checking that her car keys and sunglasses were inside, she went down to the basement car park to collect her Turbo sports car.

The three miles drive along the river road, through Cookham village, and across the Moor to Cookham Dean gave her time to think about Margaret.

She remembered her own reaction after her divorce. Revenge had been sweet and she had been overwhelmingly relieved to know that she would never have to tolerate Alan's unfaithfulness ever again. What she hadn't bargained for though was the period of abysmal loneliness and the sense of desolation that had followed.

The feeling had gradually passed because she'd pulled herself together and filled her life with other activities but, at the time, she had been glad of almost anyone's company to fill the vacuum.

An open-top sports car was already parked in the driveway of Willow House. As she pulled in behind it, Jan thought it was vaguely familiar but it wasn't until she had already rung the doorbell that she realized it was Jason Parker's car and a small ball of anger knotted inside her. This was why she found it impossible to contact him; he was here, at Willow House visiting Margaret.

I'm wasting my time coming here, Jan thought crossly. It seems Margaret isn't lonely or in the depths of despair after all.

She was still frowning when Margaret opened the door.

'Jan! How lovely to see you. Come on in. I was just about to make some coffee. Jason Parker's here.' Her blue eyes sparkled, her skin glowed, her smile was radiant, and she looked fresh, and feminine, in a cornflower blue dress trimmed with white.

She certainly didn't look like a grieving widow in need of

cheering up, thought Jan belligerently as she noticed how the finely pleated skirt swirled around Margaret's shapely legs as she walked, drawing attention to her high-heeled white sandals.

'I thought that was Jason's car outside. I've been trying to get hold of him for days.'

'Oh dear! I'm afraid I've been monopolizing him,' Margaret admitted with an apologetic smile. 'Go on into the sitting room. He's in there. I'll make the coffee while you have your little chat.'

Ruffled by her blandishments, Jan did as she was told. She stopped short in the doorway, eyebrows raised in astonishment. The floor was covered with sketches and plans, swatches of carpet, snippets of curtain material and several wallpaper pattern books propped open.

Sitting tailor fashion in the midst was Jason.

'What's going on?'

At the sound of her voice, Jason raised his head, grinned, and shrugged, widening his amber eyes and arching his brows expressively.

He was wearing a black tracksuit that hugged his firm body like a second skin. The top, she noticed, was unbuttoned halfway down his chest and his gleaming suntanned skin colour matched the gold piping and decorative embellishments.

He looked like some virile Grecian god and Jan found herself studying him as she had never done before.

She was shocked to realize that because she had discovered his latent talents and had helped to set him on the path to what was now such a successful career, she regarded him almost as her property. She suddenly felt very possessive about him and almost wished she had not introduced him to Margaret.

She had long ago decided that he was probably hermaphroditic, and that was why he had such phenomenal artistic ability and why he was able to conceive such exotic schemes.

His design skills were very masculine with strong, bold, unclut-tered lines. He combined these with a sensitive feminine flair when it came to selecting colours and textures, and choosing and blending fabrics, so that the resultant effect was always exquisite.

He never repeated a treatment; each was so beautifully suited to its location that you knew instinctively that it would not be right in any other setting. He was inordinately skilled at balancing the finished effect of a room with the personality of the owner, a fact that Jan always enthused about when recommending his work to anyone.

In the past, she had felt a sense of satisfaction when her friends were overjoyed by what he had achieved in their homes. Now, sensing the deeper affinity that existed between him and Margaret, she felt a stab of unease, and was shocked that it might be jealousy on her part.

Fifteen

Jealousy? The idea astounded Jan Porter. It was laughable. Why on earth should she be jealous? He was far too effeminate for her taste. Although she admired his style, his smooth, hairless head had always made her inwardly cringe. Even though she had been the one to give him the gold medallion that he always wore around his neck, she hated his jewelled rings, gold bracelet, and the diamond stud he wore in his left ear.

Disturbed by her conflicting thoughts and reactions, she vented her feeling of confusion on Jason. 'How on earth do you expect to make a success of your business if you hide yourself away here,' she scowled.

'Jan!' With lithe animal suppleness he unwound himself from his cross-legged position and stood up. Taking both her hands in his he regarded her at arms length. 'You look exquisite!' he breathed, looking her up and down and giving an insubstantial sigh.

Tetchily, she pulled her hands free. 'You can't win me round that easily. I've been trying to contact you for three days now; doesn't your office ever pass on messages?'

'Of course they do. It's only minutes since I tried to phone you.'

'From here?'

'Of course. They knew where to contact me.' He waved his arm expansively. 'Thanks to you, my dearest Jan, I have this

tremendously exciting project. Margaret has entrusted me with
the restoration of her entire home! Can you imagine it?'

'What's so wonderful about that? I let you do my entire flat,
didn't I?'

'True, and I enjoyed every moment and I know you have been
delighted with the result.'

'It's all right. Slightly passé now. I'm thinking of having it done
over again.'

'What a splendid idea! The moment this is completed I will
create something absolutely unique, something very special for you.'

'I fancy a complete change. I was thinking of calling in a
London consultant.'

She saw him wince, and knew she had hit below the belt. She
felt contrite but before she could say anything to soften the blow
Margaret came in with a loaded tray and Jason sprang to his feet
to help her.

Their hands touched briefly as he took the tray from her and
Jan's resentment mounted as she observed the look that flashed
between them.

How dare Margaret impinge on their friendship like this? She
wished she had never made contact with her when Reginald had
died, but it had seemed such a good idea at the time.

She'd missed Margaret over the years since they'd stopped
meeting up. Thelma and Brenda were good company but, although
only a few years older, so much more set in their ways. Compared
to them, Margaret's company had seemed a refreshing change.

It was probably because she and Margaret were nearer to each
other both in age and temperament. Even a couple of years on
the wrong side of sixty seemed to make a considerable difference
to the way people acted and looked at life.

In the last couple of years, Thelma had become a hypochondriac
and could be quite a bore about her health. And when she wasn't
complaining about her aches and pains then she was arguing about
some minor issue that she'd met up with in her role as a local
councillor. All very laudable, of course, but Jan often found it tedious.

Brenda was even worse. With her it was either her grandchildren or her awful dog. Why was it that small dogs like Brenda's
Pekinese yapped so much, Jan wondered. Its shrill bark was ear
piercing and Brenda insisted on taking it everywhere with her.

Tucked under her arm it wasn't a lot of trouble but Jan hated it when Brenda brought it to the flat. It padded its way all over her cream leather settee and sniffed at every corner and cushion until she felt like screaming. So far it hadn't disgraced itself but Jan was quite sure it would do so one of these days.

She had been more than ready to help Margaret get over her loss by picking up the threads of their friendship again, but not to this extent.

'This is quite like old times,' smiled Margaret, as she handed round the coffee and proffered a plate of biscuits to Jan and Jason. 'Remember how we used to take it in turns to have coffee mornings, Jan? I'm really looking forward to coming along to them again.'

'Mm!' Jan murmured and then took a bite of her shortcake biscuit and munched it contemplatively. 'That would be nice but by the look of it you are going to be far too busy decorating to contemplate any entertaining.'

'It won't take all that long. Perhaps when it's finished I ought to throw a party and invite everyone to come here and then—'

'Parties! Isn't that what you wanted to see me about, Jan?' Jason interrupted. 'Your birthday party; it's only a few days away.'

'Fancy you remembering when you have so much work in hand!'

'How could I forget? It's an annual event!' He laughed at his own joke. 'I've enjoyed designing something different each year. This year is extra special, isn't it?'

'If being sixty is special, then I suppose it is.'

'Of course it's special. Think of all the things that have happened since you were born. Since the end of the war there's been a revolution in ideas . . .'

'I don't need a history lesson.'

Margaret shot a quick glance at Jan, wondering why she was being so caustic. She didn't think Jason's comments had called for quite such a biting response.

'This year we must make it something really outstanding,' enthused Jason. 'Have you anything special in mind?'

'Yes.' She regarded him coolly. 'A complete break with tradition.'

'Oh?' He looked puzzled.

'I'm having it on the river. Hiring a boat. I'm engaging a

firm of caterers . . . and a band . . . and an entertainer.' As she improvised haphazardly she saw his amber eyes darken in shocked surprise.

'Great! Sounds a wonderful idea. You do want me to organize it for you?' he asked cautiously.

'There's no need. That's why I've been trying so hard to contact you, I simply wanted to let you know that everything is in hand because you usually contact me weeks in advance and this year you haven't done so.'

He looked crestfallen. 'But I always stage your birthday party, Jan. In fact, this year, because it is a very special birthday, I had some wonderful ideas. Surely you didn't think I would forget about it?'

'How could you possibly do that when it's always proved to be so lucrative for you?' capped Jan waspishly.

They're like two cats fighting, Margaret thought uneasily. She felt she ought to say something to try and restore peace, but was afraid that they might both vent their spite on her if she interfered.

'I'll go and refill this,' she murmured, picking up the coffee pot and retreating to the kitchen.

She found the gentle bubbling sound as the coffee perked soothing. From the sitting room came the rise and fall of voices, as though they were still arguing.

Margaret wondered if it was the thought of being sixty that was putting Jan in such a bad mood. It was a milestone, of course. But then, so were most birthdays. The only consolation was that everyone else was getting older at the same time. She was only a few months off her own sixtieth birthday. Brenda and Thelma had both already passed that momentous milestone.

She wondered how old Jason was. It was hard to tell. The fact that he was completely bald didn't mean a thing. She'd never known anyone without a hair on his or her head before. She knew some men even shaved their heads as a fashion statement so in their case being bald had nothing to do with their age.

Jason didn't look old. His face was unlined and he was as supple as a ballet dancer. Even his hands, with their long, sensitive fingers, were extremely youthful.

You could tell so much about a person from their hands. They were the first to show signs of age. Discolourations, raised veins, enlarged joints, brittle nails and crêpey skin were all tell-tale signs. Jason's were as soft as a woman's and fastidiously manicured.

She was still thinking about Jason when Jan burst into the kitchen like a ship in full sail. Her mouth was set in a tight line and her eyes were dark and stormy.

'I haven't time to wait for a second coffee,' she snapped.

'It's ready. I was on the point of bringing it through.'

'Not for me. Jason could probably do with another cup though. He needs strong black coffee or something to calm him down.'

Margaret bit her lip, not sure whether to commiserate, or not. It was Jason she felt sorry for; he had been the one to take the brunt of Jan's spleen.

'You'd better take the coffee on through. I'll see myself out,' Jan told her brusquely. 'I'll phone to let you know the time, and place, where I will be holding my birthday party,' she called back over her shoulder as she made for the door.

Sixteen

Jan's birthday party on board the pleasure-steamer *Castle Gold* was an enormous success. When they set off upstream from Boulter's Lock at seven o'clock, it was a perfect May evening. The sun was still high in an almost cloudless sky, and there was a soft, balmy breeze coming off the river.

Jan and her group of friends lounged or sauntered on the top deck as they steamed by the hanging gardens of Cliveden, past the weir and the Ferry Hotel at Cookham, and then on towards Marlow.

By the time the *Castle Gold* had negotiated several more locks, reached Henley and turned round to go back to Maidenhead, the sun had sunk below the horizon, a fiery ball that left the late evening sky bathed in blood.

Fortified by champagne and the mouth-watering buffet, most of the guests were now completely relaxed and thoroughly enjoying themselves.

Margaret was exhausted after dancing with Jason to the strains of the six-piece band that had joined the boat at Marlow. They had taken refuge in a quiet alcove and were content to sit and watch the others dancing while they recovered their breath.

'I find it hard to believe that Charles is actually your son,' murmured Jason, as Charles and Helen glided by in each other's arms. 'You look much too young to be the mother of such a grown man!'

Margaret smiled non-committally. She had to admit that Charles did look mature. An exact replica of how Reginald had looked when they'd first been married. Helen's black silk trouser suit, with its flared bottoms, was so reminiscent of the early seventies that, watching them dancing together, Margaret felt transported back in time by elusive, half-recalled memories.

Reginald had been much more extrovert than Charles. He'd had a presence that commanded attention, a more arrogant manner, a boldness that broke down barriers. Women were attracted to him, even when he was being chauvinistic. He'd been an exciting companion and a wonderful lover. She pushed away the memories that reminded her of how crazily in love with him she had once been.

'I'm almost the same age as Jan.' She stopped, knowing that Jason wasn't listening. Although he was looking directly at her his amber eyes had a dreamy, faraway quality. He reminded her of a great golden tiger . . . a tiger that was about to pounce.

'Margaret, I think I'm falling in love with you.'

His words struck her completely dumb. She wondered if she had drunk too much champagne. The cacophony of sound as the band played on, glasses clinked, cutlery chinked against china, and people laughed and talked as they danced, was all drowned out by the reverberations of Jason's words inside her head.

Any moment now, she told herself, she would wake up, find herself in splendid isolation in her newly decorated bedroom and know she had been dreaming. Then she would pad downstairs to her brand new ultra-modern kitchen and make herself a cup of tea. After that she would take a shower in her completely refurbished bathroom with its sunken bath and gold-plated taps.

She was conscious that Jason had moved close, that his arm was encircling her waist and pulling her towards him. She stiffened as she felt the warmth of his body emanating through his white silk shirt.

Until that moment she had felt so carefree. Jason's declaration had brought her back to the present with a jolt. She had been a widow for only six weeks. It was much too soon to be starting a new relationship. Even more to the point, Jason must be so much younger than her that it would cause a terrible scandal. Jan would be absolutely furious, she thought guiltily. She has already showed her displeasure because she thinks I am monopolizing him.

'Margaret,' his voice was honeyed and persuasive, 'admit that you feel the same way.'

'Do I?' She felt her pulse quicken.

'Of course you do! You're simply afraid of what other people will think.'

Startled, Margaret half turned, bracing herself to look at him. 'You're reading my mind,' she gasped.

'Which only proves how close we are to each other!' he persisted, his voice husky with emotion.

She shook her head feeling uncomfortable with her thoughts.

'I want to share my life with you,' persisted Jason. 'I want to be with you morning, noon and night. Especially at night! To be able to sleep with you in my arms, to find your face on the pillow at my side when I open my eyes in the morning, to spend every hour of the day—'

She laughed shakily. 'Your business would soon suffer if you did that—'

'No, I'd work twice as hard so that I could give you everything your heart desired,' he promised. Taking one of her hands he raised it to his lips, sensuously kissing the tip of each finger.

A radiance, an inner glow seemed to flow from him, so intense that it felt as if it was scorching her, melting her resistance. She pulled away from him, clenching her hands into tight fists. She felt so exhilarated that she didn't know what to say or how to handle the situation.

It felt awesome to know that she could invoke such intense feelings in another person. She was sceptical, though, as to whether it was love that Jason felt for her. She didn't love him. Margaret was quite certain of that. She wasn't even sure that she was capable of loving anyone ever again, other than her children and grandchildren.

Looking back, she wondered if she had ever loved Reginald. She suspected that what she had felt for him had been a teenage crush for her boss. A challenge because, not only was he so much older than her, but he was her boss and because of that she had thought him to be quite unattainable.

By marrying so young she had never had a chance to grow up and find out what life was all about. She'd moved from college to marriage almost overnight.

There had been no experience of living away from home, going on holiday with girlfriends, or even sharing a flat with them. Nor had there been any opportunity to date boys of her own age and discover by trial and error what falling in love was all about.

Her parents should have put their foot down. She'd been barely nineteen. They should have made her wait at least a year even though Reginald had appeared to be so eminently suitable. He was tall, good-looking, smartly dressed, well spoken, and so very confident and sure of himself. He had offered security because he had his own business. In fact, he was a very eligible bachelor indeed! They couldn't have found a more suitable husband for her if they'd tried to pick one themselves.

It had been exciting at the time. Reginald had treated her like a princess, proudly showing her off to his friends and business associates like some prized asset.

He'd provided her with the sort of lifestyle most women only dream about; one that certainly wouldn't have been possible if she'd married someone of her own generation.

When they were first married they dined out, or partied, three or four times a week. Frequently, it was an important local social function or business event and he insisted that she had all the right clothes so that she would outshine all the other wives.

It hadn't been difficult, she reflected wryly, since she was twenty years younger than most of them. She hadn't objected, though, when he sent her along to have her hair done, or to shop for a new outfit, even though her wardrobe was already at bursting point.

Reginald's business was thriving; money was plentiful. He'd

inherited Willow House so there was no question that they would live anywhere else. Not that she had wanted to because Willow House was a dream and so enchantingly different from the conventional modern house where she'd grown up.

He'd given her a generous housekeeping allowance and insisted that she should have help both in the house and in the garden. Even so, three children in less than four years, combined with a very hectic social life, had taken its toll and drained her energy. By the time Steven, their youngest, had reached five and was ready to attend day school, she had felt middle-aged even though she was still under thirty.

Reginald lost patience with her when she sometimes opted out of more and more social occasions, leaving him to go on his own.

For the sake of the children they had still holidayed together as a family. Once the children were older, though, they had abandoned holidays altogether. He had bought her a car instead, and they had led almost separate lives. She had her women friends and her own interests. He had his club, local politics and played golf more and more, not only at the weekends but evenings as well in the summer.

She had to admit, her lifestyle had been tolerable. As long as she was there when he came home he wasn't in the least interested how she spent her time. It was an enviable way of life in a prosaic sort of way, until the day Reginald had his heart attack.

Overnight, he had changed from being a self-satisfied, slightly pompous, highly successful businessman, with a recognized standing in local society, into a recluse who soon became an irritable, overbearing and demanding grouch.

What was so intolerable was that he had expected her to abandon her own social life and be his constant companion twenty-four hours a day. That, more than anything else, had extinguished what small spark of affection she had still felt for him.

Her sexual feelings for him had died soon after Steven had been born. Although they shared the same double bed there was no real passion in their love-making. She endured it out of habit. It was more a sense of duty, a kind of payment for the many luxuries he provided.

To all outward appearances they enjoyed a full life, and were admirably suited to each other. Age had barely made any difference to Reginald's frenzied social round. She'd become accustomed to being wined and dined, three or four times a week.

Few of the people they met on these occasions were close friends. Many of them were extremely boring and she tolerated them out of a sense of habit and duty. She knew them all so well that they were like an extended family. She felt confident in their company, although not as much at ease as she was with the three women who were her own close friends.

Her friendship with Jan, Thelma and Brenda was far more intimate and confined mostly to coffee mornings, shopping sprees and similar leisure activities. Only very occasionally would one or the other of them be involved in one of the political or social evenings that she attended with Reginald.

She had felt amused when, following his heart attack, Reginald had stated he intended to reprogramme his lifestyle, declaring he needed to conserve his energy. If he was giving up work then there was no need to continue with the social round he had previously supported. He resigned from local affairs and from the golf club. From now on he wanted a quieter, more private life, and he intended to spend the rest of his days in his own home.

She had been inordinately relieved when Reginald stated that he considered sex much too strenuous for a man in his condition. She had longed to suggest that they have separate beds, but she felt it would be prudent to wait a while before suggesting this.

During the early days of his illness, when it was imperative that he stayed in bed, he was restless unless she was there beside him, holding his hand and talking to him. It had been so touching that, for a short while, it almost rekindled the romantic feelings she'd had for him when she'd been eighteen.

His changed outlook on life, his pernicious manner, and constant demands for attention because he resented being ill, soon dispelled the illusion.

She withdrew into her own protective shell, creating an invisible barrier between herself and Reginald and the rest of the world. Now she had no immediate desire to change the situation.

She liked Jason as a friend, but she didn't want a deeper involvement with him, or with anyone.

She didn't want to hurt his feelings so how could she make

him understand that she wasn't ready to sacrifice her newly found freedom. It was so wonderful to be able to come and go as she chose, not to have to account for her actions, or to be at anyone else's beck and call.

Following his heart attack Reginald had needed so much nursing, had been so demanding, that sometimes she had felt like a servant. His meals had to be ready at set times, morning coffee and after-noon tea, served on the dot. The clock had ruled even the time they got up in the morning and went to bed in the evening.

His routine had been far more stringent than when he had been at work. The only difference had been that she was the one at his beck and call instead of his secretary or some other employee.

She didn't think life with Jason would be anything like that but how could she possibly know until it was too late to do anything about it? No, she decided, she had just escaped one trap, and she didn't want to jump straight back into another.

With his uncanny instinct for reading her thoughts, Jason murmured, 'I'm frightening you by rushing things. You want us to give ourselves time to get to know each other better.'

His amber gaze mesmerized her. She found herself twisting her hands together in a distracted manner.

'Well . . .' She felt uneasy, unable to explain her reasons. 'My family . . .'

'Why should they object to our friendship?' He grinned, his amber eyes glowing mischievously. 'Unless they're afraid I might take you away from them.'

'People will think that . . .'

'Take no notice. They'll soon get used to the idea.'

'There'll be talk . . .'

'Does it matter? If we shut our ears to any gossip, we won't hear it!'

She started to say, 'No! It means I'll be a prisoner again,' but the words stuck in her throat. How could she expect Jason to understand?

Sensitive to her hesitancy, he put a finger under her chin, tilting her face until he was looking straight into her eyes. 'I only want to make you happy. I want to take care of you, pamper you, cherish you, but we'll share only as much of our life as you wish. No more.'

Margaret shook her head, frissons of fear running through her as she felt the trap closing around her.

'If you need space, for a day, a week, or a month you need only say the word and I'll keep away. It's your happiness that matters to me more than anything else. Now, what is your answer?'

'I . . . I'll think about it.'

'Of course! But only for three seconds. I want your answer now, before you go home tonight, so that I can face tomorrow knowing our destinies are linked.'

'I . . . I'm not sure. I don't know what Charles . . . Steven . . .'

'Forget about them,' he whispered, softly. 'Think of yourself . . . of us. They're all living their own lives. Now it's time for you to do the same.'

Margaret felt suddenly angry.

It had been such a wonderful outing. She had been enjoying every moment; the river, the food, the music and the company. Why did Jason have to ruin it all?

Tears blurred her eyes as she stared out into the semi-darkness, listening to the water lapping against the sides of the boat, the eerie cries, and scuttling in the reeds and bushes along the river bank contrasting to the liveliness on board.

Looking up at the thin crescent of moon, the sprinkling of stars, like silver dust scattered on the purple velvet canopy of sky, she shivered, not with cold but with the realization that Jason had pricked the balloon of fantasy that she'd donned like a magic cloak. He'd brought her down to earth, to the mundane facts of everyday living.

Tonight had been a taste of the exciting new freedom that could be hers if she had the courage to remain independent.

The future had so much to offer; new friendships, travel, all the exhilarating experiences she'd missed out on over the past years. Now, as a whole new spectrum was about to open up, Jason was trying to inveigle her into a relationship that would ruin everything.

She wasn't even sure she wanted a fixed arrangement with Jason, or with anyone else for that matter, yet she felt powerless to stop it. Events were moving too fast for her.

She stared out into the darkening night, wondering how to extricate herself from the situation she found herself in. They were almost at Boulter's Lock and she wanted to call a halt to Jason's attentions before they reached there.

As the boat ground against the side of the mooring site and the gangplank was lowered, she laid a hand on Jason's arm. 'Can we talk about this some other time? I'm not sure if it's because I'm not used to so much wine, but I feel desperately tired.'

Jason was not so easily dissuaded. 'We can't let the evening end like this, I'll see you home.'

Margaret clenched the inside of her cheeks between her teeth to steady her nerves. 'There's no need, thank you all the same. Charles and Helen go right past my door they'll drop me off.'

Resolutely she moved towards Jan, who was standing by the rail of the boat next to the gangplank.

'It's been a wonderful party, Jan,' she murmured, as she kissed her goodbye.

Jan remained statuesque, unbending even as their cheeks touched and Margaret's heart sank. She suspected that it was because Jason had deserted Jan's side all evening.

Jason remained silent, contenting himself with a stiff little bow as she excused herself so that she could join Charles and Helen.

Seventeen

Charles was still incensed by his mother's behaviour when he and Helen reached home. He had not spoken a word since they had dropped her off at Willow House but Helen read the signs. The shine of his knuckles as he gripped the steering wheel, the set of his jaw, the tight frown, the tenseness of his shoulders all revealed the tension he was feeling.

He'd probably want to talk about it once they got indoors, she thought, and she debated whether she should listen or pretend she hadn't noticed that anything was wrong, and go on up to bed.

If she did that then she knew she would have to endure him tossing, and turning, beside her in bed all night. If they sat down with a nightcap and she let him talk about it that might take hours before he came to terms with the situation. Either way, she thought resignedly, she wasn't going to get much sleep.

Why on earth couldn't Margaret react to her husband's death in the normal way? she thought, wearily.

Most widows went through a brief spell of deep grief followed by spasmodic bursts of crying and reminiscing. Then, once the husband's personal effects were cleared from the house, there was a gradual acceptance of the situation. That might last for six months, or so, while readjustments were made and a new routine established. After that, except on anniversaries, the matter was rarely mentioned.

Why did Margaret have to be so different, she mused, as she prepared hot chocolate for herself and Charles, and took it through to the living room.

Charles was slumped in his armchair looking anything but his usual composed self. He'd loosened his tie, kicked off his shoes, and was scowling into space.

'It's been quite an evening, hasn't it? I thought this would help us to get to sleep,' Helen said, placing his mug of chocolate within easy reach.

'Sleep!' Charles snorted. 'I'm hardly likely to do that with what's on my mind.'

'Do you want to talk about it, darling?' Helen murmured in a low soothing voice.

'What is there to say?'

Helen sighed understandingly. 'It's certainly an odd situation.'

'It's certainly not normal!'

'That's true. You know, I would never have described your mother as hard, or callous; the very opposite, in fact. Yet she's shown no grief at all, neither when your father died nor at his funeral.'

'I know that, but I thought she was merely putting on a brave face.'

'Quite! In fact, I expected her to have some sort of breakdown afterwards,' admitted Helen, 'but not a bit of it. If anything she's seemed to take on a new lease of life. She's behaving in a way she would never have dreamed of doing when your father was alive.'

'Like trying to swap Dad's car for a Mercedes, and booking to go abroad on a packaged holiday, you mean?'

'Well, I wasn't thinking of those specific things so much as the way she acted tonight; with that Jason Parker person, I mean.'

Charles scowled. 'Don't remind me. She certainly wasn't behaving like a grieving widow.' He groaned, running his splayed fingers through his hair. 'I can't get over it. She was so light-hearted, flirtatious almost—'

'If we were aware of it then other people must have noticed her behaviour,' interrupted Helen. There was a note of triumph in her voice. She had always felt rather in awe of Margaret ever since she was first married. Now she felt secretly pleased that Charles was finding out for himself that his mother wasn't so perfect after all.

'So what can we do about it?'

Helen picked up her hot chocolate and sipped at it, thoughtfully. She wanted time to think this one through. Charles was actually asking her for her advice, something he rarely did. This was a golden opportunity to break the close tie that had always existed between Charles and his mother. It was certainly one she intended to exploit, but she felt far too tired to reason things through properly at the moment.

'Its too big an issue to go into now, darling,' she prevaricated, draining her mug and setting it down. 'We're both tired. I think we should sleep on it.' She smothered a yawn. 'Things might seem different in the morning.'

'Far worse, probably!'

'Perhaps we should have a family get-together so that you can talk things over with Alison and Steven.'

'You mean a family meeting without Mother?'

'Yes!'

'Mm!' Charles stood up and stretched. 'I'm not sure it will do much good, but it might be worth a try.'

'Would you like me to phone them?'

'You could contact Steven. He might be more willing to come if you're the one who asks him.'

'What about Alison?'

'I'll ring her.'

'Shall we invite them to come here for dinner tomorrow night?'

'No. Let's just ask them around for a drink after dinner. Say, nine o'clock tomorrow evening?'

'Are we asking Mark and Sandra to come along as well?'

'God, no! It's to be a family discussion, not a social occasion or a character assassination.'

'Its going to be very difficult to explain why they're not invited,' warned Helen.

'Oh, do whatever you like. Mark and Sandra can come along if you think it's necessary. I simply thought we would get to the heart of the matter quicker if it was just the three of us.'

'Oh, so I'm excluded as well, am I? What am I supposed to do? Sit out in the kitchen ready to bring in the drinks when you ring a bell?'

'Oh for God's sake! Look, I'm shattered. I'm going to bed. Do what you like. Make it dinner and invite them all if that's what you want to do.'

'Not at all! I'm not looking for extra work . . .'

'Then forget about the whole thing. I'll try to call round and have a word with Mother sometime and see if I can reason with her.'

'No, we'll do things democratically. This is a problem that should be shared by the entire family,' Helen insisted. 'The rest of them are probably just as concerned about your mother's strange behaviour as we are.'

'Isn't Margaret coming?' Thelma Winter looked questioningly from Jan to Brenda as she settled herself comfortably into one of Jan's white leather armchairs.

'Don't tell me she's retreated back into her shell again,' she added, as she straightened the pleats of her beige linen skirt, before taking the glass of dry sherry Jan Porter was holding out to her.

'Thelma, wouldn't you feel more comfortable if you took your jacket off?' Jan suggested, ignoring her question.

Jan herself was looking cool and sophisticated in a designer outfit of a pale green top teamed with jade green slacks which emphasized her slim hips. Her Gucci slip-ons matched the striped light and dark green leather belt that clinched her waist and was fastened by a green and gold enamel buckle that had the same elaborate design as her earrings.

'You're probably right.' Thelma put down the sherry and wriggled free of her tailored brown linen jacket.

Jan took it from her and put it over the back of a spare chair. The white silk blouse Thelma was wearing beneath it was severely tailored, its only decoration being her initials TW embroidered in heavy white silk on the breast pocket and a cameo brooch with heavy filigree gold edging.

'You still look terribly hot,' murmured Brenda, 'why don't you unfasten the neck of your blouse. It is summer, you know, Thelma, and the temperature today must be well up in the seventies.'

'You certainly seem to think it is! Dressed for the beach by the look of things.'

Brenda giggled, and hitched the flowery skirt of her sleeveless cotton dress up to her knees, displaying plump, bare legs. 'I intended to spend the day lazing in the garden and then Jan phoned. I didn't stop to get changed; it all sounded so urgent.'

'I thought that perhaps there had been some kind of disaster after the party ended last night?'

'Things went wrong before the party ended,' interrupted Jan. 'I thought you would have noticed! I asked you to come here this morning so that we could discuss it.'

'You mean something to do with the way Margaret was behaving?' Thelma took a sip of her sherry, and looked at Jan over the top of her glass.

'Precisely.'

Brenda looked from Jan to Thelma, and back again, her plump face bemused. 'I thought she was having a wonderful time . . .'

'Is that what you call it?' Jan's voice was knife sharp. 'I thought she behaved outrageously.'

'Why, what did she do?' Brenda frowned and then her blue eyes widened questioningly.

'Surely you noticed the way she was flirting with Jason Parker,' Jan pronounced censoriously.

'It was only a bit of light-hearted fun, surely. Anyway, I thought it was Jason who was doing all the chasing.'

'Margaret has changed,' Jan stated. 'I would never have expected her to carry on like that.'

'She's simply come out of her shell now she hasn't got that unbearable husband of hers breathing down her neck,' defended Brenda.

'That's the whole point, though, isn't it?' snapped Jan. 'That's precisely what I can't understand. He's only just died!'

'What do you expect her to do? Cry all the time?'

'She's only been a widow a few weeks so she shouldn't be behaving like that.'

'She didn't even cry at Reginald's funeral did she?' mused Thelma, her mouth tightening into a disapproving line.

'That's beside the point. After the miserable existence she's endured for the last five years I didn't expect her to be crying her eyes out, but I did expect her to behave with . . . with . . .'

'Decorum?'

'Precisely!' The triumph in Jan's voice made Thelma's pencilled eyebrows rise sharply and Brenda's lips purse up in protest.

'You're being rather hard on poor Margaret, aren't you, Jan?' Brenda remonstrated gently. 'I think she's been very brave to have put her grief behind her and tried to carry on as normal.'

'Grief? What grief? I've never in my life seen anyone grieve less.'

Jan's abruptness shocked Brenda. 'You don't know that for sure. When she's on her own—'

'Rubbish! You can tell she's not grieving. She acts like someone who's had a load lifted from their shoulders.'

'Well, so she has in a way,' intervened Thelma quickly. 'We all considered Reginald to be an old bore and we hardly ever saw him. Think what it must have been like living with him! He certainly put a stop to Margaret enjoying life once he retired.'

'It's no good saying that now; she should have stood up for herself.'

'You can be awfully callous, Jan. I'm sure Margaret tried to make the best of things for her family's sake.'

'Twaddle! They're all grown up and they could see for themselves what a tyrant he had become, so they would have understood.'

'Her children might have understood the situation, but what about the grandchildren?' persisted Brenda. 'Even small babies are sensitive to a discordant atmosphere. I know my Jack says that if he ever raises his voice then—'

'You can't ruin your life for them!' snorted Jan. 'In ten or fifteen years they'll all be living their own lives and they'll probably never even phone home or call on any of their family unless they want something.'

'Surely all this is Margaret's problem not ours,' murmured Thelma diplomatically. She drained the rest of her sherry and put the glass down on the table at her side.

'I agree! As long as it doesn't interfere with our lives,' Jan said quickly.

'But it won't, will it – except for the better. It's all in the past and it's lovely knowing that we will have Margaret back now. You should have invited her to join us today for a glass of sherry, Jan.'

'I've invited her along for coffee. She'll be here in about twenty minutes. I asked you both to come early so that we could settle how we are going to handle things. I'm referring to the way Margaret was behaving on the river trip.'

Brenda looked utterly confused. 'Jan dear, what on earth are you on about?'

'I'm talking about the way she monopolized Jason,' snapped Jan. 'Damn it, she's only known the man a couple of weeks.'

Thelma frowned. 'He's doing some work on her place, isn't he?' she queried.

'Yes he is and I was the one who introduced them. That's the irony of it.'

'Oh, Jan, what a giggle! You're jealous!' Brenda went into burbles of laughter, dabbing at her eyes with a tissue. 'You don't like it because he's paying more attention to Margaret than he is to you.'

'What utter nonsense! I'm referring to the way Margaret was flirting with him. I'm sure I wasn't the only one who noticed how she was leading him on.'

'It's rather a difficult situation,' murmured Thelma thoughtfully. She had noticed that Margaret and Jason had seemed to spend quite a lot of time talking to each other, but she had not given it a great deal of thought until now. She had never particularly liked Jason and had always assumed that Jan tolerated him only because he was such a brilliant interior designer. Now, from the way Jan was reacting, she wasn't so sure if that was the only reason.

'I think you're imagining it, Jan,' defended Brenda.

'Oh, no! He's been round at Willow House every day for the past two weeks.'

Thelma looked thoughtful. 'If you raise that point she's bound to tell you she's having the place redecorated and that the only reason he is there is to do with work.'

'How do you know he's there every day?' Brenda's blue eyes sharpened accusingly.

'Whenever I've driven past, his car has been parked in the driveway.'

'You've been spying on them, haven't you, Jan?'

'I've also found it's impossible to contact him by phone at his office.'

'Surely that's because he's out working?'

'He calls it that. It's always at Willow House, though!'

'If Margaret is having the entire place done up then he is bound to be there a great deal – and it could take several weeks or even months.'

'So what do you want me to do? Keep quiet until the work there is finished and then find it's too late?'

'Too late for what?'

'Brenda, you are so naive that you exasperate me sometimes. I asked you both round here in the hope that between us we could devise some sort of scheme to save Margaret from doing anything she might bitterly regret later on.'

Thelma shook her head. 'I don't really see that there is anything we can do. After all, you can hardly say "hands off". Jason Parker is a free agent, and he can be friends with whoever he chooses.'

'You mean you want us to help stop her taking Jason Parker off you, don't you?' chuckled Brenda, unabashed by Jan's anger.

'That is both uncalled for and offensive. I introduced them to each other so I'd feel responsible if she made a fool of herself with him. Don't forget he's almost twenty years younger than her!'

'Which means he is twenty years younger than you,' Brenda reminded her triumphantly.

'I am well aware of that fact. I regard him as my protégé. I'm sure Jason would agree that it's thanks to all the countless introductions and recommendations that I've given him that his business has prospered in the way it has.'

'So what are we supposed to do about it? Are you suggesting we should tell Margaret that we disapprove, and advise her to stop seeing him?'

'Or should we say he's already spoken for?' quipped Brenda.

There was an uneasy silence as Jan collected up the sherry glasses and arranged them carefully on a round silver tray.

'Well?' she demanded. 'What are we going to do about it? Have you any suggestions, or not?'

Eighteen

Willow House had received its final lick of paint. In six weeks it had been transformed from a shabby family house into an elegant, highly desirable, country residence worthy of a centre spread in *Delightful Homes* or *Top Houses*.

Margaret was entranced. The finished results surpassed even her highest expectations. She was more than satisfied with Jason's work.

It seemed inconceivable that she had toyed with the idea of moving house after Reginald had died because she'd thought that new surroundings might help to erase all the miserable memories that were blighting her outlook on life.

She'd even studied the estate agents windows and collected their handouts, but she'd found nothing of interest. There hadn't been a single property in the price range she could afford that was remotely suitable. None of them offered either the sort of accommodation, or the exclusive setting, that Willow House enjoyed.

She would have been prepared to take a smaller house if she could have found one she liked; one that was within walking distance of shops, the medical centre, library and the railway station.

The last straw had been when Charles had suggested, 'Perhaps we should think about having a granny flat built on to our place for you?'

She had been appalled at the thought of being under his watchful eye, night and day, with Helen monitoring all her comings and goings. They would even be able to vet her visitors and probably interfere at every possible chance. Added to that, she would be regarded as a built-in babysitter. Much as she loved her grandchildren, she had brought up one family and had no intention of repeating the process over again.

Compared to that idea, Willow House, even as it stood, was more suitable, she'd decided. It was secluded, yet within walking distance of all the local amenities. The rest of the family lived within easy reach, yet they were all sufficiently far away that she would be able to retain her independence.

Discounting the last years since Reginald had been ill, Willow House had plenty of happy memories, ones she didn't want to leave behind. All three of her children had been born and raised there; the garden had been a haven for them and their friends, and their very own adventure playground.

The garden had always been her special delight, too. The children had given many of the shrubs and trees now growing in it to her as a present on her birthday, or Mother's Day, or at Easter.

The willow tree, from which the house took its name, was one of the finest specimens she had ever seen. Almost a hundred foot high, its delicate waving green fronds provided a welcome shade in summer and home for a variety of birds, and squirrels, all through the year.

Reginald had never shown very much interest in the garden. He had preferred to spend his leisure time playing golf. Even after his retirement, when he had been forced into giving up golf for health reasons, his interest in the garden had remained peripheral. When the weather was warm he would sit out on the patio in summer, reading his newspaper while she pottered around weeding the borders, deadheading the roses, and tending to the flower pots.

No, she'd decided, there were no changes at all she wished to make out of doors. The interior was quite another matter.

She'd been so impressed by the work Jan had had done to her flat that staying where she was at Willow House and hiring Jason Parker to transform the interior into the sort of home she'd always dreamed of living in had seemed to be the perfect solution.

It had certainly been successful and beyond her wildest expectations. There were so many changes that she was sure if Reginald ever came back he would feel completely lost.

The kitchen had been the starting point. Margaret would have been content to simply have the mid-sixties style units ripped out and replaced by modern oak fitments but Jason had been far more ambitious.

'You will have to put in a new cooker so you may as well have one of the latest split-level models with a ceramic hob and double oven. I'll bring along some brochures so that you can choose the one you like.'

'I ought to replace the washing machine . . .'

Jason made a note on his pad. 'I'll incorporate that into the scheme. One with a built-in drier will take up less space than the two separate units you have now. And what about the fridge and the freezer? They're pretty obsolete. A fridge-freezer unit will not only look better, but it will be space-saving and more efficient.'

He'd gone on to include a dishwasher and the microwave she'd always wanted, but which Reginald had steadfastly refused to buy because he didn't approve of them.

The rest of the changes to the decor in the kitchen were fairly restrained. Jason had wanted to be more adventurous, but she had opted for a few subtle touches. She had always wanted leadlight glass doors on the main kitchen cabinet and a stained-glass panel in the centre of the large window. Now she had them and the result was stunning.

The main bathroom had been next on her list and she had let Jason have free rein. It had been a wise move. He had transformed it into an exotic retreat. The ordinary bath had been replaced with a Jacuzzi in a subtle shade of oyster pink. It was positioned across one corner of the room and resplendent with gleaming gold-plated taps and flanked by heated towel rails. The ceiling was panelled in golden oak that matched the woodwork of the vanity unit. A glass-encased sunken shower blended superbly with the decorative tiles on the walls.

By far the most satisfying transformation, however, was the main bedroom – her bedroom. Gone was the heavy walnut furniture and in its place Jason had designed fitted units in the palest possible shade of lilac with mirrored doors that were outlined with a delicate tracery of gold leaf.

The lilac, purple and grey stripes of the satin drapes matched the bedcover, and frilled cushions, piped in purple, were piled high against the bed head. Her feet sank into the deep-pile purple carpet.

There were mirrors everywhere reflecting the opulence and glamour of the setting. It was over the top; it had a Hollywood flavour, but she loved it.

So far neither her family nor friends had been allowed to see it. She had managed to put them off calling, assuring them she was fine but much too busy and that the house was in a state of complete turmoil at present.

She'd implied to the family that she was getting out and about with her friends. To Thelma and Brenda she'd made the excuse that she was busy with her family and, because she'd sounded so bright and cheerful whenever any of them phoned her, they had accepted her explanation.

Jan hadn't been in touch at all, but Jason reported that Jan was still annoyed by the amount of time he was spending at Willow House.

Margaret had spasms of guilt about Jan. It was true that every minute of her day was taken up, as she claimed, but mostly it was with Jason.

When he had first suggested that she should go with him to select paint colours, or approve the fabrics or fittings he had selected, she had hesitated, remembering his admission when they had been on the boat of how he felt about her. Since he never mentioned the episode again, however, and treated her with nothing but the utmost courtesy, she began to wonder if it had all been a figment of her imagination.

She began to look forward to his arrival each morning and she was eager to know his plans for the day. His suggestions were so varied that it was like being on a continuous holiday.

The days she enjoyed most were when they went up to London to browse over fabrics in Harrods or Liberty's, or to wander along Bond Street, or the King's Road, in search of unusual items of furniture.

Before making any important decisions Jason would often suggest they should first visit a specialist shop. Often these were in outlying country areas. He took her to Gloucester and Bath, to Evesham and Broadway in the Cotswolds, as well as to Stockbridge and Salisbury in the West Country.

Jason was a fount of information and turned each outing into a special occasion, whether they went to exhibitions, toured museums, or visited a stately home. On all of these jaunts, he knew of quaint half-hidden pubs and restaurants that all had one thing in common; they all offered superb food.

She had never been so entertained, so pampered, or so fussed over. He consulted her over the minutest detail, anxious for her opinion and unwilling to make a single move without her approval.

He employed only the very best craftsmen to work at Willow House and at the end of the day, when they returned to check on how the restoration work was progressing, he was adamant that every detail must be in accordance with her wishes.

She had only to show the slightest hesitation when he made a suggestion and he would insist she considered several alternatives. She had never felt so important, or known a man to be quite so attentive. It was all very flattering and ego boosting.

Reginald had always observed such customary attentions as opening the car door for her, holding her coat, and always walking on the outside of the pavement when they went out together. When they were at home, though, it was more usual for her to wait on him than the other way round. Not so with Jason. He was equally attentive and courteous wherever they were. If she stretched out a hand to reach a cup, or a glass, he noticed at once and immediately moved it closer. He was so attentive that she sometimes thought that if she dropped something he would spring forward and catch it before it touched the ground.

Their outings together had a sparkle; the excitement of not knowing from one day to the next what they would be doing. She played a game with herself. She would watch for his arrival from an upstairs window and try to guess what the day's excursion was to be from the way he was dressed. In the main, Jason favoured casual clothes. Tight-fitting black jeans teamed with a polo-necked shirt sometimes in black, but often in white or red or even pale blue, always worn with a black blazer. On formal occasions he would wear an amber suit the same colour as his eyes, or a charcoal grey one that made him look as dramatic as an actor.

In this he was the complete opposite of Reginald who had always dressed formally in impeccably tailored suits, crisp white shirts, and expensive silk ties. Even his casual wear had been flawlessly cut, and in discreetly muted colours.

At first, Margaret had felt self-conscious about the way heads turned and people stared when she was out with Jason. Aware that her greying hair made her look much older than him she took to wearing a hat.

'I should be the one to cover my head, not you,' he grinned, misinterpreting her intention. 'Does it bother you that I have no hair?'

'No, no of course it doesn't. Why should it?'

'You've never commented on it, but I could tell from the expression on your face the first time we met that you were taken aback.'

She coloured uncomfortably. 'I don't think I'd ever seen anyone so . . . so completely bald. Except Kojak on television. I always assumed that he shaved his head for effect. Yours is too smooth to be shaved. Have you always been—'

'Bald?' He ran his hands over the golden expanse of his skull. 'Yes, ever since I had glandular fever when I was in my teens. If it bothers you I could always wear a toupee or a hairpiece when we go out?'

'Good heaven's, no!' She laughed uneasily. 'It's part of your character.'

They hadn't mentioned the subject again but Margaret wore a hat less and less. People staring no longer troubled her. They could think what they liked. There were so many other things in life to take her attention.

The men working under Jason's direction were transforming Willow House. Each day there seemed to be some new development that struck like an electric shock, sending her senses spinning, yet at the same time giving her a feeling of satisfaction.

She was so excited by all that was taking place that she decided that, once all the work was complete, she would throw a party. She would invite all the family as well as Jan, Thelma and Brenda.

'If the weather holds we'll make it a barbecue,' Jason insisted, assuming without her asking him that he was also invited. 'That will be much more sensible since there will be quite a number of small children running around.'

'And what if it rains?'

'If it has to be indoors then everyone will have to be confined to the garden room until the food is out of the way. That should minimize the risk of any damage to the new decor.'

'Perhaps a sit-down meal would be better?'

'Quite out of the question,' he told her, emphatically. 'There's far too many people coming. It has to be a barbecue or a buffet.'

'Depending on the weather!'

'Either way, we'll keep the doors to all the rooms closed. No one will be allowed inside the main part of the house until after they've eaten. Then, when the children have had their hands and faces washed I will take everyone on a guided tour. Now won't that be splendid?'

Margaret tried not to laugh. Even though Charles had been married for sixteen years he still treated Willow House as home. The thought of Jason telling him, or any of the others who were coming, that they were not permitted to wander wherever they wished would certainly cause an outcry.

Determined that she would be free to enjoy the occasion Margaret decided to call in the same caterers who had provided the spread after Reginald's funeral. When she mentioned this to Jason he looked most perturbed.

'No, No, NO!' he protested, his amber eyes gleaming, his lower lip pouting. 'That would spoil everything.'

'I don't want to have to spend days and days baking, and preparing everything,' Margaret said firmly. 'Anyway, I'm out of practice.'

She hadn't organized anything on the scale she was planning now since well before Reginald had retired. And she'd been ten years younger then, she thought ruefully.

'Simply leave everything to me,' Jason told her. 'I shall enjoy every minute of it. I adore cooking and it will give me a chance to try out the kitchen and see if any changes are required.' His bald head glowed and his face shone with delight, like that of a gleeful cherub.

Margaret knew when she was beaten. Having grown accustomed to not fighting battles she was unlikely to win she gave in with a smile. In the days that followed, though, as Jason arrived armed with lists of the dishes he was planning to cook and even longer lists of the ingredients required, she wished she had been more resolute. It was too late now to change the arrangements, she reflected. Jason was as excited as a child promised his first bicycle.

'It's going to be fabulous,' he enthused, his amber eyes glowing. 'My flat over the studio is far too small to hold a full-scale party. The nearest I've ever got to staging something like this has been arranging Jan's parties. That's been tremendous fun, but nothing compared with what I am going to do now.'

At the mention of Jan's name, Margaret felt faintly alarmed. There was still a marked coolness between them because Jan felt she was monopolizing Jason's time, so would letting him organize her party make things worse, Margaret wondered?

Nineteen

'That was some party!' puffed Hetty Chapman, collapsing into a chair, and looking across the room at her husband. 'I don't think I've ever been to one I've enjoyed so much in my whole life.'

'Mm. It was certainly different.'

'And the house! Old Reginald wouldn't recognize it.'

'Mm.'

'You don't sound very impressed.'

'I was impressed alright, but I'm a bit worried about what it's all costing. I do hope Margaret isn't overspending.'

Hetty yawned and loosened the belt on her dress. 'I shouldn't let that worry you. Charles will be keeping a tight hold of the purse strings.'

'I most certainly hope so. I've no idea how much Reginald left but Margaret has a long stretch of years ahead of her with no source of income. It isn't as though she has a job of any kind.'

'Reginald would have left her comfortably off. She's probably got more money than we'll ever see. He was pretty shrewd and he inherited Willow House remember. I imagine he invested his money well and he probably had a hefty life insurance policy. Mark my words, you can bet Charles will be keeping an eye on her financial affairs.'

'Will she listen to him though? From the way she was carrying on tonight I would think the only person likely to have any influence over her at the moment is that decorator fellow Jason Parker.'

'Her toy boy!'

'Hetty!' Joseph's grin softened the condemnation in his voice.

'Well, you've got to admit he's years younger than her. And that bald head!' Hetty shivered. 'It's almost like seeing him without any clothes on.'

'Mm. Odd sort of chap, I thought.'

'I'm sure he's kidded Margaret into letting him do Willow House up exactly as he wants it because he's planning on moving in with her.'

'You could be right about that. Willow House must seem like a very desirable residence compared to that poky little flat over his studio in Cookham High Street.'

'That large bedroom, the one he called a leisure room, I wouldn't mind betting that if he does manage to move in there he's planning to make that into a permanent studio for his own use.'

'You could be right but I hope not. If Margaret gets herself saddled with a bloke like that she'll have the devil's own job to get free of him.'

'Perhaps she won't want to? It's a big house to rattle around in on your own.'

'Yes, it would have been much more sensible if instead of spending so much money having Willow House done up she had moved to something smaller. A flat, or a cosy little bungalow, would have been more suitable for her and so much easier to run.'

'Well, it's too late to talk about that now. After all the money she's spent on Willow House she's hardly likely to want to move.

'Mm. Well, let's hope she doesn't have to do so, but if she goes on spending her money in such a reckless way it may well come to that.'

Joseph and Hetty Chapman were not the only ones concerned about Margaret's financial future. Charles was aghast by what was happening.

'She's had the place done out from top to bottom! Not only decorated but new furniture and fittings, as well. It must have cost a small fortune,' he ranted as he and Helen drove home from the party.

'It's a long time since they had anything at all done to the place, it was all a bit shabby,' Helen protested. She sighed enviously. 'I absolutely loved her new bedroom. And that Jacuzzi . . .'

'Stop right there! It's no good you getting any ideas about having one of those installed at our place because we can't afford it.'

Helen's lips tightened. 'If your mother can then I don't see . . .'

'She can't afford it, either! First thing tomorrow I shall be going to see her and putting her straight on one or two points.'

'Is that necessary? Surely your father has left her comfortably off?'

Charles bit his lip. He had no intention of telling Helen the true state of affairs. He was anxious, however, to nip in the bud any ideas she might have about them redecorating, or buying new furniture.

'If Mother goes on spending in this manner then she will end up absolutely destitute in a couple of years' time. It's not advisable to spend your capital when you are not in a position to earn any more.'

'That may be true but it's a one-off outlay, surely? She's hardly likely to have the house done over again, now is she?'

'I'm not so sure about that. I have a feeling that if that Jason fellow has his way it's quite possible that in a year or so she'll change it all for something quite different,' pronounced Charles gloomily.

'He did seem to be very much at home there, didn't he?' Helen murmured. 'For a design consultant, or whatever he calls himself, I mean. You would have thought he was the man of the house the way he served the drinks and ordered us all around.'

Charles's mouth tightened. 'Shutting all the doors before we arrived and then taking us on a conducted tour and opening them one by one . . .'

'It was almost as if we were strangers or prospective buyers . . .'

'We should all have taken a stand and refused point blank to take orders from him.'

'How could we! It would have ruined everything for your mother.'

'Better that than let that gigolo run the show,' Charles muttered angrily.

Anger flared in Helen. It was the one thing that infuriated her, the way Charles held a post-mortem on everything and decided in retrospect on the course of action that should have been taken.

'Then why didn't you speak out? After all, you are head of the family now,' she reminded him.

As they waved the last of the guests off and began to clear away the remains of the buffet, Jason looked questioningly at Margaret.

'Was it a success?'

'Success! It was absolutely brilliant.'

'They certainly seemed to enjoy the spread,' he persisted as he stacked up the plates and glasses.

'And so they should! The food was absolutely delicious. I had no idea you were such an excellent cook, Jason.'

'It's one of my hobbies but it's not very much fun cooking for one. I like to have someone to appreciate the results.'

'You should have got married.'

'I never met the right person . . .'

His voice drifted off and Margaret wondered if she had touched on a raw spot. She wasn't sure that he liked women, leastways not in the way most men did.

She felt embarrassed that she had broached the subject. She didn't want him to think she was prying. After all, it wasn't any of her business. She had hired him to advise her on redecorating Willow House and his personal preferences were really no concern of hers, whatsoever.

She already felt uncomfortable about how much of his time she had taken up recently. As Jan had pointed out on more than one occasion, over the past weeks he had devoted most of his creative energy exclusively to the work he had been doing for her.

The many outings to select fabrics, furniture, and fittings, the visits to exhibitions, and trips to London were, she was sure, over and above what he normally arranged for a customer.

She assumed he didn't think of her as a mere customer any more than she thought of him simply as a designer. He had been so kind and understanding that a warm friendship had blossomed between the two of them. She would miss him now that all the work was finished.

Turning round from the sink he took her hands in his. 'I have a lot of friends but I've never felt as close to anyone as I do to you,' he told her softly.

Margaret remained silent, her mind racing, remembering his declaration of love when they'd been on the *Castle Gold* on the night of Jan's birthday party. Suddenly, with a sense of shock, she realized that their frequent outings, his constant attention, had not been the actions of a professional man selling his services. They had been more in the style of old-fashioned courting.

She didn't know what to say, or even how to act, for fear of spoiling everything. She was quite happy for their relationship to continue along its present lines, but she suspected he wanted more.

Although she hadn't grieved over Reginald's death she had to admit that she did sometimes feel lonely. With the passing of time, the things he had done which had irritated her became shadowy, almost as if they were figments of her imagination.

In the past she had longed to have time to herself, to be able to do as she liked, to go wherever she wished without having to consider anyone else. Now, after a couple of months of being on her own the novelty of being a free agent had begun to pall.

More and more she found herself remembering the good times she'd enjoyed with Reginald. She began to dredge up memories buried so deep in her subconscious that they were like vignettes from another life. Nuggets of happiness no longer coated in the nervous tension that had so often marred the actual event. Now they shone like polished stones, a rosary of precious moments that she counted over and over again.

She enjoyed Jason's company, but in many ways Reginald was still as dominant an influence in her life as he had been when he was alive. Anyway she wasn't ready for a deeper commitment.

Apart from that, she reminded herself, Jason was far too young for her. Twenty years age difference may be acceptable when it is the man who is older but not when it is the other way round. Especially when he looks so much younger.

Being completely bald would have aged most men, but in Jason's case it made him look almost juvenile. The smooth golden skin of his head, together with his soulful amber coloured eyes, plump cheeks, and pouting mouth gave him a cherubic look.

When he wore a formal suit it was in mohair or linen, smoothly emphasizing his slim build and highlighted by a contrasting shirt and an outrageously colourful tie.

He was a head-turner in every sense and that, to her mind, made it all the more incredible that he seemed to be so interested in her.

True, her figure was as slim, and trim, as it had been when she was in her thirties, but her blonde hair was showing rather more than a mere hint of grey. And when she applied her make-up each morning she was only too aware that there were age lines around her mouth as well as at the corners of her eyes.

She had never been one to pamper herself with facials, or expensive beauty creams but now she wondered if perhaps she should take professional advice from a qualified beautician and hope that she hadn't left it too late.

She hadn't visited a hairdresser in years so perhaps the time had come for her to do so. She kept her hair shoulder length by snipping an inch or so off the ends when it became too unwieldy to roll up into a French pleat. That, and a twice-weekly shampoo when she was taking her shower, was the only attention she had given it since Reginald retired.

Having set her home in order, perhaps it was now time to do the same for herself. After her dramatic clear out, she ought to start by replenishing her wardrobe and not with quality, classic styles that would last a lifetime and classified her as a sensible middle-class woman but with up-to-the-minute styles.

It wasn't merely clothes; her mental attitude also mattered. She ought to get a job. The thought haunted her. It was as if there were three heads on her shoulders, each screaming a different answer.

Before she did either of those things though she intended to buy a small car. She had been without far too long and now that Jason had finished working on her house she would have plenty of time on her hands and would need her own transport.

She missed having her own car so very much. She might not be able to afford the open-top sports car of her dreams but she still had enough of her savings left to buy a smart little runabout.

She wouldn't tell anyone, not Jason, her friends or her family about it until the deed was done. Charles would say she couldn't afford it and everybody else would be offering advice that she didn't want.

She certainly wouldn't be going to the garage in Maidenhead that Reginald had favoured because she was pretty sure they would get in touch with Charles and tell him what she was doing before she could complete the deal.

For the next few nights she scanned the small adverts in the newspaper hoping to spot something suitable.

It was quite by chance that when walking home from the village she saw the bright yellow sports car in the driveway of one of the houses. It had a home-made FOR SALE notice in the back window and as she stopped to read the price she was delighted to see that it came within her budget.

'Fancy trying it out?' asked a young man who had obviously noticed her interest and came down the garden path to meet her.

Margaret smiled hesitantly. 'I'm not sure if it's suitable,' she prevaricated.

'Who is it for? Your son?'

'No!' She felt irritated. 'It's for me!'

'I see. Well why not sit in it and see if you like the feel of it?'

Again she hesitated knowing full well that she would like it. It was almost exactly what she'd dreamed of owning. She knew so little about what to look for, though, that even though she'd found it and wanted it she felt someone ought to take a look at it before she bought it.

She wouldn't ask Charles, of course but Steven had said he would help her if she needed him to do so.

'I am interested and I do like it,' she admitted, 'but I would like to have it checked out.'

'That's fine by me, so why don't you bring your mechanic round? I'll be here all evening.'

Margaret smiled. 'I might do that,' she promised.

Twenty

It was over forty years since she had worked, Margaret reflected. The moment they had set the date for their wedding Reginald had insisted that she should resign from her job as his secretary.

She'd been so infatuated by him and in such a state of euphoria that she hadn't dreamed of arguing. It had all seemed like a dream when Reginald Wright, managing director of Wright Engineering, actually asked her to marry him. He was so handsome, so worldly and the fact that he'd proposed marriage to her, a shy eighteen-year-old, had seemed unbelievable.

Margaret recalled how nervous she'd been when she'd first joined the company and Reginald had called her in to take dicta-tion. She had been afraid to lift her eyes from her pad in case she missed getting something down.

It wasn't until an hour or so afterwards, when she had taken in the batch of letters for his signature, that she had really looked at him.

Reginald had been in his late thirties, a tall, imposing man with a shock of well-groomed dark hair. He had a strong face, clean-shaven with a straight nose, strong cheekbones, and a firm, square chin. His smartly cut dark charcoal suit sat well on his broad frame. With it he was wearing a crisp red and white striped shirt and dark red tie.

His compelling dark grey eyes, under wide dark brows, had unnerved her. His penetrating gaze had made her knees feel weak. She held her breath as she waited for him to sign the letters she'd brought in, her fingers crossed, silently praying she'd not made any errors. When his wide firm mouth relaxed into a smile of approval after he had signed each one and handed them back to her to send out, her heart had pounded wildly with relief.

She'd done everything after that to try and impress him. She'd invested the whole of her first month's salary on a smart grey suit, high-heeled black shoes and two crisply tailored white blouses to try and make herself appear more sophisticated. She'd painted her finger nails with pale pink varnish and sought advice about make-up. She'd abandoned all her pieces of junk jewellery in favour of plain gold ear studs and a discreet gold necklet.

She checked her work meticulously. The slightest error and she retyped the whole letter. For the first few weeks, because she was so nervous, her waste-paper basket was full to the brim each evening. Afraid that someone else in the office might notice she took to secreting the spoiled sheets and smuggling them out at the end of the day so that she could dispose of them in the dustbin at home.

She had been working at Wright Engineering for about two months when Reginald asked her if she could stay late to type up some reports that he needed urgently for a meeting first thing the next day.

'Leave them on my desk and I'll call in and collect them later on this evening,' he told her as he left the office.

He returned earlier than she had expected. She was still typing the last page.

He had changed out of his formal business suit, and was wearing a tweed sports jacket, grey slacks and a black polo-neck sweater. In her eyes he looked even more devastating and there was a catch in her voice as she answered his questions about the work she had almost completed.

When he came and stood behind her chair, reading the page over her shoulder, her heart thudded so loud against her ribs that she was sure he must be able to hear it.

'I've kept you very late,' he apologized. 'You must be starving!'

'Yes, I am rather hungry.' She smiled awkwardly.

He frowned. 'Have you let them know at home that you're working late?'

'Oh yes. I phoned my mother.'

'So what time is she expecting you home?'

'I . . . I didn't say a specific time because I wasn't sure how long it would take me to type the reports . . .'

'Good! Come on then, I haven't eaten either so we'll have a quick snack together.'

He'd taken her to a Chinese restaurant and ordered a selection of dishes without asking her what she wanted. She'd been too nervous to say anything. The food had been new to her but delicious and she had eaten in silence, letting him do all the talking.

Later, relaxed by the food and wine, she had answered his probing questions about her background, telling him about the rest of her family.

She told him about her brother Joseph who had only recently married and was trying to build up his own business as a market gardener. She even spoke about her sister Vivienne who was ten years older than her and wanted to leave home and share a flat with her friends.

'So what about you, Margaret? What are your plans for the future?'

She took a deep breath before answering. 'To go on doing what I'm doing now,' she finally told him.

'Working as a shorthand-typist!'

'That's right. I . . . I'm very happy . . . I love my work.'

Two months later, Reginald had appointed her his private secretary. That had been a milestone in her life.

Although she hadn't realized it at the time, it had marked the end of her independence as Margaret Chapman.

Their whirlwind courtship had swept her off her feet. Within the year they were married and Reginald had installed her in Willow House.

Built on the edge of the Chilterns, within walking distance of Cookham Village, it offered the best of all worlds, yet it was only six miles from the house she'd grown up in outside Windsor.

Before the novelty of being a full-time housewife had time to dim she had found herself pregnant with Charles. Alison followed him two years later and she was barely out of the pram before Steven arrived. Even with full-time help in the home and a live-in nanny, Margaret found that having three babies in four years kept her fully occupied.

She saw less, and less, of Reginald. He worked long hours, and quite often his business meetings extended late into the evening. At weekends he unwound on the golf course.

In the space of four years he had become a family man, yet basically he had not changed his bachelor ways one iota. Under the banner of business commitments he left himself free to lead an independent life.

He had been astute enough not to neglect her. On the occasions when they dined with some of his business colleagues he seemed to be inordinately proud of the fact that despite several pregnancies she had managed to retain her svelte figure. That and the fact that she was only half the age of most of the other women who were present had other men eyeing him enviously

She was the one who had become disillusioned. More and more she felt that Reginald treated their marriage as he would one of his business transactions and was glorying in the fact that he had achieved the desired result.

Although she had a beautiful home, a delightful young family and a very handsome husband she sometimes felt lonely.

She had her own car and plenty of money to spend on clothes and personal needs. She lived in luxury, yet in some ways she had nothing.

They rarely went out as a family because during the week Reginald was always too busy and at weekends his golf took priority over everything else.

Reginald rarely told her anything about what was going on in his business life and when she did attend official functions other wives looked at her in surprise because she appeared to know so little about his business affairs. Some of them seemed to think it was because she wasn't interested; others were sure that she knew but was refusing to disclose any details.

As the children grew older and began to make lives of their own Margaret attended fewer and fewer of Reginald's business functions. Instead she began to make a life of her own and she took refuge in the friendship that had developed between herself, Brenda Williams, Thelma Winter and Jan Porter.

Twenty-One

Margaret listened with wavering attention as Charles tried to explain her financial situation now that everything to do with Reginald's will had been settled. Unease clutched at her insides like a clammy hand.

The realization that she still had to pay Jason Parker for all the work he had arranged for her to be carried out on Willow House was uppermost in her mind. She had no idea how much this would amount to. She had given him a free hand, told him that money was no object. Her only criterion had been that everything must be top quality, especially the standard of workmanship.

Accordingly, he had engaged only the most skilled tradesmen and craftsmen and used only the finest materials. She suspected this meant that everything had been extremely expensive.

It was no good telling Charles that every room in the house

had needed to be redecorated and refitted. It wasn't true. She had insisted on having it done because at the time she had wanted to exorcize the past. She wanted Willow House to have the stamp of her personality on it, not Reginald's. Now she wasn't sure that it had been necessary, or that it had been successful.

There was no denying that the work had completely trans-formed the house and she loved all the new colour schemes and furnishings, but Reginald's presence was still there.

She found herself thinking more and more about him and the life they'd spent there together, Not constantly, but in flashes. It was like turning a corner and suddenly catching a glimpse of a scene long forgotten, or seeing someone in the distance and remembering the occasion when you last met.

It seemed to happen whenever she was in the house alone, and she attributed it to the fact that until now she had rarely been there on her own. For the last ten years Reginald had rarely left the house. When he did, it was to visit the doctor or the hospital and she had always gone with him. Before that, even though he had been out a great deal, there had always been the children and their countless friends.

She sighed contemplatively. In those days the house had resounded to voices, laughter and music. Now the house was practically deserted and only the echo of her own footsteps broke the overall silence.

Four bedrooms, and she occupied only one of them. Three large reception rooms as well as a huge family kitchen and a big square hall and she was the only one using them.

While the workmen had been in and out, measuring up, painting, wallpapering, rewiring, hanging curtains, laying carpets, and the hundred and one other tasks they had carried out, the place had been alive. The sound of their banging and hammering, their constant chatter and occasional bursts of singing had filled the air.

When they'd been there she had even looked forward to the evenings when she would at last be alone and everything would be peaceful.

While the work had been in full swing, Jason had been around much of the time. On those days when they were not out together, on some buying or viewing excursion, he would be at Willow House overseeing the work in progress.

Since his declaration that his feelings for her transcended mere friendship she had avoided being alone with him whenever possible. She didn't feel ready for such complications of that sort. Instead she had thrown herself back into family life.

It wasn't the same though.

The easy camaraderie that had always existed between her and Alison seemed strained. Whenever Alison came to visit it was as if she was walking on eggshells, trying desperately hard not to criticize, or say anything that might upset her.

Alison seemed to measure her words carefully as if afraid to bring her father's name into the conversation. She had obviously cautioned Christopher to do the same. Whenever he was about to say something about his grandfather, Alison distracted him by changing the subject. It made things so strained and so uncomfortable that Margaret wanted to scream.

She longed to tell Alison that she didn't mind his name being mentioned; she wanted to talk about him and the past. Yet she didn't do so. Instead she condoned her avoidance by pretending not to notice.

In the past she and Alison had freely discussed anything under the sun. There had been no holds barred. Sometimes their criticism of each other had led to sharp words and even tears but they had always made up with hugs and kisses. Now, they were so restrained it was as if there was an invisible wall between them.

Mark was aware of it, Margaret was quite sure. Whenever the three of them were together he did his best to keep the conversation on general topics. If he did mention Reginald's name he did it in a matter-of-fact way.

On the few occasions when that happened Alison would visibly wince and give him a pained look.

If she wasn't careful, thought Margaret, this state of affairs would lead to a quarrel between Mark and Alison. She didn't wish to be involved so she kept away from them.

Things weren't much better when she dropped in uninvited on Steven. It was something Sandra had never liked her to do. Her explanation was that she might be at work and it inconvenienced her mother if she was there looking after the children.

Margaret accepted this excuse even though she knew that when Matthew and Hannah were babies and Sandra was at home all the time, she had still preferred visits to be prearranged. By the time she arrived Sandra would have made sure that her home was in apple-pie order and the kettle on the boil or even the tea or coffee prepared ready.

It had made Margaret feel so uncomfortable that her visits were regarded as an inspection that she had rarely visited them. Instead, Steven had called in at Willow House two or three times a week and brought the children along to see her at the weekends.

Now, sheer loneliness had driven her to seek their company and Sandra's cool reception made her feel unwanted.

She began to feel sorry for Steven. He was such a warm, friendly person, bubbling with good humour. He was the sort of man who enjoyed an open house. She was sure that if he had his way the place would be full of friends, and echoing to laughter.

As it was, their home had the atmosphere of a show house; immaculate with not a thing out of place, presided over by Sandra in the role of being the perfect mother and the children as spic and span as two dolls. Margaret wondered if they ever had runny noses or dirty hands.

Even during meal times they behaved perfectly. Hannah, who was now five, had eaten neatly and drank without spilling from the age of two. Margaret wasn't sure whether this was Sandra's influence or the strict training imposed on the children by the German au pair Sandra had installed so that she could continue her career as a model again.

Sensing that her uninvited visits were a source of annoyance to Sandra, Margaret resolved not to impose again.

She turned instead to her old friends, Jan, Brenda and Thelma. Even their company, though, had lost something these days.

She had invited the three of them for coffee a few days after the party and received very mixed reactions about the changes she had made to Willow House.

Jan was sharply critical. 'Not content with filching my designer from under my nose you've pinched my ideas as well,' she'd commented acidly.

'You should be flattered that Margaret thinks you have such good taste,' Thelma had interposed quickly, trying to cool things.

'I didn't steal him, you introduced us all to him and so when

I wanted to make some changes I automatically thought of him,' defended Margaret.

'And you've had him working exclusively for you for months!'

'Well, I think it's all very lovely,' murmured Brenda, 'just the right blend of old and new. Beautifully done!'

'Well, it would be with Jason giving it his undivided attention,' Jan snapped at her.

'The same as he did when he worked on your place! I'm sure its one of the secrets of his success,' enthused Brenda.

'He put forward ideas, and he supervised the workmen, but he didn't make it his sole enterprise,' Jan retorted.

The electrifying tension between herself and Jan worried Margaret. It had stopped her from inviting either Brenda or Thelma over on their own in case that made matters worse. It was ridiculous, of course, but she didn't want to give Jan the impression that she was stealing her friends as well as her decorator.

It made her feel more out on a limb than ever.

'Mother, are you listening to me?'

The sharpness of Charles's tone brought her back to the present.

'Of course I am, darling.'

His face was so serious. She forced herself to pay attention.

'I'm telling it to you exactly as it is, Mother,' he stated forcibly. His mouth was a thin grim line, his dark brows drawn together in a worried scowl. He had never looked more like his father than he did at this moment, Margaret thought, as she stared back at him across the imposing mahogany desk that had once been Reginald's.

'But we've always been so well off. Your father never stinted . . . leastways not until he retired. Since then, of course, he's acted so parsimoniously that it's been difficult living with him. Even so . . .'

'Why do you think he had a heart attack, Mother? Why do you think he gave up the social round he was so much a part of and stopped playing golf when he enjoyed it so much?'

'It was his doctor's orders. After his heart attack he was told to take things easy. Golf is a very strenuous game . . .'

'I know he was told to take things easy and not to play golf, but he could still have retained his membership at the golf club. As a social member he would have been able to meet up with all his friends there.'

'You know very well he didn't want to have anything to do with any of them once he knew he couldn't play.'

Charles shook his head. 'He couldn't afford to do so any more; that was the real reason he shunned them all.'

'What on earth are you talking about, Charles? Absolute nonsense! Your father has always been able to afford to do whatever he wanted to.'

Twenty-Two

Margaret walked away from Charles's office in a daze. She had thought he was a clever realistic businessman like Reginald had been but it now looked as though he hadn't got his finger on the pulse at all. All this talk of being hard up was utter nonsense. It was no good him trying to pull the wool over her eyes simply so that she would agree to move out of Willow House so that he could sell it and enjoy making a profit from it.

She wished there was someone she could discus it all with. She didn't want to involve either Alison or Steven because it might lead to a family row and since they would also benefit from the monies from Willow House they might even side with Charles rather than with her.

She was tempted to talk to Thelma, Jan and Brenda about it when they next met for coffee but then decided it wouldn't be wise to confide in them over such a personal matter.

An hour later when she met up with them and watched Brenda cuddling her little dog on her lap, half concealed by her coat in case anyone spotted she had brought it into the café, she wondered if perhaps a dog would be the answer for her.

If she had a dog then she could sort things out in her mind by talking to it without any fear of it divulging what she had said.

She quite liked the idea; that was something she could discuss with the other three, she decided.

When she mentioned aloud that she was toying with the idea of getting a pet because she found it was rather lonely living at

Willow House on her own they all had quite separate opinions on the subject.

Jan deplored the idea. 'You've only just had the place re-decorated so why on earth do you want it all messed up by some animal?' she demanded.

'I've already explained. At times I feel lonely.'

'Well, it's your choice but if you have a dog then you must expect some damage as well as hairs all over the furniture,' Jan pointed out.

'Oh, I think a cat is much better, so warm and they love to be petted,' Thelma intervened.

'Cats are all right if you don't mind them wandering all over your work surfaces in the kitchen or clawing the arms of your favourite chair.'

'Well, at least you don't have to exercise them,' Thelma said with a laugh. 'The very idea of owning a dog and having to take it for a walk two or three times a day puts me right off having one.'

'You don't have to do that if you have a small one like I have. You can even train them to use a soil tray,' Brenda said as she smoothed the silky coat of the little animal on her lap.

'What you've got is a lapdog not a proper dog,' Thelma said with a laugh. 'The sort of dog Margaret needs is one that is big enough to be real company and also to act as a guard dog.'

'I suppose it might be a good idea,' Jan agreed grudgingly. 'I wouldn't like to live in a place as large as Willow House all on my own. It might be all right during the day but at night I would be on edge and worried by every sound I heard.'

They spent a long time discussing what sort of dog Margaret ought to buy and exactly where she ought to go to get it.

'I think you should buy one from a rescue centre,' Brenda said firmly. 'That way you will be giving love as well as receiving it.'

'You mean one that has been abandoned?' Margaret said in surprise.

'Exactly.'

'If it's been abandoned then doesn't that mean there is some-thing wrong with it? Possibly that it has attacked someone and that's why they don't want it?'

'That's not always the case. The previous owner may have

moved house to somewhere smaller, perhaps a flat, where they are unable to accommodate it, or gone abroad and can't take it with them.'

'Or the owner may have died and there is no one in the family who is prepared to take on a dog.'

'It might even be a stray. Dropped out of a car by someone who is fed up with looking after it.'

'Surely no one would do a thing like that,' Margaret said in a shocked voice.

'You'd be surprised,' Brenda said indignantly. 'People can be very cruel, that's why I said you should go to a rescue shelter and pick one from there.'

Margaret sighed. 'I wouldn't have any idea what sort of dog to pick.'

'Yes you would; in fact if you walked down the line of kennels the dog would pick you. They'd probably all want you to take them home but one of them will touch your heart and you won't be able to resist it.'

Margaret frowned. 'I'm not at all sure that I would want the responsibility of looking after a dog though. It would be a bit like having a child . . .'

'Or a sick husband,' Jan said waspishly.

'I would like to be able to give the idea a trial. You know, have a dog for a couple of weeks to see if we got on together.'

'I'm sure there are plenty of people who would welcome the chance of letting you do that. Someone to look after their dog for a couple of weeks while they went away on holiday,' Thelma said thoughtfully.

'Perhaps I should put a notice in the newspaper or in the newsagent's shop?'

The matter was still in the air when they parted but Margaret couldn't put the idea out of her head. She mulled it over for another couple of days and, as her feeling of loneliness increased, so the idea of having a dog became more and more desirable.

Finally she resolved that she would write out a card and take it along to the newsagent's and ask him if he would put it in his window.

'Of course I will, Mrs Wright,' Gordon Bond said with a warm smile.

'Thank you!' Margaret returned his smile gratefully. He had been delivering their newspapers for over twenty years but she hadn't seen him to speak to since his father had died several years ago and he had taken over the business

'It doesn't indicate what breed of a dog or even what size you'd consider,' he said as he scanned the card she'd handed to him.

'That's because I don't really know,' Margaret said with a sigh.

He reread the card tapping the edge of it thoughtfully against his chin.

'Am I right in thinking that you have never owned a dog Mrs Wright?'

'Never!'

'Then why do you want one now?'

Margaret hesitated. 'I'm lonely. As you probably know, my husband has recently died and now I'm finding that living at Willow House all on my own is rather quiet and lonely.'

Nodding his head thoughtfully Gordon Bond studied the card again. 'I tell you what, Mrs Wright, I think I can help you over this. I'm going on holiday at the end of the week so why don't I leave my dog with you and you look after him until I get back in two weeks' time?'

'Oh!' Margaret looked startled. 'I've never met him, he may not like me!' And I may not like him! she thought.

'I'm sure the two of you will get on like a house on fire. He's a very sedate old boy and he'll be on his very best behaviour.'

'Well . . . If you think it would work then I'm willing to give it a try but what happens if I find I can't manage him.'

'You will be able to, after all it is only for two weeks, remember,' Gordon Bond told her confidently.

'As long as you feel happy about the arrangement.'

'Oh I do. I'll bring him round on Friday afternoon together with all his paraphernalia. His name is Bellamy and I'll make sure he is happily settled in. We're not leaving until mid-morning on Saturday so I'll phone you in the morning to make sure the pair of you like each other and that he has settled in and everything is OK,' he promised.

'I won't need you to display that then, will I?' Margaret murmured holding out her hand for the card she had given him.

'Not at the moment, so I'll pop it in the drawer until I come back from my holiday and we'll see then what you want to do,' he told her.

Twenty-Three

Margaret had no idea what sort of dog Bellamy would be and it came as a shock when Gordon Bond arrived late on Friday accompanied by a large black Labrador.

Nervously she stretched out a hand to pat it.

The moment the dog saw Margaret's hand coming towards him he began to bark. It was a deep growling bark that scared her stiff and she pulled her hand back quickly.

'Now now, that will do,' Gordon Bond reproved the dog. 'This is Mrs Wright and you're going to live here at Willow House with her for the next two weeks so settle down and be friendly.'

Again Margaret made an attempt to pat him and this time he sat quietly, staring up into her face enquiringly.

'Aren't you going to come in?' Margaret held the door wide so that they could enter.

The dog pushed past Gordon as though eager to be there. Once inside he began sniffing everywhere as they went into the living room.

'He's just making himself at home,' Gordon Bond explained as he unclipped the leash from the dog's collar and the dog shook himself vigorously as if to make sure that he was no longer restrained.

'I'll go fetch all his equipment from the car while you get acquainted,' Gordon said turning to leave the room.

'Stay!' he ordered, as Bellamy barked again and began to follow him.

Left alone with the dog Margaret stared at him unsure what to do. The dog stared back at her. She stood there petrified as he sniffed at her feet and then looked up at her again as if waiting for her to do or say something.

She had no idea what he wanted but to her great relief at that moment Gordon Bond returned with the dog's basket which he told her was also Bellamy's bed, a plaid blanket, a carrier bag of food, and a drinking bowl as well as a feeding bowl.

'Shall I put this lot in the kitchen?' he asked.

'Yes, I suppose so. Thank you.' She wasn't too sure about the dog's basket being in there but she could always move them later on, she thought.

'What about his basket? Remember that is also his bed. Do you want him to sleep in the kitchen? I think he would be better in the hallway or even underneath the stairs.'

'Oh do you! Very well, if that is what you think is the most suitable place.'

'Right! Leave it to me.'

Watched by the dog Gordon found a suitable spot to put the large wicker basket and after sniffing round it for a minute or two Bellamy barked his acceptance.

He barked again as Gordon handed over to Margaret the plaid blanket that he had brought. 'That's his blanket and I advise you to put it over the chair he will be using in your living room to protect it from hairs.'

'Chair?' Margaret frowned, completely perplexed. 'You mean he sits on a chair?'

'That's right; he likes to have his own chair. I'm surprised he hasn't laid claim to one of the armchairs already. He's probably being polite and waiting to see which one you sit in,' he added with a laugh.

Margaret tried to laugh as well but found it impossible. She had never envisaged there would be all this fuss made over Bellamy coming to stay with her. She had thought you kept a dog out in the back yard in a kennel.

'Right, I think we've done everything we can to make him feel at home. Now he hasn't been fed yet because I thought it would help him to settle better if he started off with a meal in your house. Let's go into the kitchen and I can show you what to give him.'

As he unpacked the carrier bag on to one of the work surfaces Margaret stared at the selection of cans of dog food and bags of biscuits laid out there. She listened as Gordon explained which ones Bellamy had in the morning and which in the evening and how important it was to get the mix right.

Then Gordon prepared an example and handed the feeding bowl to her and told her to put it down on the floor for Bellamy.

She did so and stood back. The dog stared from one to the other of them expectantly.

Gordon half filled the dog's water bowl with cold water and handed it to Margaret. 'Put that down for him as well. You need to keep that topped up all the time because he likes a drink of water at odd times during the day.'

She placed the water bowl alongside the food and stood back. Nothing happened. Bellamy continued to look from his food to her and then to Gordon and then back to his food again.

'He has been trained to wait until you give him the order, "Eat,"' he told her.

'I see! My goodness he is very well trained,' she commented as she issued the command and Bellamy immediately went to his dish and began devouring what was there with gusto.

While the dog ate his dish of food Gordon went over his daily routine to make sure Margaret knew what was expected of her. At the conclusion he handed her a card. 'It's all written down there not only how often each day you take him out for a walk but also his menu for each day. You will see he likes his tins of food to be rotated so that he has something different each day. Now is everything clear?'

'Yes, I think so,' Margaret said.

'Nothing to it, really,' Gordon Bond assured her as he headed for the door.

Bellamy looked from his bowl and started to follow him but Gordon held up a finger. 'Stay!' he ordered. 'You are going to live here with Mrs Wright for a couple of weeks.'

He came back into the kitchen and patted Bellamy, held the dog's face between his hands and let the dog lick his own face and then he was gone.

Bellamy gave a sharp bark, looked at Margaret and then went back into the kitchen to make sure that he had eaten every scrap from his bowl. Satisfied that he had done so, he wandered into the sitting room and stood there looking around. As soon as Margaret sat down he bounded up into one of the other armchairs and happily settled himself down.

Margaret knew she ought to move him and cover the chair

with his rug but she still felt rather nervous of him and decided
that as long as he was quiet it was best to leave him alone.

Twenty-Four

Living with Bellamy was a whole new experience for Margaret.
Some days were good and she enjoyed the dog's company; others
were disastrous and she wondered if she was going to be able to
hold out until Gordon Bond returned from his holiday.

She had to admit in all honesty that she and Bellamy did not
see eye to eye. She was sure that he didn't mean to be disruptive
and cause trouble. When he did, which was frequently, and she
reprimanded him he sat staring at her as though completely
puzzled by her harsh tone and hard words.

In some ways he was good company. He enjoyed being petted
and he was always eager for any scraps of food she fed him in
between his scheduled meal times.

'You should be called "Belly" not "Bellamy",' she told him
reproachfully after he had devoured some slices of cold chicken
she had left out on a plate on the worktop while she went out
into the garden to collect a lettuce to make a salad.

He also exasperated her by the way he followed her round.
He would even follow her upstairs unless she ordered him to stay
down in the hallway.

When she did this he would wait patiently at the foot of the
stairs and watch her every movement as she came back down
them, then dog her footsteps as though afraid to let her out of
his sight. It was the same as Reginald had done so she would try
and ignore him until she could stand it no longer. Then she
would shout at him to 'stay' or ordered him into his basket in
the hallway.

The devotion and bewilderment in his eyes when she did this
made her feel guilty and she usually ended up rewarding him
with a biscuit or treat of some kind. She knew this was strictly
against Gordon Bond's instructions but it appeased her conscience.

Taking Bellamy for walks was often a nightmare. He would

walk along docilely at her side until he spotted another dog and then the sudden jerk on his leash as he darted to make its acquaintance was so strong that often she was in danger of losing her balance.

Then there was the occasion when he almost pulled her into the duck pond. She had simply had to let go of his leash and inwardly pray that he wouldn't attack the ducks. They had squawked wildly as he swam towards them and flew up into shrubbery at the far side of the pond where he couldn't reach them.

When Bellamy emerged from the muddy water he had shaken himself so vigorously her legs and skirt had been so badly spattered that she'd had to go straight home and change.

After the first few days she decided that it might be better to let him loose in the garden instead of going for walks. The problem was that invariably he simply settled down on the lawn and did nothing. In order to make sure he had exercise she had to go out there and throw a ball for him to chase after.

Sometimes he enjoyed this; at other times he simply ignored her efforts. He either put his head down on his paws and went to sleep or else roamed round the garden disappearing out of sight so that she was in a panic in case he had escaped and wandered off towards the main road.

The grandchildren's reaction to Bellamy was very mixed. The boys enjoyed throwing sticks for him to retrieve or chasing after him until he tired of such antics and turned his back on them and ignored them. When this happened they walked away in disgust saying he was a stupid dog anyway.

Petra was the only one who seemed to really like him and who spent hours simply talking to him. Bellamy responded by listening intently and then raising one of his paws to shake her hand. Margaret sometimes wondered if he actually knew what Petra was saying to him.

'I do wish he was yours, Gran,' Petra said. 'Are you going to get a dog of your own when Bellamy goes home?'

'I'm not sure. They are rather tying, you know. I don't like going out and leaving him on his own.'

'Why ever not? He's supposed to be a guard dog isn't he?'

'I'm not too sure about that. He certainly barks loud enough when people come to the door.'

'Well, there you are then. He's trying to protect you. That's exactly what you need when you are living on your own.'

'Yes, but I have a feeling that he doesn't stay in his basket but wanders round the house because I find dog hairs everywhere.'

'Does that matter?' Petra laughed. 'I think he must be wonderful company. You can't possibly be lonely with Bellamy around. Does he sleep on your bed?'

'Good heavens no!' Margaret exclaimed. 'I certainly wouldn't want that. No, it's the fact that he chews things. He ruined one of my slippers the other day while I was out and on another occasion he practically devoured a leather belt I left lying on the chair in my bedroom.'

'That's a sign of his affection for you,' Petra explained, her young face very serious. 'It's because he was missing you and he could smell you on those items that he chewed them.'

'I see!' Margaret didn't really but Petra sounded so positive that she let the subject drop.

Both Charles and Helen thought she was mad to be looking after Bellamy when they discovered that she was doing it for nothing.

'That newsagent is taking advantage of you,' Charles told her. 'If he'd had to put the dog in kennels it would have cost him hundreds.'

Alison claimed she didn't like dogs and shuddered every time Bellamy went near her.

Steven was enthusiastic but mystified as to why she was considering having a dog now. 'You'd never let us have a dog when we were kids,' he said reproachfully.

By the time Gordon Bond came to collect Bellamy and all his paraphernalia Margaret was feeling that the strain of looking after a dog was more than she could stand.

She was extremely grateful to him for giving her the opportunity of finding out first hand if she wanted to have a dog or not.

Nevertheless she breathed a deep sigh of relief when Gordon Bond returned from his holiday and came to collect Bellamy.

It had certainly been an experience, she thought, as she watched him and an excited, yelping Bellamy walk away down the path. It most certainly wasn't one she wanted to repeat, she told herself as she closed the front door behind them.

Twenty-Five

'What on earth do you mean, Charles?' Margaret felt frustration and anger welling up inside her as she faced her eldest son.

Charles frowned in exasperation. 'You still can't accept it, can you? The company has been in financial trouble for years and things have got worse. We're on a knife-edge! Everything is mortgaged up to the hilt. Even Willow House and my home. We rent the factory; we lease all our cars including the BMW that Dad was driving. Even the new computer system we had installed is on rental. Now do you understand the situation?'

She shook her head bewildered. 'But I've got to have a car, Charles! How on earth can I get around?'

'I don't know, Mother, but there certainly isn't any money to buy you one at the moment. Dad used up all his personal capital years ago trying to bail out the company.'

'I need money to live on,' Margaret protested. 'You're not going to stop the cheque that's been paid to me from your father's account each month to cover the housekeeping are you?'

'Not completely, but I will have to reduce the amount.'

'Reduce it! Don't talk nonsense, Charles. I'll be at starvation level if you do that. I simply can't economize any more.'

'It would help if you moved into something smaller.'

'Leave Willow House!' Her eyes widened in horror. 'You must be out of your mind. Do you really expect me to give up my home, where I have lived for forty years, where you were all born and brought up and that I have just had completely redecorated and refurbished and move into a flat?'

'It doesn't have to be a flat. There are some attractive little cottages . . .'

'Poky little one-up one-down places with rooms not large enough to swing a cat in.'

'There are some delightful Elizabethan-style cottages in Wooburn Green that would be ideal for someone living on their own,' Charles went on ignoring all her protests.

'Move from Willow House to one of those!'

'Alright, alright!' Wearily Charles raised a hand to stop her tirade. 'We'll leave things as they are at the moment, but do remember it may come to that. There's no spare cash at all, and unless there is an upturn in business we may be forced into liquidation.'

'That's out of the question! Wrights have been an established name in engineering since Reginald's father, your grandfather, started the business on the Slough Trading Estate fifty years ago. It must be something to do with the way you run things.'

'Mother! You've not listened to a word I've said, have you? It's nothing to do with the way we run things at all. Ninety per cent of the engineering firms on the Slough Estate are in the same predicament.'

She shook her head as if refusing to believe what he was telling her.

'Come to that,' Charles went on, 'so are most of them in the rest of the country. We've all got to pull our horns in and hope things will pick up again soon.'

'Of course they will. It's always a question of swings and roundabouts in business, isn't it?'

He shrugged. 'Perhaps! In the meantime, the coffers are practically empty. There's no money to buy you a car, and there's a possibility that your monthly income will have to be cut in the very near future. If we do go under and things are put into the hands of the receiver then there will be no alternative but for you to move out because Willow House will be repossessed,' he told her harshly.

Margaret stared at him in silent disbelief. Perhaps it was a good job she hadn't mentioned that she was planning to use her own savings to buy a car. By the sound of things she might need her little nest egg in order to survive.

'I didn't intend to be quite so blunt,' he told her apologetically, 'but it seems to be the only way to impress upon you the seriousness of the situation.'

'I see.' Margaret picked up her handbag from where she'd laid it down on the desk. 'Perhaps I'd better go and look for a job,' she muttered scathingly.

'I'm afraid you wouldn't find it very easy to get one,' Charles told her wryly.

'Don't be too sure. I was a first-class secretary when I married your father.'

'Shorthand and typing are as dead as the Dodo. These days, Mother, you need to be able to use a computer. That was something else that put a terrible strain on Father. Your generation find today's skills far too demanding for them.'

Margaret bridled. Why did Charles always have to put her down; to ridicule whatever she said or suggested.

'You're saying I'm past it, are you?'

'Frankly, as far as a business career is concerned, I'm afraid it's the truth.'

She bit down on her lower lip to stop it trembling. 'So what do you recommend I do?'

'You could always take in a lodger.'

'A lodger?' She looked puzzled. 'Why ever should I do that?'

'To help pay the overheads of Willow House if we do manage to stay afloat and it's not repossessed.'

'That's not even amusing, Charles.'

'It wasn't meant to be. I was deadly serious.'

'Yes. Very well.' Margaret looked at her watch. 'I must be going. I'm having coffee with Jan and the others at eleven.'

'You've plenty of time. It's only half past ten.'

'I want to call at the nursery, I ordered a plant for Jan, and I must collect it to take with me.'

'Mother! You can't afford gestures of that sort.'

'Nonsense! Joseph always lets me have them at trade price. That's why I ordered it from there.'

'Well, don't spend any more money, not until we receive the end-of-year figures from the accountants and know exactly where we stand financially.'

'Very well. Now, will you call me a taxi?'

'A taxi! You're going to take a taxi after all I've told you about the state of our finances?'

'Since I haven't a car I have no alternative, have I? Perhaps you'd like me to buy a bicycle?'

Charles shook his head in despair. 'Come on!' He stood up, picked up his car keys, jangling them impatiently. 'I'll run you to Maidenhead to Jan Porter's place.'

'Thank you. We must go to the Chapman Nurseries first,' she

reminded him. 'Still, it is on our way if you take the Hedsor route.'

They drove in silence. Margaret's thoughts were occupied by what Charles had been telling her.

Was she really too old to get a job, she wondered. Charles obviously thought so. It might be amusing to prove him wrong. It would give her something to do. Take her out where she could meet new people. She might even be able to get a job where they provided a car. Now that would be something! That would certainly show Charles she was not the outdated, empty-headed old woman that he so obviously thought she was.

As he sat in his car outside the Chapman Nurseries waiting for his mother, Charles contemplated the situation.

He was very much afraid that although he had tried his best to outline their financial position he hadn't made much impression on his mother and it worried him.

He had already discussed the matter of his mother's extravagant lifestyle and his concern about how she was going to manage in future with the company accountant.

Jack Winter not only handled Wright Engineering's affairs and knew how grave the situation was but Charles knew that he had also handled his father's personal affairs.

It might have been better if he had let Jack Winter be the one to talk to his mother, Charles reflected. She might have taken more notice of him. It irked him that she still seemed to think of him as a small boy who knew nothing about business matters and didn't take what he said seriously.

He was extremely worried about how she would react if they did go under. Then, whether she wanted to or not she would have to sell Willow House.

There wouldn't be a lot he could do to help her because his house was also mortgaged up to the hilt and they would have to downsize. Furthermore both he and Helen would lose their company cars. He was worried, too, that they might not even be able to afford the fees for Petra to be able to take up the university place she'd attained and Amanda's future education would also be affected.

Neither of them mentioned the subject when Margaret came

out of the nursery, nor when he pulled up on the forecourt of the block of luxury flats in Maidenhead where Jan Porter lived.

As he drove away, he studied the flats in his rear mirror and prayed his mother wouldn't decide that she wanted to live there. The upkeep of one of those would be even higher than Willow House.

Twenty-Six

The plant that Margaret had brought for her delighted Jan and she kissed her friend warmly.

'You really shouldn't have done that,' she said contritely as Margaret handed it over, 'but it is lovely. I ought to be the one giving you a present as I was rather a bitch about Jason the last time we met.'

'Let's forget about it,' Margaret murmured with a bright smile.

Despite Margaret's air of false cheerfulness, Jan was quick to notice her preoccupation.

'Something on your mind?' she asked, as she refilled Margaret's cup.

Margaret shrugged her shoulders and gesticulated helplessly with her hands.

'Are you still feeling lonely? Pity you don't like the idea of having a dog; they can be such good company. Have you thought about having a cat instead?'

'No, I don't want a cat. They're almost as much trouble as a dog, hairs everywhere, on the cushions and so on. They jump up on to the worktops, too.'

'Well, that's true. So, if it's not loneliness then what is it that's upsetting you? I saw Charles drop you off so I assume that means you still haven't got your own car? Is that the problem?'

'Partly! According to Charles there's no chance at all of my ever getting one,' she said bitterly.

'Oh?'

Thelma and Brenda were now listening avidly. Margaret tried to explain in a light-hearted way about Wright Engineering's financial plight, but the pressure of the morning exploded inside her, and everything came bubbling out in a torrent.

'You are quite sure Charles is telling you the truth?' mused Jan. 'He's a very shrewd businessman. Reginald trained him from a very young age remember. He might just be telling you a hard luck story to keep you from spending too freely.'

'I don't think so. I've already had a letter from the bank manager telling me that the joint account I had with Reginald is frozen.'

'That's the normal practice . . . until after the will has been sorted out,' Brenda assured her. 'I remember when Jack died . . .'

'I would have thought Reginald would have had a small fortune stashed away in shares in his own name or yours,' interrupted Thelma.

Margaret shook her head. 'I thought so as well because he was very thrifty but it seems there is absolutely nothing like that at all. What's more, absolutely everything that I thought we owned like the house and car belongs to the company and is mortgaged in some way to the bank.'

'That's dreadful! So you really think that Charles wants you to move out of Willow House?'

'Either that or take in a lodger.'

'That's certainly a pretty grim thought but if it saves you from having to move then I suppose it's not such a bad idea,' Thelma said briskly.

'I took in a lodger after Jack died,' Brenda reminded them. 'She was a schoolteacher. Such a nice young girl and from a good background.'

'She wasn't with you for very long though, was she?' stated Thelma.

'That's right!' Jan's eyebrows lifted quizzically. 'What exactly happened?'

'It became rather difficult. She wanted to have her boyfriend to stay at the weekends and there was no spare bedroom.'

'So she left simply because of that?'

'Well, I wasn't having them sleeping together like she wanted. Not under my roof, I mean,' Brenda defended herself. 'I didn't think it was right.'

'You've never had another lodger since then?'

Brenda shook her head, a tremulous smile on her plump

face. 'I find I prefer to be on my own. Such a nuisance and a responsibility having to consider someone else all the time.'

'My sentiments entirely,' agreed Thelma with a hearty laugh. 'Two women never get on in the same kitchen and if you take in a man he wants waiting on hand and foot. Either way, they're far too much trouble.'

'If you're lonely then it's better to have a dog, I always think,' Thelma said with a laugh.

'I've already tried that,' Margaret reminded them and once again recounted her interlude of looking after Bellamy for Gordon Bond while he was away on holiday for two weeks.

'It's not simply a question of loneliness, not in Margaret's case,' Jan mused. 'It's a question of putting some cash in her pocket.'

'Mm! Well, for my part I'd sooner take a job than do that,' Thelma affirmed. 'Much more rewarding financially, and far more satisfactory in every other way.'

'That's all very well for you, Thelma. You've always worked and you have a job you like,' protested Brenda. 'What chance has Margaret of finding work when she's been a housewife for the past forty years?'

'Don't you start!' Margaret rounded on her angrily. 'I've just been through all that with Charles telling me that not only am I too old to get a job because I'm not computer literate but that shorthand and typing are things of the past.'

'Unfortunately, he's probably right,' affirmed Jan.

'Maybe. I still didn't enjoy hearing him say so.'

'Computerization has a lot to do with it, of course. At one time as long as you could read and write you could find work. Age didn't seem to matter.'

'No, they were quite happy to employ older women as receptionists, just as long as they looked smart and had their wits about them,' agreed Brenda.

'They certainly aren't prepared to do that today,' stated Thelma.

'Now, you even have to go on a course of instructions if you want to help out as a voluntary worker in one of the charity shops,' said Brenda, laughing.

'That's true, I got the shock of my life when I went along and offered to do one morning a week and they told me I'd have to go on a three-day course,' Thelma said gloomily.

Margaret looked interested. 'What did the course entail? Do either of you remember?'

'I've no idea. I didn't bother to go,' Thelma said. 'I couldn't do with all that nonsense. I thought it was so unnecessary. At my age I'm perfectly capable of handing things over the counter and taking their money and I told them so.'

'Anyway,' Brenda chuckled, 'I don't know why we're bothering to talk about it since they don't pay. You can't afford to waste your time doing anything like that, now can you, Margaret?'

'It will have to be the lodger,' agreed Thelma brusquely. 'Now, do you want us to scout around and try and find someone suitable?'

'No, no!' Margaret felt alarmed. 'Not for the moment, anyway. I need time to think about it. I'll have to psych myself up for it.'

Twenty-Seven

Margaret found that managing without a car was even more restricting than having to ask Reginald to drive her everywhere.

She wished she'd gone ahead, and used her savings to buy the yellow sports car. She'd had every intention of doing so, but after the way Charles had gone on about the state of her finances, it had seemed prudent to wait awhile.

For one thing, there was still the question of Jason's bill to be sorted out. She had meant to talk to Charles about it but in the end decided not to do so.

After Charles telling her what dire straits they were in she'd felt apprehensive about what he would say when he saw how much it was. She decided that the best thing to do was send it on to Charles at the office. She wouldn't even put a note in with it. She'd keep her fingers crossed that he'd pay it without any comment.

If he did and she didn't have to use her savings to settle it, then she certainly would go ahead and buy a car even though she had probably left it too late to buy the yellow sports car that had taken her eye.

In the meantime she'd have to resort to public transport and take a taxi when necessary. It wasn't as though she was stranded. The railway station was within walking distance and there was a bus service to Maidenhead and from there to Windsor, High Wycombe, and to countless other places.

It took much longer than by car, though, and if it was raining there was the inconvenience of having to carry an umbrella. Coming home was even worse. Tired, laden with shopping, struggling in and out of trains and buses, took away all the enjoyment of a day out. A taxi might be extravagant but it was so much easier and brought her right to the door.

She found that supermarket shopping was the greatest problem. She was used to making a monthly trip and stocking up with everything from meat and vegetables to soap powder and cleaning items. She soon found that this was far too big a load for even the most friendly taxi driver to help her with. They didn't even open the car door for you these days, she reflected, far less carry your groceries inside the front door for you.

'Of course I'll take you to the supermarket, Mother. You only have to ask,' Charles promised when she mentioned the matter to him. 'We'll collect you next time we go. I usually take them as soon as I've finished work on a Friday.'

The trip had been a disaster.

Too late Margaret had discovered that Helen went to a different supermarket to the one she normally used so she had felt disorientated and unable to locate half the items she needed.

Added to that, Petra and Amanda had gone with them, and Petra had insisted on helping Margaret load her trolley. This had proved to be a tremendous distraction. Helen and Charles were through the checkout and waiting to go home long before she had finished traipsing up and down the aisles.

Impatiently, Helen had helped her unload the items at the checkout and had then packed the items into bags while Charles took their shopping out to load in his car.

Normally, Margaret stopped for a coffee at the supermarket cafeteria before she went home but Helen wouldn't spare the time. She wanted to get home as soon as possible because she had frozen items that she wanted to put away in the freezer as soon as possible.

'We'll drop you off first,' Charles told her as they struggled to stack her bags of groceries into the boot of his car.

'Wouldn't it be best if you took Helen and the girls home first? She seemed anxious about getting her frozen items stored away.'

'No. We'll do it my way, Mother. Please don't argue.'

His patronizing tone infuriated her. Tight-lipped, she squashed into the back seat between the two girls. They were both fed up but their faces lit up when she produced a ten-pound note for each of them.

'Give that money back,' ordered Helen from the front seat, glaring over her shoulder at them.

'Oh, Mum, must we?' they grumbled in unison.

'Yes! Granny should have known better.'

'But Mummy . . .'

'That will do,' barked Charles. 'Hand the money back to your granny this minute.' Reluctantly the girls complied.

Margaret placed a comforting arm around each of them. 'I'll give them to you next time I see you,' she whispered.

She sensed Charles was watching her in the driving mirror and knew he disapproved. There was a brusque coldness in his manner when they reached Willow House.

As she fumbled with her door key he unloaded her shopping from his car and dumped it all on the doorstep.

She waved and blew kisses to the two girls as he roared away. Their response was pathetic. Helen didn't even wave.

'I'll certainly not ask Charles to take me shopping ever again,' she told herself aloud as she unpacked the shopping bags and stored things away in the freezer and cupboards.

Next time she was low on supplies she phoned Steven.

'He's away, up North somewhere,' Sandra told her. 'He went yesterday so he won't be back for two or three days. Can I give him a message?'

'No, it's not important,' Margaret told her. She waited for her daughter-in-law to enquire how she was but she didn't.

'I'll tell him to ring you when he gets back,' Sandra said airily, replacing her receiver even before Margaret had time to ask after Matthew and Hannah.

Choked by frustration and self-pity, Margaret poured herself a gin and tonic. There was still Alison, of course. She would probably be willing to arrange a regular monthly shopping trip. Or would she?

Alison had her own family commitments too. For one thing, there always had to be someone at home to answer the phone in case Mark was needed at the hospital. Still, it was worth a try, Margaret decided.

At one time they had spent a day together at least once a week, window-shopping, or buying clothes. They'd certainly not done anything as mundane as shopping for food.

Mark answered the phone. 'Alison's not here at the moment. I'll leave a note for her to ring you the moment she comes in.'

'No, no, it's alright. It's not terribly important. I simply wanted to ask her to come shopping with me.'

'Women!' Mark's cynical laugh jarred on her ears.

That was it, she decided. She would never again ask any of the family to help her. How could they all be so selfish, she wondered.

Looking back, it made Reginald seem almost caring the way he had always been willing to take her to the supermarket. Once the routine had been established and he confined himself to loading the car and then bringing all the bags indoors when they reached home, it hadn't been too bad.

It seemed pathetic that she couldn't cope on her own, she told herself severely. How on earth did she think she was ever going to get a job if she couldn't even organize her own monthly shopping trip?

The more she thought about actually going out to work the more it began to lose its attraction. There was no doubt at all that she had lost confidence in herself and in her ability to cope.

So what was she to do if there was no money coming in, she wondered? Stop shopping for a start, she thought wryly.

There was only one answer to her problem, she decided, and that was to do as Charles had suggested and take in a lodger.

She wasn't sure how to set about finding one and she didn't intend to ask the family to advise her or help her, not after the shopping fiasco.

She didn't want to ask Jan, Brenda or Thelma. She'd prefer to tell them once it was all accomplished.

It shouldn't be all that difficult, she told herself. She had pleasant rooms to offer and they could have a bedroom and a sitting room if that was what they wanted and they were prepared to pay rent to cover both.

Or, if they merely wanted a bedroom then she could take in two lodgers. That might be a better idea because they would be company for each other.

She found a pen and paper and began listing what it would cost to have them there. If she intended to give them breakfast and a main meal in the evening, then she would need to work out how much the food was going to cost. Then there was the laundering of the bedclothes.

She realized that she might find looking after them and keeping their rooms clean too much work for her so she needed to include daily or weekly help into the overall sum.

She supposed she ought to make a charge for general wear and tear. She would probably have to have rooms redecorated more often and then there were repairs to be considered. Other people were not always as careful when they were living in other people's homes. Furniture might be accidentally damaged.

In addition to all this she ought to make a list of do's and do not's. No pets, for example, no parties, no coming in so late at night that they disturbed other people in the house. She didn't want them playing music late at night either.

She remembered Brenda's experience of visiting boyfriends and decided she would have to take a stand about visitors. She didn't want young children there, even for a visit, if they were going to make a mess or too much noise. She most certainly didn't want a widow or unmarried mother with young children.

When she totalled everything up Margaret was amazed at the high rent she would need to charge if she was going to make a profit out of letting rooms. She wondered what sort of single person was going to be able to afford to come and live at Willow House. Obviously it would have to be a high-earner, probably a professional man or woman. She'd have to be extremely careful in how she worded her advert, she decided.

In the end she felt so exhausted she resolved to put off deciding on anything or writing out the advertisement until the following day. She needed to sleep on it; she was no longer all that sure that having a lodger was such a good idea.

When she woke next morning she thought it through again while drinking her first cup of tea of the day and decided that perhaps finding a job would be a far better move after all.

Twenty-Eight

For the next few days, now that she had decided to get a job rather than take in a lodger, Margaret mulled over what sort of work she wanted to do.

She wasn't qualified to be a teacher or for any other professional calling so that meant that if Charles was right and shorthand typists were no longer used then the only sort of work that she could apply for were run-of-the-mill jobs.

She didn't want to do factory work, cleaning or cooking or caring for old people. She wouldn't mind being a receptionist at a doctor's or a dentist's surgery; or even for a business concern as long as she didn't have to use a computer.

The only other kind of work would be in a shop. Not on the till in a supermarket because the continual pinging as the goods passed through the checkout would drive her mad after a time. She certainly didn't want to stack shelves either. She didn't fancy a food shop of any description. Possibly a chemist's or a hairdresser's, as long as she wasn't expected to make the coffee and sweep the floor.

She quite liked the idea of working in a florist's. Joseph would give her a reference and say how clever she was at arranging flowers and how much she loved them.

Perhaps the most suitable would be as an assistant in a dress shop, but there were precious few independent ones left and she certainly didn't want to work for one of the large chain stores.

The other possibility was a bookshop. She liked reading and it would be interesting knowing what new titles were being published and which authors were the most popular.

That weekend Margaret studied the vacancies columns in

the local newspapers hoping to spot the sort of job she felt capable of doing. The only one that caught her interest was in a card shop and she decided to apply for it. She knew where the shop was and didn't have to take it if she didn't like the owner there.

An hour later she was in Maidenhead. The card shop was in a side street just off the main shopping area. There were two customers already in there when she walked in so she began to browse the stands holding the cards to see what sort of stock they carried.

There were greeting cards and birthday cards of every description. Some of them shocked her they were so lewd. She wondered if she would be doing the buying, if so, then that type of card would disappear in double quick time.

The man behind the counter looked middle-aged and studious. He barely glanced up from the sheaf of papers he was sorting through as she went up to the counter after the other customers left.

'Good morning. I've come about the vacancy.'

'Vacancy?' He looked at her so blankly that she wondered if she had come to the wrong card shop.

'The one in the local paper.'

'Oh that! It's been filled.' He turned back to the forms he had been filling out.

'It only appeared today.'

'Filled before the paper came out,' he said tersely not even looking up this time.

Margaret left the shop feeling deflated. She made her way back into the High Street and went into a small café. As she sat sipping the latte she had ordered she watched the overweight waitress hobbling to and fro serving other customers. She was middle-aged and obviously from the way she was walking she had a bad hip or knee and was in a good deal of pain.

For a minute Margaret wondered if she ought to ask if they needed a replacement. Then as she looked again at the woman and saw the strain on her face she decided that it wouldn't be fair on the poor woman to take her job off her and that it wasn't the sort of work that she wanted to do anyway.

Having almost an hour to wait for a bus Margaret decided to go into the public library. There would be up-to-the-minute newspapers in there and she might spot a suitable job in one of them. If it was in Maidenhead then she could apply for it there and then and save having to come back into town again.

To her surprise and annoyance the space normally set aside as a reading space and where the newspapers were usually to be found was now filled with computers.

She stood for several minutes staring fascinated by what was on the screen. She was startled when a smartly dressed young librarian assistant appeared and asked, 'Are you here for a lesson?'

'Good heavens no! I thought this was where the reading room was and where I would find the newspapers. I wanted to see if there were any local jobs advertised,' she added by way of explanation.

The assistant looked at her with raised eyebrows. 'We haven't had a reading room here for almost a year. As you can see we now utilize the space to house computers. Are you sure you wouldn't like to sign up for a series of lessons? We do have special sessions for absolute beginners.'

Flushing with annoyance because the woman obviously sensed she knew nothing at all about computers Margaret made a hurried exit.

It was a thought though, she mused as she went to the bus stop. If she couldn't find a job then she might consider taking a computer course.

As she approached the bus stop a large Vacancies sign outside what looked to be an office caught her eye. Tentatively she went in.

Inside there were three desks manned by very efficient looking young women. 'Can I help you?' one of them asked, looking up with an enquiring smile.

'Your sign outside said "Vacancies". I am looking for a job. What sort of position do you have available?'

'We haven't any vacancies here. We are an agency. We have a variety of jobs on our books. What sort of work are you looking for? We can offer you a wide range of professional positions and of course clerical work, shop assistant or even home care and nursing jobs.'

Margaret felt at a loss. 'Have you any vacancies for receptionists?'

'Is that the sort of work you have been doing?'

'No, not exactly. I haven't been working for a while but it is the sort of job I want.'

'I see! Take a seat and I'll check.'

Margaret sat down in the chair facing the desk as the woman rose and went over to a filing cabinet at the other side of the room. As she waited Margaret noted that a framed card on the desk gave the woman's name as Daphne Robins.

In a matter of minutes Daphne Robins had returned, smiling brightly and carrying two cards.

'Right. Well, there's one at a beauty salon and one at a private clinic. In both instances, as well as welcoming clients, you will be expected to keep records of their treatment and note appointments on the computer and send out reminders and render accounts and ensure that they are not behind with their payments.'

Daphne Robins looked up enquiringly at Margaret, 'Do you think you will be able to do all that?'

'I am sure I can,' Margaret said confidently, 'but not on a computer. I would prefer to record everything in ledgers and . . .' Her voice trailed off as she saw the frown on Daphne Robins's face.

'Do I take it that you are not computer literate?' she asked crisply.

'I'm afraid not; well, not at the present moment. I am thinking about taking lessons.'

Daphne Robins shook her head and pursed her lips. 'I'm afraid then that those sorts of jobs are not for you.' She smiled brightly. 'I am sure we have others that you would like to consider.'

She rose and returned the two cards to the filing cabinet and came back with two others.

'What about working as a companion to an elderly person? It would mean helping them to wash and dress in the morning, preparing their meals and taking them out shopping or for short walks. Possibly that would be in a wheelchair.'

'No! Most certainly not,' Margaret said firmly.

'I see! I suppose you wouldn't be interested in child care, while their parents are at work? If you were looking after small children then of course you would have to be checked out by the police and social services.'

'I don't think so!'

'No, you are probably right. It really needs a much younger

person for that sort of work. Well, in that case, Mrs Wright, I don't think we have anything suitable for you on our books at the moment,' Daphne Robins said dismissively.

Deftly she tore in two the card she had started to make out in Margaret's name and dropped it into the waste-paper basket at the side of her desk. 'Never mind; do call in again because we are constantly adding new vacancies to our lists.'

Margaret left the agency feeling a mixture of annoyance and dismay. Daphne Robins had made her feel not only old but useless.

By the looks of things it was back to the drawing board, she reflected as she rode home on the bus from Maidenhead. It would seem that taking in lodgers was about the only thing she was capable of doing; the only means she had of earning money.

Even to do that she felt she needed some help and advice. She didn't want to ask her family and she didn't want to involve her friends, so who was there left, she wondered despondently.

It left only Jason.

Her heart lifted. Of course, Jason would be able to help. He might even know of someone who was looking for somewhere to live. And he could certainly recommend Willow House. He knew every inch of the place and could list all the advantages of living there in glowing terms.

She grimaced. She would hate having other people at Willow House, especially now when she'd had it so beautifully redecorated.

Still, she told herself, it had to be done and the sooner she accepted the idea the better.

Twenty-Nine

Jason appeared flattered when she phoned and told him that she had a problem and would like his help.

'Of course I'll help in any way I can . . . I'm on my way . . .'

'There's no need to come over, I can explain over the phone.'

'Nonsense! I need a tea break. It will be an opportunity to get out of the office for an hour.'

She hardly had time to lay up a tray with cups and saucers and a plate of biscuits before Jason was at the door.

'How are you managing on your own?' he asked solicitously.

'Quite well,' she answered guardedly as she poured out the tea and passed a cup to him.

His amber eyes narrowed a fraction as he studied her carefully. 'No problems at all?'

'Well . . .' she hesitated, trying to avoid his penetrating gaze. Then with a little sigh she gave in. 'You've heard, I suppose?'

'Heard what?'

'That Reginald was practically broke when he died.'

'Really!' He regarded her speculatively.

'I'm afraid so.'

'You settled my account promptly enough.'

She looked at him quickly. 'You've been paid? Oh that is a relief. I was worried in case Charles had put it on hold.'

'Charles? What did he have to do with it?'

'I passed it over to him to pay. Reginald left powers of administration in his hands. Didn't you notice it was his signature on the cheque?'

Jason shook his head. 'It wasn't a cheque. It was paid by bank transfer.'

Margaret shrugged. 'You've got your money, that's the main thing.'

'And now you're broke?'

'I was broke before, apparently. The company has been in trouble for years. It was all the worry and insecurity that caused Reginald's heart attack, or so Charles claims. After his retirement Reginald spent all his personal savings. That was what we were living on.'

'So that was why he sold your car, was it,' mused Jason.

Margaret looked startled. 'You mean to get money to live on?'

Jason nodded. 'I think that's quite possible, don't you?'

Margaret hid her face in her hands, appalled as she recalled the way she had carried on at the time. Then her heart hardened. If Reginald had confided in her, if he had explained the true state of their affairs, she would have understood why it had to be sold and not made any fuss at all.

As it was, she had taken it as just another sign of his chauvinism.

She had thought he had sold her car simply because he wanted to deprive her of her independence.

He was still managing to do that even now, she thought angrily. Her newly found freedom was being eroded because she might have to give up her home because he hadn't left enough money for its upkeep.

'What on earth am I going to do?' She turned to Jason, her face creased in despair.

Forty years of being looked after, cared for, provided for and protected from the harsh realities of life had sapped her initiative. Charles was probably right she thought bitterly. Her inability to cope with her own domestic crisis hadn't augured much hope of her landing a worthwhile job.

'Finding the right person to have as a lodger is going to be the problem,' she told Jason. 'I'm not keen on having strangers moving into Willow House with me, yet what else is there? All my friends have their own homes. The only person who might be prepared to give up her own place and share with me is my sister, Vivienne.'

The trouble was, Margaret thought, she didn't like Vivienne. They had never got on all that well and she felt sure that having to live together permanently would be unbearable for both of them.

Jason reached out and took both her hands in his. 'Stop worrying! I think I can solve your problem,'

His tone was gentle but reassuring. Margaret looked up into his face, taking strength from the compassion in his amber eyes.

'I know who will make the perfect lodger.'

'Is it a man or a woman?'

'Does that matter?'

'Not really, I suppose. Whoever it is will probably be out most of the day. A man will need more looking after. He'll expect his meals to be cooked and his washing done, that sort of thing.'

'Not this one. He's fully house-trained,' he told her gravely.

'And he's looking for accommodation?'

'Well, he has got somewhere at the moment, but I know he would prefer Willow House to where he's living at present.'

'I shall be charging an exorbitant rent,' she warned.

'He'll pay whatever you ask.'

'Really! I find it hard to believe. So who is it?'

His amber eyes gleamed teasingly. 'Can't you guess?'

'You don't mean . . .' she stopped aghast. The look on Jason's face told her all she needed to know.

'But you can't move in here with me!'

'Why ever not? You are looking for a lodger. You've just said so.'

'I don't know what my family will say.'

'Does it matter? You are the one who's going to share your home with me, not them. Come on, Margaret, you know it's the perfect solution. We enjoy each other's company so this will be a wonderful arrangement for both of us.'

Alarm bells rang in her ears. 'If you come it will be strictly as a lodger, remember,' she demurred.

'I know, I know and I accept your conditions – for a start at any rate.'

Margaret frowned. 'What happens if we find it doesn't work?'

'You have only to say and I'll move out of course. Now, does that set your mind at rest?'

'Well, it's such a shock that I don't know what to say!'

'Say yes! And now tell me when I can move in.'

Margaret hesitated. 'I must explain the situation to the family first.'

He frowned. 'Why do you need to do that? If you had advertised in the local paper would you have consulted them about the applicants or would you have taken a decision on your own?'

'Charles warned me about doing that. He gave me a list of questions to ask and said he would have any applicants vetted before anything was agreed.'

Jason's mouth tightened and his amber eyes darkened angrily but his tone was controlled as he said: 'OK. Then he can vet me if it gives him peace of mind.'

She knew he was waiting for her to say it didn't matter in his case and she felt embarrassed because she couldn't go back on her promise to Charles.

Deep down she was uncertain about having Jason as a lodger because there seemed to be something inevitable about it; almost as if he had planned it.

Right from the start he had taken such a personal interest in the work he was carrying out on Willow House. The meticulous attention to everything, his insistence on supervising every detail, had been excessive.

Had their visits to London to tour furniture stores and their numerous expeditions to art galleries and exhibitions been as much for his benefit as hers? she wondered. Had he wanted to make sure that everything that went into Willow House was in accordance with his taste?

It had been pleasant to be wined and dined, especially by a younger, handsome man who hung on her every word. It had been a novelty to have her opinion valued but had it really been necessary, or had it been a way of flattering her and winning her confidence.

After so many years of enduring Reginald's carping, listening to him grumbling about everything from the state of the country to the weather, it had been refreshing to be in such genial company.

Looking back, Margaret wondered if she had been too forthcoming. Jason had put her so much at ease and listened so willingly that she had told him things she wouldn't have dreamed of confiding to anyone else. Knowing he knew so much about her affairs now made her feel extremely vulnerable,

So was it sensible to let him move in? Was it courting trouble to have him living under her roof? If she was honest, she had to admit that she enjoyed his company but, even so, she didn't want their relationship to go any further.

As if reading her thoughts, Jason said quietly, 'It would be the ideal opportunity for us to get to know each other better at our own pace. I still have a living to earn, a business to oversee, so I would be out of the house a great deal.'

'But you would be living here . . .'

'I would keep to my own rooms unless you invited me to join you.'

Margaret nodded uncertainly.

'The great advantage for you would be that you'd be able to afford to go on living at Willow House,' he persisted.

Margaret felt herself weakening. Her resolution not to let anyone encroach on her freedom ever again was creeping away like a whipped puppy.

'I'll have to think it over,' she prevaricated. 'It sounds like a possible solution,' she added cautiously.

Jason gave a desultory shrug but his amber eyes were bright with the pleasure of knowing he had won. His lips curved in a restrained quirk of triumph. He looked so happy that, once again, alarm bells sounded inside her head.

What was she doing! She would have to tell Charles and she wondered if he would approve of her decision. If only Reginald was here to advise her.

She comforted herself with the thought that it was Reginald's fault she was in this predicament. If he had been more prudent or at least told her what a sorry state they were in it wouldn't have all come as a shock. Furthermore she would have been thriftier and she certainly wouldn't have spent the money she had on refurbishing Willow House.

As a result of all this she was now so hard up that she was being forced to do what Charles had told her and take in a lodger.

Thirty

Unable to settle, Margaret wandered out into the garden while she waited for Jason to return. Whenever her nerves were on edge or anything worried her she found it calming, restorative even, to potter in the garden. If it had been light enough she would have pruned back some of the overgrown bushes, pulled up weeds or even deadheaded the geraniums and roses.

As it was, she simply wandered up and down in the semi-darkness, enjoying the moon-soaked peacefulness. The rustling from the bushes where birds were roosting or nesting, the scampering of voles and field mice in the borders, the prickly scuttle as a hedgehog came out from under the garden shed in search of food were all overshadowed by the thunderous rumble of heavily loaded passenger jets leaving Heathrow airport on the first leg of their outward journey.

They passed so low overhead it seemed they almost scraped the top of the willow tree, their cabin lights shining like a string of stars. As she wondered where they were bound for she felt a momentary regret that she hadn't been able to take the holiday she'd promised herself.

She heard Jason's car draw up, heard him call her name as he went into the house through the front door that she had left ajar, but she made no effort to follow him.

She kept her mind a blank waiting for him to come and look for her. She didn't know whether she wanted him to stay or leave. It was weak of her, she knew, but she felt it had to be his decision.

She had laid down the ground rules, if he accepted them of his own free will, then she would feel happier than if she nagged or coerced him into doing so.

Her own feelings were in turmoil but she was still resolved not to give in. She wasn't prepared to live with Jason, not in the fullest sense of the word.

She didn't want to live on her own so if he decided not to move in as a lodger then she would look for someone else. Next time, though, she'd do as Alison had advised and let Charles handle the letting, She would put the onus on him to vet the new tenant and set down the house rules.

Perhaps it would be better if she did have a woman to share with her. She thought of Jan and Brenda and Thelma and immediately dismissed all thought of anyone like that. Jan was so bossy that she would probably be the one making the house rules. Brenda was too fussy and disorganized. She shuddered. All those knick-knacks and ornaments, she couldn't bear that. She didn't want someone of Thelma's type either. She was so dominant. It would be like having a man in the house without all the advantages of a man's strength and his technical knowledge when it came to hanging pictures, changing fuses and putting new washers on taps.

If only Steven was still a bachelor, she thought wistfully. She would have enjoyed having him living at home. It would have been such a good life for the two of them. Together under one roof, yet content to live individual lives without any interference on either side.

She always felt so comfortable with Steven. They thought alike about most things and even when her opinion differed from his, he never censured her.

'Coffee?'

Margaret swung round. She hadn't heard Jason come into the garden yet he was standing right besides her holding a tray with a jug of coffee and two mugs on it. Without waiting for an answer, he set the tray down on the wrought-iron garden table as if it was the most natural thing in the world for him to be bringing her coffee at this time of night.

'Come and sit here.' He patted the cushions on the garden seat beside him. As she sat down he poured out the coffee into the mugs and handed one to her.

It was all so incongruous that she wanted to laugh. He was acting as if he already lived there and as if the acrid discussion over the house rules and which rooms he should have had never taken place.

That's what he wants me to think, she told herself. It's a mental sweeping it under the carpet syndrome. It left her nonplussed. Her thoughts were so conflicting that she couldn't decide how to react. She wanted him to move in but could she trust him to behave like a lodger and not to encroach on her privacy or try to change the way she lived?

As she turned her head to look at him, Jason smiled back, as though he was reading her thoughts.

His smooth gleaming head, that was almost the same colour as his evenly tanned cheeks, was luminous in the moonglow. He flicked imaginary specks from his black polo-necked shirt and white jeans and then crossed one suede-clad foot over the other as he leaned back and placed his empty cup on the table.

'Perfect, isn't it!' His amber eyes gleamed like a cat's in the dim light.

Margaret looked away quickly, unnerved by his closeness. It had all happened so suddenly. Far too quickly! It was as if some invisible presence was pushing her forward, ensnaring her, not allowing her time to think.

Everything else she had attempted since Reginald had died, like changing the car and her holiday abroad, had all met with resistance from her family and fallen through. Yet everything to do with Jason moving in had rushed to a positive conclusion. Was it fate?

A sudden swoosh in the air around her startled her. She let

out a scream as a whirring black shape narrowly missed her face, circled over her head and then made another swoop in her direction.

As she ducked down, covering her hair with her hands, Jason placed his arm around her shoulders protectively.

'It's only a bat!'

'I know! I hate them, though. I'm always afraid they'll become entangled in my hair.'

'They're far too clever for that. They fly on a sort of radar system.'

She shivered. 'In that case, why can't they keep their distance!'

His laugh was warm and reassuring. 'They're attracted to you . . . just as I am.'

His arm tightened. His long fingers moved slowly up and down her spine in a slow, soothing caress as if he was counting every vertebra. It was very sensual and she found herself unable to control her shivering response.

His touch deepened. His hand moved lower down her spine until he was caressing her hip and then his fingers were kneading into the soft flesh between her hipbone and groin.

The bat swooped again, but this time Margaret didn't even flinch. All her thoughts were focused on the incredible sensations Jason's touch was arousing in her.

She tried to analyse what was happening, why she was feeling so physically disturbed by his closeness. It wasn't as though it was their first meeting. She'd been out with Jason countless times on their visits to exhibitions and showrooms. They'd eaten together, shared so many intimate moments, yet never once, not even at Jan's birthday party on the *Castle Gold* when he'd told her that he thought he was falling in love with her, had she felt as emotionally disturbed as she did now.

Her thoughts buzzed like an angry wasp trapped in an empty beer glass as physical needs, submerged for too long, came to the surface. She deplored her own foolhardiness in inviting him to live at Willow House. If this was what it was going to do to her then it would be best to tell him right away, that it had all been a mistake.

He'd be annoyed at being asked to leave. He'd have every right

to be after moving most of his personal belongings from his studio
flat to Willow House. Even so, it would be better to upset him
now than to leave him under any false illusions.

Jason mistook her sharp intake of breath, as she struggled to
bring her feelings under control and find the right words to tell
him what was in her mind, as an expression of emotion.

Margaret felt incensed as the pressure of his hand increased.
Gritting her teeth she pushed his hand aside and stood up.

'I think it's time we were going indoors.'

'You're probably right. I do have to be at work in the morning,'
he agreed in a low, diffident voice.

Margaret felt confused His tone was so smooth, so unemotional,
that she wondered if she had attributed far more to his action
than he'd intended.

'Surely you don't open your showroom all that early?'

'I like everything to be ready for customers by nine o'clock
and that means I need to be there about half eight at the latest
to make sure everything is presentable.'

Margaret collected up their coffee cups and placed them on
the tray. As she picked it up and began walking towards the house
he took the tray from her and carried it into the kitchen.

'So you get up about seven o' clock do you?' she queried as
she rinsed out the two mugs under the hot water tap and turned
them upside down on the draining board.

She bit her lip, realizing that her voice was sharp and terse and
that she was haranguing him almost like a schoolteacher.

'Seven, half past, something like that, Why?'

'I was just wondering what sort of arrangements we ought to
make about breakfast.'

'It's no great hassle. I don't bother with a cooked breakfast. I
only have orange juice, a bowl of cereal and a slice of toast and
marmalade if there is any available.'

'So you can see to that yourself.'

His eyes widened in surprise.

'Of course . . . if that is what you wish. I had rather looked
forward to us having breakfast together.'

'No . . . I think it would be better if we made our own
arrangements in the morning.'

He shrugged. 'That's fine by me.'

'Sometimes I get up very early. At other times, if I don't sleep well, I am quite late,' she added vaguely.

She waved a hand towards the fridge and the toaster. 'You know where everything is?'

'I'll manage!'

'Good . . . then I'll say goodnight. I'll lock the front door before I go upstairs. Will you put out the lights?'

'If that's the way you want it.'

His slow, amused smile made her feel uncomfortable. She suspected he was laughing at her and she wasn't sure why. Tight-lipped she began to ascend the stairs.

'So I won't see you at all in the morning?' he called after her.

She paused, holding on to the banister rail as she looked back over her shoulder. 'Probably not.'

'You will remember to invite Jan and the others to dinner.'

'Tomorrow night?'

'That's what we agreed.' He came to the foot of the stairs, and stood looking up at her. 'You do still want me to be the one to tell them that I'm moving in as your lodger, don't you?'

She hesitated, knowing that this was an ideal moment to tell him that she wasn't sure and that she needed more time to think about it but instead found herself saying: 'Yes . . . yes, of course I do!'

'So you'll phone the three of them tomorrow morning?'

'Yes! Will eight o'clock suit you?'

He frowned, rubbing his hand slowly over his bare skull so that the tanned skin rippled like soft golden sand as the tide recedes from it.

'It would be better if you made it earlier. Then you can enjoy a drink, and a chat with them, while I'm cooking the meal.'

'While you cook the meal?' Margaret stared at him, her eyes widening in astonishment.

'I'll break the big news to them over a welcoming drink the moment they arrive. Then I'll leave the four of you to chat while I get on in the kitchen,' he told her.

'I . . . I haven't decided yet what we are having.' Her tone was tetchy. She wanted to remind him that it was her kitchen, her friends and, above all, her home.

He beamed magniloquently. 'Don't give it another thought. I'll shop for what I need and bring it home with me.'

Margaret made one final effort to retain control of the situation. 'Perhaps I should . . .'

Jason held up a hand imperiously. 'Not another word! My treat, my surprise.'

'But they're my friends,' she exploded, 'I should be the one to . . .'

'You can supply the wines,' he conceded. 'Chilled white to start and perhaps a Claret for the main course.'

At a complete loss for words, Margaret went on up the stairs. Jason taking such a decisive stance brought back memories of the way Reginald had always dictated what she must do and she found it very disturbing. She knew that this was yet another opportunity to tell him she had changed her mind about him coming there to live but the words wouldn't come.

None of this had been covered by the house rules that she had compiled so carefully. She had never dreamed that he would want to cook or that he would try and organize her life. It made the list she had given him about coming in late, always locking up if he was last in, bringing down any laundry first thing on a Monday morning and countless other household rules seem like petty domestic trivia.

Was Jason simply trying to be helpful, Margaret asked herself as she undressed and prepared for bed. Probably all he was trying to do was be cooperative and she was grossly misinterpreting his actions.

Living on her own was making her paranoiac, she told herself ruefully. The more she thought about it the more foolish her anxieties seemed to be. The truth was she was not used to others taking over her household chores and she resented the intrusion into what she considered to be her territory.

It was her own fault; she had no one but herself to blame. Welcoming Jason to Willow House and making sure that he felt at home there constituted more than merely handing him a door key. She'd lost the right to consider the kitchen her sole domain the moment she'd told him to fend for himself in the mornings.

She suddenly felt uneasy as she heard him moving about on the landing. There was no lock on her bedroom door, or on any of the interior doors, apart from the bathroom and the downstairs cloakroom.

Feeling rather ridiculous she struggled to move the armchair that stood by the window across the room so that she could wedge it tight against her bedroom door. It weighed a ton. She dropped it on her instep at one stage and the pain was so excruciating that she could barely stop herself from screaming out loud.

Thank heaven her room had an en-suite bathroom, she thought, as she hobbled through to soak a flannel in cold water and apply it to her foot to try and stem the swelling.

With the chair blocking the door against intrusion she felt more sanguine. At least she'd be able to sleep in peace.

An hour later she began to wonder if she was going to be able to sleep at all. She had never felt so edgy and the question still uppermost in her mind was how was she going to make having a lodger work?

She wasn't prepared to admit to Charles and the rest of the family, that they were right and she was wrong. Furthermore, she'd never be able to face Jan and the others, if she had to admit to them that she'd made a bad move by having Jason as a lodger.

Since they didn't know as yet, then if she didn't invite them to dinner tomorrow evening, they wouldn't have to know anything at all about it.

I'll tell Jason first thing in the morning that I don't think sharing Willow House with him is a good idea, she decided.

The thought played over and over again, like a dominant chord, as she tossed and turned, trying to settle. Sleep eluded her as she speculated about the future.

At any other time she would have gone down to the kitchen and made a hot drink but now she was reluctant to do so in case Jason might hear her and come to investigate what she was doing.

She heard the night planes droning overhead, the distant sound of a car door slamming and the sudden sharp bark of a disturbed dog. Even the faint ticking of her bedside clock disturbed her, keeping sleep at bay and turning her fears and misgivings into growing uncertainty.

It was almost dawn before Margaret drifted into a nightmare-ridden turmoil; mid-morning before she woke again feeling irritable and out of sorts.

She struggled out of bed feeling disgruntled at having slept so late. Bleary-eyed, she showered and dressed, hoping that once she'd had a coffee she would feel more normal.

It wasn't until she was ready to leave her bedroom and found the armchair pushed tight up against the door that she thought about Jason. She checked on the time. At least he would be out of the house by now and she'd have the place to herself, she thought with relief.

Downstairs there was no sign of him. If he had eaten breakfast before he went off to his studio then he had not left any traces whatsoever.

She wandered through the rest of the downstairs rooms. They were all in the same pristine order as they'd been the previous day.

Feeling more reassured she went upstairs to the room Jason was planning to use as a studio. At first she felt it would be prying to go inside, invading his privacy. Then she reminded herself it was her house so she had every right to do so.

She flung open the door not knowing quite what to expect. The silence mocked her. The room was completely empty; utterly bare.

She walked along the landing towards the room that had been Steven's, the room she'd decided that Jason was to use as a bedroom. Her hesitation was momentary; she had to see if that room was also empty. If so, did it mean Jason had once again read her thoughts and sensed she wasn't happy about sharing her home with him? Or had he, too, decided that both of them living under the same roof wouldn't work?

As she opened the door she could feel his presence. It was everywhere. She looked around hesitantly, half expecting to find him sitting in there waiting for her,

His dressing gown was on a hook behind the door. Socks, underwear and shirts were piled on the armchair. She wondered why Jason hadn't put them away in the chest of drawers. She'd made sure it was ready, even relined each of the five drawers with crisp green and white perfumed paper.

Propped against one wall was a stack of unframed sketches, drawing and paintings. On the floor alongside them were boxes of paints, pencils, palettes and other art equipment.

The dressing table looked bare; not even a brush or comb, only an electric razor, a flask of expensive aftershave and a matching can of spray deodorant.

One of the wardrobe doors was ajar, and she could see his suits and jackets, hanging there. She stood looking at them, remembering the different occasions when he had worn each one. Remembering their many trips to London, their visits to exhibitions, studios, workshops and stores.

She'd enjoyed every one of those visits, she reflected. Jason had been so attentive, so knowledgeable, so entertaining.

At first she'd felt self-conscious, afraid that people might be wondering why on earth someone as young and handsome as Jason was escorting a plain, middle-aged woman.

Their age difference had galvanized her into buying new clothes. Up-to-the-minute styles, the sort of clothes that a year or two earlier she would have thought of as avant-garde and unsuitable for her mode of life. It had been because Jason had been so distinctively different that she'd had the courage to change her own image.

In that respect, knowing him had been tremendously good for her ego so why did she now feel so threatened, she wondered?

Right from their first moment of meeting there had been empathy between her and Jason; a sexual chemistry that stirred both of them. He had made no secret of his feelings for her so why was she holding back? What was she afraid of, she wondered? She was behaving like a Victorian virgin, not someone who had married at nineteen over forty years ago!

Resolutely she turned and left the room, closing the door firmly behind her. If she had to have a lodger then surely it was better to have someone she knew rather than a complete stranger.

She had made it clear that he would be living there as a lodger and nothing more and Jason was the perfect gentleman so what was she worrying about?

Thirty-One

The dinner party went incredibly smoothly, although there was no doubt at all in Margaret's mind that it was Jason who dominated the entire evening. It was his party not hers.

Jan's autocratic features had hardened when she found Jason was already installed at Willow House and she made no secret of the fact that she disapproved of him being there as Margaret's lodger.

His effusive greeting, however, helped by the large gin frugally laced with tonic that Jason handed her almost before she had stepped inside the door, overcame Jan's initial annoyance.

Thelma and Brenda seemed to be surprised by Margaret's action but not unduly concerned. Brenda welcomed him enthusiastically, calling him 'dear boy' and patting his arm. Thelma was more restrained but she, too, seemed delighted to see him, and expressed the opinion that she thought it was an excellent arrangement that he was going to live at Willow House.

'I'm sure you will be very happy there,' she enthused. 'It's a lovely house, especially now that Margaret has had it all redecorated and installed modern furniture. Then, of course, you know all about that don't you,' she added with a coy smile.

At Jason's suggestion they all took their drinks out on to the patio. As soon as they were all sitting comfortably and relaxed in the deeply cushioned wicker armchairs, he excused himself. 'I'm going to disappear into the kitchen for a little while so I'm leaving you here to either go on happily chatting to each other or you can wander around the garden and admire Margaret's clever work there. I'll call you when everything is ready.'

The meal was simple but superbly cooked and served. He tempted their palates with iced soup, delicately flavoured with fresh herbs, followed by lamb cutlets, grilled with rosemary from the garden and served with tiny new potatoes, baby onions and tender green beans. To follow, he piled strawberries into individual melon boats, and topped them with whipped cream.

The evening was hot and sultry so they returned to the coolness of the patio to enjoy freshly perked coffee and a heady liqueur that none of them had ever tasted before. Jason refused to tell them its name, claiming that it was one of his secret discoveries.

Surrounded by her closest friends, replete with food, and pleasantly soporific from the various wines and spirits she'd been drinking, Margaret felt agreeably content.

Why couldn't life always be relaxed and friendly like this, she wondered. If only one could freeze such a moment not simply as a memory but to actually be recaptured at will.

In some respects she had done exactly that, she told herself. Or, even better, she had turned the clock back. The dinner party that had just taken place could well have happened ten years earlier, before her friendship with Jan, Thelma and Brenda had been put on hold. The only difference was that Jason hadn't been there then.

She allowed herself a blissful sigh. It looked after all as if she had made the right choice deciding to let Jason come to live at Willow House. He was proving to be excellent company and far better than Reginald had ever been. Reginald would never have sat entertaining her friends with amusing anecdotes, nor would he have cooked a meal for them!

Once she was used to having Jason around the place, had time to adjust to his ways and idiosyncrasies, they'd live in perfect harmony. As long as he was prepared to let things take their natural course and didn't try to rush her their relationship might well develop along the lines he hoped.

A half smile played at the corners of her mouth. She'd been celibate for so long that it would be like taking a lover for the first time. She looked forward to being coaxed and charmed out of her shell of reserve.

It was almost midnight before Jan and the others left. After the sound of their car engines died away it was as if the world was wrapped in a blanket of silence. The moon hung like a shining gold shield in the star-studded velvet sky, the air was redolent with the perfume of roses, late honeysuckle, lavender and evening primroses.

Margaret felt hesitant about going indoors; reluctant to bring such an idyllic evening to an end.

Attuned to her mood, Jason lingered too, his fingers entwining with hers as they sauntered back towards the house. Margaret made no protest when he deviated from the gravel drive, and led her towards the massive century-old willow tree from which the house took its name.

Beneath its green canopy, the whisper of the fluttering fronds was the only sound. Her senses responded to the heady smell of his aftershave and the heat that emanated from his body as he took her in his arms.

She didn't resist as his lips found hers in a light, tender kiss. It seemed to be a fitting culmination to the evening.

As his kiss deepened, his tongue prizing her lips apart, invading the warmth of her mouth, she breathed a soft sigh of pleasure. Carried along by her own tumultuous urges, Margaret lost all sense of place or time. She felt as though she had found the fulfilment that had been missing from her life for longer than she cared to remember.

As Jason deftly undid the fastenings at the front of her dress the chill night air sent a shiver through her and she moved closer, instinctively seeking the warmth from his body. His arms tightened and passion flashed between them like the connecting sparks of an electric current.

To Margaret's chagrin Jason suddenly pulled away.

'Sorry!' he murmured apologetically. 'I was forgetting you'd laid down house rules about this sort of thing!' His short, dry laugh implied that she, too, had forgotten them.

Trembling, as much with anger as frustration, Margaret ran her hands over her hair, smoothing it back into place and refastened the neck of her dress. She was relieved that the moon had slipped behind a cloud and was no longer bathing the garden in a luminous glow so Jason was unable to witness her embarrassment. Without a word, head held high, she left him standing under the willow tree and hurried indoors.

Upstairs, in the privacy of her own bedroom, Margaret sat down on the upholstered stool in front of her dressing table. Her heart was beating a crazy tattoo as she studied her reflection in the mirror.

It was like looking into the face of a stranger. Her cheeks were flushed, her eyes wide and brilliant as though she was in a drug-induced trance What did she want, she asked herself over and over again. This time they had kept their sanity but next time, and there would be a next time she was quite sure of that, it would be very different.

As she stared at her reflection the years seemed to roll away. She was nineteen again, her mind a jumble of romantic notions. Then, just as she was doing now, she had come home from work, rushed upstairs to her bedroom and stared at herself in the dressing table mirror, asking exactly the same question.

Then, it had been because the gleam of interest in Reginald's eyes, and the realization that she was madly in love with him, had caused her such soul-searching. The outcome of that encounter had been emotionally disastrous. A few years of hectic love-making followed by a lifetime of restrictions and domination by Reginald.

The romance between them had waned quickly, obliterated by his concentration on the commercial success of his business. The almost total submersion of every aspect of his life in business matters had excluded her, left her isolated. He used sex merely as a mechanical release for tension.

The children had been her compensation but they, too, had dominated her life. Even as a small child Charles had been able to make her feel inadequate by spurning her affection whenever he decided to do so.

In her constant endeavours to win his approval, she had on many occasions overlooked the emotional needs of Alison and Steven. Alison had resented this; Steven had striven all the harder to please her, to show her love and affection.

She had learned the hard way the meaning behind the old adage that in every relationship there is one who loves and one who is loved.

It was one of the reasons why she was so scared of starting a relationship with Jason. Which way would it be with them? Which of them would be the one who loved to distraction and never had the satisfaction of knowing their love was fully reciprocated?

It was no consolation that fate had deemed they should meet and had inevitably set in motion a kaleidoscope of events.

She knew that nothing she could do would change the predestined way the shapes and colours fell or the patterns they formed.

That night Margaret didn't bother to drag the heavy armchair across the room and place it against her bedroom door.

Despite her troubled thoughts and many misgivings she fell into a deep, dreamless sleep almost the moment her head touched the pillow.

Thirty-Two

Next morning, Jason had already left the house when Margaret went downstairs. His bedroom door was closed and she made no attempt to look inside.

She pottered about in the garden most of the morning, weeding the borders, trimming the edges of the lawn, deadheading the roses and tying back bushes which had become weighed down with their profusion of flowers.

She felt content and hummed to herself as she worked. She was enjoying the feeling of having the place entirely to herself and to be able to do exactly as she pleased.

Still in her jeans and sloppy white T-shirt she made a cheese and pickle sandwich for her lunch. She took them out on to the patio and sat in the sun to eat them and drink a mug of coffee.

Afterwards, she showered and changed into one of the new summer dresses she had recently bought; a pretty blue cotton with white flowers embroidered on it. Then she went to Maidenhead to shop for an hour and meet Jan, Thelma and Brenda for coffee at the Italian cafe in the High Street.

When she came home again shortly before five o'clock, Margaret deliberately didn't do anything about preparing an evening meal. Instead she sat out in the garden reading a book until the sun dipped below the horizon and a chill evening breeze sent her indoors.

She was just starting to make herself a snack when Jason arrived home. He gave no reason for being late and she didn't ask. He greeted her in a mildly friendly manner and asked what they were eating.

Feeling guilty because there wasn't a meal ready, Margaret tried to make excuses.

Jason dismissed the matter as of no importance. 'Don't worry about it,' he laughed. 'You go and watch television and I'll bring in something on a tray for both of us.'

'No, no! I'll do it,' she protested. 'It's my responsibility to prepare the meals.'

Laughing, he shooed her out of the kitchen. 'Preparing a snack for us both will help me to unwind.'

Defeated, Margaret did as she was told and retired to the sitting room.

The news had just started when Jason came through with two trays. He placed one on her lap. Sandwiches, salad, fresh fruit salad topped with cream and accompanied by a shortbread biscuit.

'Have you got everything you want?' he asked before settling himself down in an armchair and balancing the other tray on his knees.

'Yes thank you. It looks lovely.'

Margaret ate in silence, her eyes alternatively looking at her plate and then at the screen. Reginald had hated anyone to speak or pass any comment while the news was on so she was taken aback when Jason began commenting on everything the newscaster said.

Edward Stourton was reading the news and it amused her when Jason butted in, expressing his own opinion, or arguing with what he said, almost as if the man was in the room with them.

Later, though, when she settled down to watch the evening play, Jason's continuous running commentary and witticisms about the plot and the characters annoyed her. She found it so distracting that eventually she pleaded a headache and went upstairs to finish watching it on the portable television in her bedroom.

Being so unsociable worried her and as she lay there listening for Jason to come up to bed she wondered if she ought to go down and apologize. After all, she reminded herself, he had made her a delicious supper.

She fell asleep still trying to summon up the effort to get out of bed and slip on her dressing gown and go downstairs.

By way of apology the following night she went to considerable trouble to have a tempting cooked meal ready for Jason when he arrived home. She even went as far as to phone his office and leave a message asking him not to be late but to be home by seven thirty.

So that there would be no repetition of the television incident she laid the table in the dining room, using her best china and cutlery and the treasured crystal flutes that had been one of her wedding presents and reserved for very special occasions.

Jason arrived home promptly at seven thirty bringing with him a bouquet of freesias.

Margaret accepted them with delight. 'How clever, they're my favourites.'

'Really!' He looked pleased. 'I had difficulty finding something you didn't already grow.'

'I've tried to grow freesias often enough but sadly not with any success. I've never managed to grow freesias, anemones, sweet peas or nasturtiums and I love all of them,' she added wistfully.

'Then I must grow them for you. I have green fingers, did I tell you?'

She shook her head, smiling. Trust Jason to be able to do things she couldn't.

'I'll put them in water. They'll make a lovely centre piece for the table.'

There were so many of them that as she carried them into the dining room she wondered if their fragrance might be overpowering.

Jason raised his eyebrows in surprise when he saw the elegant table display.

'Are we celebrating something special he asked?'

'No! You prepared the meal last night so I thought I ought to do it tonight.'

'Nice thought but you shouldn't have gone to so much trouble.'

'It was no trouble, I enjoy eating in here.'

'When we are on our own a snack on a tray in front of the telly is quite alright for me,' he told her firmly.

'I always eat my main meals in here,' she told him.

'Not when you are on your own, surely!'

'Yes, even when I'm on my own. Reginald was very particular about not letting standards slip.'

Jason placed his hands on her shoulders and swung her round to face him. 'Reginald's not here now,' he said gently. 'You don't have to live by his rules any more.'

'I know that! Even so, I think it's important to maintain standards.'

Jason made no answer but he looked annoyed and the imperceptible shrug of his shoulders implied that he thought she was making an absurd fuss.

He'd regained his good humour by the time they sat down to eat. He praised her cooking, asked for a second helping of the apple crumble she had made for dessert and insisted on helping her clear away afterwards.

'Having a dishwasher is so labour-saving.' She smiled. 'I've never had one before. It never seemed to be a justifiable expense. Reginald always claimed it wasn't necessary for two people.'

'And did he do the washing up?'

Margaret shook her head emphatically. The thought of Reginald washing or drying dishes was something she could barely comprehend.

'No, of course not,' she chuckled. 'Once he'd finished eating he adjourned to the sitting room with his newspaper. I cleared away and washed up, while he enjoyed a brandy and watched the television, or read his newspaper until I took in the coffee.'

Jason scowled. 'Things are going to be different from now on. Very, very different, you'll see,' he assured her softly.

His eyes glowed as his gaze locked with hers and Margaret felt a slow heat building up inside her. Alarmed in case Jason sensed how much he affected her she turned away quickly and began sorting the china Jason had just dried and putting it away inside the glass-fronted cupboard.

She felt mortified that she kept reacting like a lovesick schoolgirl to his blandishments and innuendos. Why on earth couldn't she handle the situation in a cool, mature way?

She tried to picture how Jan would treat him, how she would reply to his banter, but quickly gave up. It was a pretty foolish comparison, she reasoned. Jan's personality was entirely different to hers and Jason obviously didn't have the same feelings for Jan as he had for her, or else he would have moved in with Jan long ago.

It was as pointless comparing herself with Jan as it was comparing Jason with Reginald. In each case they were opposing personalities. The washing up incident was only one of their many dissimilarities. Reginald would never have dreamed of making his own bed, or hanging up his clothes, any more than he would have returned the newspapers to the paper rack after reading them, or rolled them up neatly and placed them into the waste-paper basket when he'd finished with them. Those were the kind of things he had always expected others to do for him.

She felt resentful that for almost forty years she had done all those sorts of things with such slavish docility. She had never had a word of thanks, nor had she ever questioned whether or not it was her responsibility. Jason had opened her eyes to the fact that there was no god-given law that said it was her duty to wait on other people.

Even so, although she was grateful to Jason for a good many reasons, including the fact that his outlook on life had changed her own opinion about so many things, not least her own value, he was only a lodger. It was her home she reminded herself, so she shouldn't permit him too much freedom to air his views or encourage him to change her lifestyle.

As it was she was perturbed by the sexual tension between them. He was good looking and charming; he had a thriving business and good prospects, so why was he interested in a woman twenty years older than himself?

To her mind it didn't make sense.

Thirty-Three

Over the next few weeks Margaret found every aspect of her life undergoing change. Jason was a tornado of energy and so full of surprises that she didn't know what to expect from one day to the next.

He was so anxious to please her that he was always startling her with unexpected bouquets of flowers, gifts of chocolates, unusual meals, or spontaneous outings to places she would never have dreamed of visiting, or hadn't known existed.

Some of their trips left her gasping with delight. Attending Henley Regatta had been one such an occasion. She'd felt like a million dollars in a new full-skirted red and white summer dress, white jacket and a flower-trimmed, red straw hat. Jason had sported a black blazer, white flannels and a cream panama hat.

They'd enjoyed the hospitality of one of Jason's clients on board a luxury cruise boat moored near Henley Bridge. It had afforded a magnificent view of the entire stretch of the river and they'd been able to watch the races while being wined and dined in style.

Other outings, such as the trip to a steam fair at Knowl Hill, where she'd stumbled around in mud that ruined her shoes, had left her wondering why Jason had brought her to such a place. She certainly hadn't shared his interest in the noisy, oily tractors and engines or the rides that he found so exhilarating but which had petrified her.

Her reaction hadn't pleased him. She'd quickly found that beneath his cool, laid-back manner he had an iron will and couldn't tolerate any opposition or dissension of any kind. He always expected things to go his way and once his mind was made up nothing could move him.

Jason was the same as Reginald in that respect and it troubled her.

In most other aspects, though, he was the exact opposite of Reginald. He was full of geniality and charm, a sophisticated urbane man of the world. No one had ever paid her so much attention, or been so solicitous, so determined to make her feel happy.

Whenever Jason was in the house things buzzed. His energy left her breathless. For so long she had been attuned to living with someone much older than herself who demanded peace and quiet. Now she had to contend with the reverse side of the coin and often she found herself exhausted simply trying to keep pace with Jason.

It astonished her the way he asked her opinion about so many diverse things. She felt flattered when he not only listened attentively to her answer but also drew her into lengthy discussions. Verbal debate was something of a novelty to her and she was so out of practice that at first she felt whatever she said sounded trite. It also disconcerted her to find that in most of their exchanges she ended up agreeing with him.

Margaret also found it unnerving that Jason noticed even the minutest change she might make around the home. A photograph moved to a different spot while she was dusting, fresh flowers in the hall, a change round in the sitting room, a new magazine on the coffee table, even a different brand of biscuits, were all noted and commented upon.

It was the same with the way she dressed. She had discarded most of the contents of her wardrobe, the drab clothes she had worn over the past ten years. She had replaced them with smart new outfits in brighter colours since she'd decided they did so much more for her appearance than muted beiges and browns.

Jason had accompanied her on several of her shopping trips and to her embarrassment had insisted she went in for shorter skirts.

'You've got good legs so why not show them off,' he'd protested when she demurred.

He had certainly provided plenty of opportunities for her to do so. They went out to eat several times a week and always to a different restaurant. He favoured Indian, or Chinese, but he loved to surprise her and sometimes he took her to one of the quaint riverside pubs, or one of the many plush eating-places dotted around the Thames Valley.

He was always willing to take her anywhere she particularly wanted to go. At her request they had gone to Hampton Court and the Chelsea Flower Show and numerous times to the theatre in Windsor.

As she'd suspected right from the start their relationship deepened. Yet even after the inevitable happened and they became lovers, she refused to let him share her bedroom.

He respected her wishes over this. Even when they did sleep together he returned to his own room before morning. Since they never met at breakfast time any misgivings she might be feeling had time to clear from her conscience before he arrived home in the evening.

She knew she was living a lie by keeping quiet about their relationship but it was the only way she could bring herself to look Charles and Alison, in the eye. Not that she had seen very much of either of them since Jason had become her lodger.

They had both vociferously disapproved of him moving in so they kept away. On the rare occasion when they invited her over to their homes Jason was not included. On the few occasions when Charles was forced to bring over documents concerning

Reginald's will for her signature he always came around mid-morning, knowing that he was bound to find her at home on her own.

Qualms about her life with Jason didn't worry her when it came to facing Steven. She didn't discuss the matter with him, but she was quite sure he knew how things stood between her and Jason and accepted it without question or comment. Unlike his elder brother and sister, Steven never had criticized her actions. Even as a teenager he'd respected her judgement.

As summer gave way to autumn and the golden days became shorter, the chill winds of winter reminded Margaret that time was passing. Although her social life was hectic and every other aspect of her life had changed she'd still not undertaken any of the special things she'd been looking forward to so much.

Jason had taken over her life so completely that it was as if she'd been reprogrammed. Temporarily, or at least she hoped it wasn't permanent, she seemed to have lost her sense of direction.

It was as if she was suspended in a kind of limbo, watching herself experimenting with a lifestyle so completely different from anything she'd previously experienced. It was almost as if she was behaving like a puppet.

Her first sexual encounter with Jason had tapped a well of passion deep within her, bringing to the surface such an intensity of feelings that she had felt overawed.

Reginald's love-making had centred on his own gratification; selfish in the extreme. It had been legalized rape bordering on brutality!

Jason, by comparison, was tender and considerate. He was always fervently concerned about her enjoyment. His exciting foreplay aroused her so intently that her whole being cried out for a release of the passion pent up inside her.

His touch set every fibre in her body trembling. As they clung to each other, his breath caressed her face as shivers of desire engulfed her. If she closed her eyes, and lay very still, the fire spread deeper. As he held her close, his flesh burning against hers, her need of him had a desperate urgency. She was unable to control the eagerness of her body as she felt the muscles of his back rippling beneath her hands. Then the strange, wondrous rhythm took over.

As he possessed her body and the last delicious, shuddering moments came over them simultaneously, she was both excited and appalled by the intensity of her emotions.

During the first few weeks after they became lovers, over-whelmed by her own needs and eager for even greater revelations, she had been avid for their daily encounters.

She hungered for Jason's arms. Their love-making was so import-ant to her that it blinded her to the many minor irritations that living with him imposed on her. It was only later that she became aware that her addiction to his love-making had become bitter-sweet torture. Too late she realized that gratification for him lay in tantalizing and teasing her to a point almost beyond endurance.

Gradually, she began to despise herself for letting him use her in such a manner, for her lack of control over her own feelings. She felt ashamed of her need of him. Time and time again she tried to curtail their sessions of pleasure.

One touch and she became inflamed by his closeness. It was as if both of them had found some wonderful treasure trove into which they must constantly dip, gorging on the delights it afforded them. It was as if they were on a constant diet of exotic food or rich chocolate and eventually they were surfeited – or at least Margaret was – by such extremes.

Thirty-Four

As she slowly came to her senses, Margaret began to resent Jason's persistent demands. It was as though they were engaged in some sexual marathon, aiming at an excess of gratification. As Jason became more and more possessive Margaret felt as trapped as she had been in the days when Reginald had been alive.

Jason insisted on doing the cooking when they ate at home so she couldn't even indulge in the foods she preferred. She had grown used to Reginald's preference for plain English cooking. Now she had to re-educate her palate to accept pasta and rice, Greek and Italian foods as well as exotic Indian and Chinese dishes.

Part of her dissatisfaction with life, she suspected, was because she was putting on weight.

Jan had been the first to openly mention the subject.

'You're getting quite plump, you know, Margaret. You want to watch your diet,' Jan observed, frowning in a disapproving way when at one of their midweek coffee mornings Margaret had accepted a second wedge of chocolate gateau.

'I put on a lot of weight after Jack died,' sighed Brenda. 'I was eating for comfort, using food to try and compensate for my loneliness because I was missing him so much.'

'Well, Margaret doesn't need to do that! She certainly can't be lonely, not with Jason living at Willow House with her,' snapped Jan.

'I saw him the other morning when I was out shopping and I noticed he's putting on weight, too,' observed Thelma. 'In fact, he looked so plump and smug that he reminded me of a marmalade cat who'd found a ready source of cream.'

'He's probably enjoying Margaret's company. It must be so nice for him to have someone mothering him after leading a bachelor existence all these years,' mused Brenda.

'Mothering?' Jan's carefully pencilled eyebrows rose questioningly.

Margaret felt as if the chocolate fudge topping on the chocolate cake she was eating was turning sour in her mouth. They were laughing at her. Obviously Jan had guessed the truth and despised her for having a relationship with Jason.

She tried to tell herself that Jan was only reacting in this way because she was jealous. She and Jan were virtually the same age, and since Jan had known Jason first she was probably still piqued because he had not shown a similar interest in her.

Or had he? Had Jan been having an affair with Jason, and was that why she was now regretting having introduced him to me, Margaret pondered.

Far from improving matters that only seemed to make the situation worse. Having been a one-man woman all her life the realization that she might be taking on someone else's cast-off was disturbing. It was like buying clothes from a charity shop knowing that someone had discarded them because they were tired of them.

If Jan had been having an affair with Jason then why had she let him go? She was so strong willed, so very dominant, that Margaret was sure she would have fought tooth and nail to hold him and that she would have succeeded.

Unless, of course it was because Jan had grown tired of him? That was quite possible. She could well understand Jan breaking off their close relationship because she found Jason's domination or even some of his habits intolerable.

The thought niggled away at the back of her mind. She found herself mentally listing the numerous ways in which Jason annoyed her. Giving him the complete run of the house had been a mistake, she decided. Now it was too late to do anything about it. He even wandered into the bathroom of her en-suite while she was in the bath, as though he had a perfect right to do so.

The first time he had done it she had screamed and grabbed at the flannel to try and cover herself.

'I didn't mean to startle you,' he chuckled, sitting down on the side of the bath.

When she had said, 'Please go away! I'm not used to people walking in on me while I'm taking a bath!' he had merely laughed.

'Now I'm here I may as well stay and wash your back,' he teased. 'Sit up!'

Taking the flannel from her trembling hands he had begun sponging her shoulders, letting a stream of warm soapy water cascade down over her breasts

His insistence angered her. Who did he think he was! If she'd been dressed and sitting in a chair she would have got up and walked out of the room. Naked and half immersed in water, she not only felt humiliated but powerless to do anything other than try and placate him.

She breathed a sigh of relief when he stood up and dried his hands on one of the fluffy pink bath towels. If she kept perfectly calm he would leave now, she told herself as she slid down lower into the cooling water.

But he didn't. Instead, he picked up the bottle of scented oil from the ledge over the bath, and unscrewing the top poured out a liberal amount into the palm of one hand. Replacing the bottle he rubbed his hands together, and then bending over began massaging the upper half of her body with his oil-drenched hands.

Inflamed by his touch she tried to wriggle free. His hands grabbed at her shoulders, but they were so slippery with oil that he was unable to hold her. He upset her balance, though, and she slithered down into the water, gasping as she inhaled the bubbles floating on the surface.

Choking, and struggling to get her breath back, she grabbed at the side of the bath and pulled herself up out of the water. She was so furious that she made no attempt to keep her anger in check. He had invaded her privacy, intimidated her and almost made her drown and she rounded on him vehemently.

Jason rocked with laughter as she tried to snatch hold of the towel he was holding.

From that moment on, Margaret's dissatisfaction with her new lifestyle grew apace. She knew she should have considered herself unbelievably fortunate over the way things had turned out yet she was far from happy. She might have everything most women dreamed about. A lovely home, plenty of friends, a fulfilling sex life with a handsome man and yet she still felt edgy.

There were days when she even went as far as to admit to herself that she longed for the quiet uneventful life she had known when Reginald was alive. She wished there was someone she could confide in. It was impossible to speak to Jan about it. By mutual consent Jason's name was avoided whenever possible.

Charles was the obvious choice but she couldn't talk to him because she knew he would be so censorious. He even disapproved of the fact that she had taken Jason as a lodger without having any legal contract between the two of them.

'How can you be sure that he is trustworthy, Mother?' he had asked on more than one occasion.

'He pays more than his share of the overheads,' she assured him.

Charles was by no means content with this argument, and she was almost tempted to say, 'because we're lovers' in order to see the shocked expression on his face.

'I still think you would have done better to have sold Willow House and found something more compact and less expensive to run,' he grumbled.

'I'm happy where I am and as long as I can afford to stay here I shall.'

He immediately made it clear that the present arrangement would only be valid as long as the bank was happy with the arrangement. He made it quite clear that under no circumstances would he be prepared to subsidize her.

Alison should have been her natural choice of confidante and yet Margaret felt she was less able to talk to her daughter about such matters than almost anyone.

Alison had the same cold, clinical approach to personal problems as Reginald had shown. In Margaret's opinion she would have made a highly successful businesswoman. She had never understood why Alison had gone in for nursing. Compassion and patience weren't her strong points. She wondered if she derived some masochistic pleasure out of making herself do something that must surely be anathema to her.

If she talked to anyone about what was bothering her then Margaret knew it would have to be Steven. He understood her so well. Yet how could she bring herself to confide in him about her sexual relationship with Jason? It seemed improper to discuss such matters with your youngest son!

Every day brought some new revelation of Jason's character that disconcerted her. He consulted her over the most trivial details. After years of being virtually dictated to by Reginald, of having to fit her lifestyle around whatever he chose to do, it unnerved her. Furthermore she worried endlessly about whether she was giving Jason the answers he wanted, or did he agree with her decisions in order to please her.

She became confused and depressed. While Jason was at work she spent hours wandering in the garden, mulling over the situation, seeking a solution. More and more she regretted that she had deviated from her initial resolve to treat him strictly as a lodger.

At night, long after Jason had sunk into a deep sex-induced sleep, she lay there at his side, exhausted but sleepless, knowing this was not really the sort of life she wanted. It was the other side of the coin. After years of celibacy she now was being offered such a surfeit of sex that she felt satiated.

Above all it troubled her that she was distanced from her family. It would soon be Christmas, and she couldn't bear the thought of spending it alone with Jason. She wanted to be with her own family, to share in their celebrations, to enjoy the company of her own children and her grandchildren. It would be a difficult situation because they wouldn't invite Jason and how could she leave him at home to fend for himself during the season of goodwill.

The end of the year was also a time for reflection. She thought again of all the things she had planned to do once she was free to do them and so far, apart from refurbishing Willow House she had done none of them.

She had planned to travel, to see places in England, Wales and Scotland that she had never seen, yet she still had not done so.

Thirty-Five

The moment Margaret finished her breakfast the next morning she found a biro pen and a pad of lined paper and began to write down all the things she wanted to do and places she would like to visit.

She started by listing all the National Trust houses. She gave each of them a separate line so that it would be easier to tick them off when she had visited them. So far she had only been to Cliveden, which was virtually on the doorstep, but she also wanted to see Waddesdon Manor, Stourhead with its wonderful gardens and lakes, Hidcote, the Fox Museum at Laock Abbey, The Vine, Harwich Hall and a dozen other properties.

Next she listed the seaside places: Brighton, Bournemouth, Hastings, Llandudno, Rhyl, Scarborough, Robin Hood's Bay, Swansea, Torquay and Whitby. The list went on and on until she'd filled an entire page. There were also the towns: Cardiff, Leeds, Chester, Edinburgh, Aberdeen, Worcester, Truro, Penzance, Exeter and Chester; the list seemed endless. Then she added castles: Rhuddlan, Harlech, Kidwelly, Chepstow, Conway and Caerphilly. On the next page she listed all the beauty spots that she had heard about and wanted to visit. Finally came all the other things she wanted to do including joining the Women's Institute or Townswomen's Guild and becoming a member of an amateur dramatic society. She would also like to take a computer course, learn to play chess, try her hand at painting and join a walking group.

When she'd finished, she put the pages aside knowing that the list was far too long and that she would have to edit it down because there simply weren't enough days left in her life even if she lived to be ninety to do everything she wanted to include.

She'd committed all her thoughts to paper so now she would leave it for a day or so and then go through it and highlight the ones she thought most important.

She hadn't intended letting Jason see it but she had left the pad on top of the bureau and it caught his eye when he came in that evening.

'What's all this?' he asked as he looked through the pages and studied the long list of items. 'Is this a New Year's resolution or simply a hundred and one things I want to do before I die?'

'Something like that,' Margaret murmured wishing she'd had time to whittle it down to reasonable proportions before telling him about it.

He studied the list again, commenting out loud about those that drew his attention or interest.

'I can teach you to play chess,' he told her, 'and I can certainly tell you which of the seaside places you've listed are worth seeing and take you there whenever you wish. We can also visit the National Trust places together and I can make sure that you understand about the antique furniture and the importance of the pictures that they may have hanging there. I'm not all that interested in the castles though. Most of them are mere shells; ruins that are on the point of falling down.'

He went through the list again. 'You haven't included any churches. Aren't you interested in cathedrals, old churches or even monuments? Surely they are important?'

'The list is not complete, simply a hotchpotch of things that came into my mind,' she mumbled.

'Hotchpotch yes, I agree with that!'

Margaret frowned as he picked up a pen and began scoring through some of the places on her list.

'What do you think you are doing, Jason?'

'Sorting it out and deleting some of the ones that are unimportant.'

'They are all important as far as I am concerned,' Margaret retorted, trying to keep the anger out of her voice.

'Rubbish! I'll draw up a proper list and then I'll start making plans to take you to all the places I think you would enjoy.'

Margaret bit down on her lower lip trying to quell the anger inside her. How dare he alter her list; how dare he take over. She wanted to do these things and visit these places on her own.

'We probably should allocate one day a week for sightseeing. Mind you, if we want to visit places like Aberdeen and Torquay then we will have to spend at least one night there because they are so far away. Perhaps we should do these over a weekend. Anyway, don't worry about it, I'll plan it all out,' he told her, confidently. 'It may take a while though because at the moment I'm very busy and so I'll have to hire some additional staff to be on hand at my studio when I'm taking you out.'

She didn't answer but watched in silence as he folded up the pages of lists and put them into the inside pocket of his jacket.

'Will you also accompany me to the Women's Institute meetings or to the Townswomen's Guild?' Margaret asked in a tight voice as Jason started to walk away.

He stopped and regarded her with raised eyebrows. 'I think those are a little out of my league and I can't imagine you would enjoy them either.'

Margaret felt herself bristling with annoyance. 'Why ever not?'

'All those tedious discussions about cooking and sewing won't interest you and you're not really into do-good ideas. In fact, I am at a loss to understand why you want to engage on such a hectic round of activities at all. I thought you were happy with your life as it is.'

'I am but since we're on the brink of a new year it seemed to be a good idea to make a note of some of the other things that I have always wanted to do,' she said lamely.

Jason shook his head and looked at her indulgently as if she were a child that had to be humoured.

'Excellent idea; leave it all with me and as I've already said I will take care of it all,' he told her, patting her shoulder reassuringly.

That night Jason was even more loving as if he was trying to recompense for annoying her earlier in the day.

Margaret still felt annoyed though. She had been thoroughly enjoying making out her list and thinking about each place she planned to visit and deciding for herself which ones she would put at the top of the list and which ones at the bottom. Now they would be in the order Jason decided and which suited his taste.

She knew she was being childish but it had been so long since she had been in control that she resented having to take a back seat.

As if reading her mind Jason said sleepily, 'You don't like it, do you, if someone muscles in on your ideas?'

'I don't mind in the least as long as they agree with what I want to do,' she retorted quickly.

He laughed sardonically and then turned over so that his back was towards her leaving her to lie there feeling angry and now so wide awake that she knew she wouldn't get to sleep.

After a few minutes she got out of bed and went downstairs to make herself a cup of tea and see if she could find a sleeping pill to take.

When she returned upstairs the bed was empty

She woke extremely late the next morning feeling tired and disgruntled. Her list, with half the places she'd planned to visit now scored out lay on the breakfast table. She read it through while she drank a cup of tea and then with a resigned sigh tore the pages in half and put them in the trash bin.

For the next couple of weeks leading up to Christmas there was a truce between them. They both seemed to be trying to make amends and be on their best behaviour although neither of them would bring out into the open what was worrying them.

Two days before Christmas Jason suggested going away for a few days. 'I thought Torquay might be nice. They call it the English Riviera so it might be quite warm and sunny there and since it was on that list you compiled and which now seems to have vanished I thought it would be a good start.'

'It will be Christmas in a couple of days' time. I can't go away now!' Margaret exclaimed in exasperated tones. 'I have all the presents for the grandchildren to wrap up.'

'That shouldn't take long. I'll give you a hand with them and help you to deliver them.'

'I want them all to be here with me on Christmas Day; I want to see their faces when they open them.'

'So you are planning to entertain your entire family here for a meal are you?'

'Of course I am! We always spend Christmas Day together. It's about the only time in the year when the entire family is gathered under one roof.'

'Very well, if that's the way you want it then we'll delay our celebration until later. Tell me what the numbers are going to be on Christmas Day and I'll plan the menu.'

'Oh no! This is my family and I intend to be the one to entertain them.'

'You mean you intend to do all the cooking?' he asked in surprise.

'As I have already said, it is my family so naturally they will expect me to do the cooking.'

'Am I invited or don't you want me here on Christmas Day?' he asked quietly.

She hesitated so long before answering that his face darkened angrily. 'If you would rather I wasn't here then say so!'

Margaret took a deep breath. 'Well, it is a strictly family affair so it might be better if you were not here,' she said quietly.

Jason looked so angry that for a minute she wondered what he was going to do.

'This is your way of repaying me for interfering in your list, isn't it, Margaret? How childish can you be.'

When she didn't answer he walked away and she heard him going upstairs to his room. She wondered if he was sulking or whether he had gone up to pack his belongings and leave.

She felt uneasy. Could she afford to go on living at Willow House if he left permanently? She wondered if she ought to run up and apologize.

The truth was, though, that she didn't want him sitting down to their family Christmas dinner. It wasn't simply that he would take over as if he was the man of the house – she knew that her family wouldn't like that at all.

But things between them really must change and the New

Year would be a good starting point, she told herself. Jason was, after all only a lodger.

Thirty-Six

The New Year certainly did bring changes; ones that Margaret had not foreseen. Gradually she realized that Jason was using her home, her beloved Willow House, as a showcase for prospective clients.

It all started quite innocently. He asked if he could invite a couple who had recently bought a house in their area round to supper so that he could show them the changes he'd made at Willow House.

Margaret shook her head. She knew he was proud of his work and anxious to show it off but she didn't like the idea of entertaining strangers especially as a business project.

Jason assured her that it wouldn't be a sales pitch at all. He intended it to be a cosy evening. He'd do all the food preparation and buy in the drink and they were such nice people that he was confident she would enjoy their company.

The discussion went on for several days until finally she capitulated.

They were a very pleasant middle-aged couple but Margaret felt prickles running up and down her spine as they went round her home studying the improvements and interrogating Jason as to how much this or that had cost.

A couple of weeks later when he again asked if he could entertain some prospective clients she refused.

'Why ever not? You are always saying how much you love your home so surely you enjoy showing it off?'

'To my friends and family I do but not to people I don't know and will never meet again. It's my home not a show house,' she said sharply.

He'd looked at her with pursed lips. 'I understand what you are saying but unfortunately I've already invited these people. Will it be all right just this time? I can hardly put them off now.'

Reluctantly she agreed. 'Very well, but I don't wish to meet them so you must entertain them on your own.'

His mouth tightened but he gave her a smile and a small bow. 'Yes, ma'am, message received and understood,' he said in a teasing voice.

She spent the evening in her bedroom watching television with the sound turned down so that she could hear every movement in the house and know where they were and what they were looking at. It had meant that he was unable to show them the master bedroom or the luxurious en-suite bathroom he'd installed there.

Next morning she hadn't mentioned their visit and neither had he.

It hadn't stopped him from using her home as a showpiece but afterwards he had done so in a far subtler manner. Without a word to her he arranged for clients to visit whenever he knew she was going to be out at a coffee morning with her friends or a shopping trip.

Once when she'd popped back to collect a letter she'd forgotten to post she found three cars parked in the driveway as well as Jason's car. Inside the house several smartly dressed men were gathered in the dining room laughing and talking and all with glasses of wine in their hands. On the dining table were piles of brochures that they were picking up and stuffing into their briefcases.

She wasn't sure if Jason had seen her but she was so annoyed by what was taking place that she had to restrain herself from flinging wide the dining room door and ordering them all to leave.

Instead she collected the letter and left without a word to anybody.

Jason said nothing about the meeting when he returned hone that evening but as soon as they had eaten their meal she had taken him to task about the matter.

He had listened to her in silence, his face darkening with every word she uttered.

'Are you asking me not to bring clients here or are you telling me that I can't?'

Margaret shrugged. 'It amounts to much the same thing doesn't it?'

'No, not really. I consider this my home and as such I feel I am entitled to entertain whoever I like.'

'No, Jason! It's not your home, you are only here as a lodger.'

'A mere lodger? Are you quite sure about that, Margaret?'

His tone was both caustic and scornful.

As he stared hard at her she felt the colour rising in her face. She knew this was her last chance and she must stand her ground. She must make him realize that she had no intention of giving in to his demands but she couldn't find the words to clarify all that was in her mind.

'So I'm merely a lodger, am I?' he repeated.

There was an extended uneasy silence as the question hung in the air between them; each of them waiting for the other to speak.

She didn't know what to say or how to handle the situation. She knew she was the one at fault because she had been far too lax over their relationship. It was something she now deeply regretted. She should have been firm and rejected his advances from the very first moment.

Once he had overstepped the line after moving into her home there had been no going back. He had taken advantage of the fact that she was so compliant. Unless she took a firm stand now then she would always be at his mercy. He would encroach more and more on her life, take more and more liberties and finally dominate her and take her over completely.

She must make it perfectly clear, she told herself, that she had no intention of letting him entertain his clients there. Willow House was her home and was most definitely not going to be used as a showcase.

The impasse lasted for several weeks. Jason took advantage of the situation. He brought clients to the house more and more frequently. He no longer exercised any discretion, such as waiting until she was out of the house, but brought them alone without warning at all times of the day.

Her nerves became frayed. Willow House lost its charm. It was no longer her beloved home because he had turned it into a mere show house.

Jason even took liberties with the furniture and furnishings, changing them round to suit the taste or requirements of different clients whenever he felt it was to his advantage to do so.

The situation reached its peak the day she went into the drawing room to look for something in the bureau. There had been three men, all strangers to her, in there talking to Jason. She had deliberately ignored them all as she made for the bureau.

Jason excused himself from his clients and came over to her his mouth set in a hard line. 'Will you please leave. Can't you see that I am entertaining some important clients,' he said in an angry whisper.

'I need to collect something from . . .'

'Later, later. I'll be out of here in an hour or so.' He seized hold of her arm and steered her towards the door.

After he had pushed her through into the hallway he had turned back to his clients and apologized profusely for the interruption. She drew in her breath sharply as she heard him say with a deprecating laugh, 'Servants, they have no sense of propriety these days, have they!'

As the loud masculine laughter spilled out in the hallway she cringed, then all the pent-up fury of the past months welled up inside her and she knew the time had come to do something decisive.

Her first instinct was to go back into the room and tell them all, Jason included, to get out of her house immediately.

Realizing that this was childish she went back up to her bedroom and sat there brooding about the best way of stopping Jason from entertaining his clients at Willow House.

There was really only one way to do this, she decided and that was to send Jason packing, tell him that he could no longer remain there as her lodger.

She realized that it was a drastic step and that he would probably put up a fight. Her mind was made up though and she had to get her life back and her independence.

It wouldn't be easy, she was well aware of that, but she was determined. Everything had turned sour and she wanted to put an end to their relationship and draw a line underneath everything that had happened so far.

She didn't want any comebacks or a prolonged argument

about him leaving. She intended to be strong-willed and make it impossible for there to be any reunion.

She owed him nothing. He had been paid for the work he'd done for her on Willow House and now, as far as she was concerned, the friendship that had existed between them was over; their mutual attraction completely exhausted.

She thought long and hard about what was the best way to go about it because she not only wanted it to be permanent but she wanted it to be done legally if that was at all possible.

She felt the need to talk about it to someone but realized that was impossible. No one in the family would really understand. because none of them had wholeheartedly agreed with her having Jason as a lodger.

The obvious confidants were her three friends but here again she suspected that they had considered she was foolish to have agreed to him becoming a lodger in the first place. Jan certainly had.

No, she decided, it must be her decision, hers and hers alone. And she had to be sure that when she told Jason to go there would be no way he could ever come back.

She thought of nothing else until eventually her mind was made up. She had to completely sever her connection with Jason if she was ever to be her own woman again. She felt desperate to claim back her independence.

There was only one way she could achieve that and she intended to do it; she was not only going to turn Jason out of Willow House but she was determined to banish him from her life completely.

It would take a good deal of courage and she was bound to meet up with all sorts of opposition not only from him but possibly from friends and family as well. It was going to be diffi-cult to explain the situation to them after she had been so adamant that she was doing the right thing in taking him in as a lodger but she knew deep down that it was the only answer.

Margaret put off confronting Jason for as long as she possibly could, trying to clarify in her own mind exactly what she was going to say to him.

She didn't want to become involved in an argument because

she was pretty sure that Jason would counteract anything she said, and she was well aware that Jason was a past master at winning arguments.

No, she resolved, she would tell him straight out that she could no longer tolerate him living there as a lodger and that everything between them was finished and that she wanted him out of her house and out of her life.

She went over and over in her mind what she would say until she was word perfect. She contemplated phoning him at his studio and doing it by telephone; that would be the easiest way since she could simply replace the receiver and cut off his protests if necessary.

Even as she dialled his number she decided that would be a cowardly way of handling things; she must tell him to his face.

When he answered she took a deep breath and in as steady a voice as she could muster told him she needed to see him.

'What right away?'

'Yes! Right away,' she said firmly.

'What's so urgent that it can't wait until I get home this evening?'

'No, now, Jason. Be here in half an hour.'

She had thought she would feel relieved now she had taken such a drastic step but instead she felt nervous about their upcoming meeting.

Shivering, she ran upstairs to her bedroom and changed into a thick black sweater and comfortable grey slacks; it was the sort of outfit Jason hated to see her in.

She came back downstairs and plugged in the coffee percolator and set out two mugs and a plate of biscuits on a silver tray. She may as well be civilized over this, she told herself.

Jason arrived half an hour later dressed with casual smartness in dark trousers, a pink open-necked shirt, and a navy blazer. He was carrying a large bouquet of flowers which he handed to her with a sweeping gesture.

She smiled briefly as she took them from him and turned away quickly in case he attempted to kiss her. She took the flowers into the kitchen and stood them in the sink. Then she poured the coffee and carried the tray through to the living room.

He was standing looking out at the garden but he spun round

and took the tray from her and set it down on the low table in front of the settee. Then he sat down on the settee and patted the seat beside him, holding out a hand to her.

She moved back quickly and sat down in one of the armchairs facing the settee. He passed one of the mugs of coffee to her and took the other himself, frowning slightly as he did so.

'What's all this about,' he asked. 'Is something wrong?'

Margaret bit down on her lower lip, then took a deep breath and said in a firm unwavering voice. 'No, nothing is wrong. I want to tell you that I no longer want you here as a lodger.'

Jason looked at her in astonishment. 'I'm not sure I follow you?' he parried.

'I want you to leave Willow House immediately. I don't want you as a lodger or in my life in any way,' Margaret said harshly. 'We're finished, Jason; completely finished.'

His eyes hardened and the smile went from his face. 'You can't mean that, not after all I've done for you.'

'Your time here is over, Jason. I want you out and I want my life back.'

'Your life back,' he scoffed. 'What life? Until I came on the scene you were a lonely, miserable old woman living in a drab rundown house. What are you going to do without me? I turned your life around and brought you into the twenty-first century.'

Blood rushed to Margaret's head, flooding her cheeks and neck, causing her to tremble with a mixture of anger and humiliation.

She took a gulp of her coffee; it was too hot for comfort but the sudden stab of pain in her mouth and throat focused her mind.

Jason sipped his coffee. 'Who put this idea of getting rid of me into your head?' he asked coldly. 'Was it Jealous Jan or that spiteful son of yours?'

'It's entirely my decision and I have no intention of arguing about the matter or discussing it any further,' Margaret said stiffly.

Jason banged his half-full coffee cup down on the table so hard that the liquid slopped over, but he made no attempt to mop it up.

'You may not want to discuss it further but I certainly do.' He waved an arm dramatically. 'You owe me an explanation or an apology Margaret. My artistic flair has transformed this house and I designed every bit of it with loving care to provide a setting that I felt reflected your personality.'

'You were hired to update Willow House,' Margaret said drily.

'I put my heart and soul into the work and your debt to me is—'

'That will do Jason, I've heard all you have to say and some of it was most unflattering. As for owing you anything, your exorbitant bill for the work you did was paid in full.'

'I'm not talking about mere money,' he said scornfully.

'You have used my home like a hotel even to the point of entertaining clients and treating me as if I was merely a servant here. I am no longer prepared to tolerate that, so hand back your keys and remove your possessions immediately.'

'Margaret!' He gave a forced laugh. 'What's got into you? You don't mean it.'

'Oh I do. I want you to leave.' She stood up and looked at her watch. 'Right now!'

Jason also stood up.

'Margaret,' he reached out to take her hands but she stepped back out of reach. 'What's got into you?'

She didn't answer but met his furious gaze calmly, although inwardly she was quivering. She thought of the story of King Charles the First wearing two shirts when he went to his execution so that no one would think he was trembling from fear if it was cold, and smiled to herself that she had changed into a thick sweater for much the same reason.

'Come on, I don't know what I've done to upset you but it will blow over.'

'Jason, I'm deadly serious. I want you out of this house and out of my life.'

'And what if I won't go?' he asked in a soft, wheedling tone.

'Then I shall have you evicted because I am leaving Willow House.'

'You can't do that. It's your home and mine,' he blustered.

'Not any longer. I've decided to sell Willow House and to move right away. I intend to make a completely fresh start.'

Thirty-Seven

Margaret decided to let Charles handle the sale of Willow House.

'Now that my mind is made up I want it done as quickly as possible so that I can put it all behind me and start afresh,' she told him firmly.

Charles shook his head in disbelief. 'Are you sure you know what you're doing? A few months ago you refused to even consider selling.'

'I know but I've changed my mind. You were quite right after all. It really is the best thing for me to do.'

'Are you quite sure you've thought this through?' he repeated, as if unable to believe she was serious. 'Are you sure that you're not acting on some sort of impulse and repeating the same mistake you made when you called in that Jason Parker to redecorate Willow House?'

'Yes, I know that was rather impetuous and I should have talked things through with you first,' Margaret admitted contritely.

Charles ran a hand over his chin. 'I think you are once again rushing ahead, instead of sitting down, and considering all the various aspects of what you are doing, and what long-term effects they might have. Why not go home and make out a list—'

'I know what I'm doing, Charles, and my mind is made up,' Margaret interrupted firmly.

'You thought that last time and look where that got things! A massive bill which meant I had to go crawling to the bank manager and extend the company overdraft, in order to be able to pay it.'

'Well, if you handle the sale of Willow House, then you'll have an opportunity to repay the bank, won't you?'

'I certainly hope it will accomplish that and more. I hope there will be enough from the sale to put the company back in the black. Without Willow House as collateral the Bank is unlikely to grant the company an overdraft the size of the one we have now!'

'Try looking on the bright side, Charles, the value of Willow House has trebled, or even quadrupled, since your father used it to get a loan, so there should be no problem. I expect it to fetch a price that will not only clear off your overdraft but provide me with a flat and a car and ensure I have a nest egg for my future as well.'

'Don't count on that happening in a hurry!' he sneered. 'Properties like Willow House don't sell overnight. It could be on the market for months and months. And you'll have to be prepared to show any prospective buyers round, remember.'

'It will sell much faster than that, if you handle it the way I want you to do it.'

'Really? You're a property expert now, are you?'

Margaret gave him a withering glance. At one time she would have been mortified by his sarcasm, but now she let it slide off her like hailstones off a gable end.

'Yes, I know what I want done, Charles, and it is only out of courtesy that I am asking you to be the one to handle it. I know that the deeds are lodged at the bank, so if you don't want to comply with my wishes then I shall go straight to the bank manager myself. I thought that to do so behind your back would have been humiliating for you, Charles, which is why I am approaching you first.'

She felt breathless after her long speech but also gratified when she saw the look of utter surprise on his face.

Taking a deep breath she went on, 'I've already found a flat that I like.'

'I'm sure you have! One of the half-a-million pound jobs along the riverfront where your friend Jan Porter lives? Or is it one of those ultra-superb conversions at Nashdom Abbey?'

'Neither! It's in Windsor, A retirement block, not far from the river and quite near the town centre, and it's only two hundred and fifty thousand pounds.'

'Only two hundred and fifty thousand pounds!' Charles puffed out his cheeks in exasperation. 'And where are you going to find that sort of money?'

'I'm not, you are. You'll sell Willow House, buy me the flat, and a car and provide me with a nest egg like I outlined earlier. I'm sure there will be enough left to clear the company's overdraft. Furthermore, I'll still let you use my flat as collateral against your overdraft if you need to do so.'

Charles gave a harsh laugh. 'And what if the bank manager doesn't agree with your hare-brained little scheme?'

'I see no reason why he shouldn't. He will still have the deeds of a two hundred and fifty thousand pound flat to hold as security.'

'A flea-bite in comparison with the size of the overdraft.'

'You are talking about the existing overdraft. Remember, you will be able to reduce that by a very considerable sum once Willow House is sold.'

'When it sells! As I told you before, that may take months and months. And your precious flat may be gone by then.'

'Not if we put a deposit down on it right away.'

'And where is the money for that coming from? I don't suppose you've given that any thought?'

'If you go and talk to the bank manager and explain what we are proposing to do, I'm sure he'll cooperate.'

Charles shook his head in disbelief. 'You honestly believe that, don't you! You think he's going to advance a loan right now on the possibility of Willow House selling sometime in the next six months – if we're lucky.'

'Yes. Once you tell him it's to be sold at auction.'

'At auction! Are you completely mad? Unless the advance publicity is handled skilfully the whole thing could be a disastrous fiasco. It might only fetch a quarter of its value.'

'Rubbish! You put a reserve price on it. Make this known from the start, and then you only attract the sort of buyers prepared to go higher.'

'We are talking about Willow House not a modern mansion with a swimming pool and tennis court and treble garage,' he retorted mockingly.

'I know that. Stop and think of all the advantages there are to a property like Willow House. It's near to London; handy for Heathrow Airport; and the M4, M40, M25 and M3 are all within a few minutes' driving time. All the leisure and social activities of Henley, Marlow, Ascot and Windsor, not to mention some of the best eating places in the south of England, are all on the doorstep.'

'And you've tried them all out, have you? You can personally recommend them?'

Margaret ignored his jibe. She had spent a great deal of time studying advertisements and putting her plan together and she wasn't going to let a few wisecracks from Charles undermine her confidence.

'So what sort of reserve price are you planning to put on Willow House?'

'Six hundred thousand pounds,' she told him coolly.

'Six hundred thousand pounds? Are you mad?'

'I've been studying the market and in my estimation, that is its current value; exactly what it should be. It's in pristine order because it's been newly decorated and modernized throughout, remember!'

'How can I forget when I've just had to pay a whopping bill for Jason Parker's services?' he muttered.

'Which you will soon be able to recoup,' she retaliated sharply. 'Now, are you going to get cracking and organize things, Charles, or do you want me to do it myself?'

She picked up her handbag from where she had placed it on the corner of his desk, and stood up. 'I'll call into the bank and explain the situation now on my way home, if you like.'

'No, Mother! No! That's *not* the way to handle it! I'll need to take the manager out to lunch and explain the whole set up to him diplomatically and then ask his advice . . .'

'We don't need his advice,' Margaret interrupted crossly. 'My mind is made up. I've told you what I want to do and that is to put Willow House up for sale by auction. If you don't want to go ahead and organize it then say so and I will do it myself.'

'Leave it with me, I'll see to it,' Charles said wearily. He rose from his chair and opened the door for her. 'Leave it with me.'

'And you'll do something about it right away?'

'I'll put it on today's agenda.'

'Make it this morning's agenda. If you have to discuss it over lunch then ring the bank manager now and fix the time and place. I suppose he will want to use one of his cronies as the auctioneer?'

'Well, he probably does know who is the best one in the area . . .'

'Get on with it then, Charles.' She pushed his hand away from the door. 'I can see myself out. I shall expect to hear from you with details of what is happening later in the day.'

Without giving him a chance to answer she swept out. Her knees were shaking, and she felt as breathless as if she had run a half marathon. She had never spoken to Charles like that in her life before. Ordering him around as if he was a child. Insisting he did things her way. Refusing to take his advice. She had astonished herself and she was rather proud of what she had achieved. If the outcome was only fractionally as successful as this initial foray had turned out to be, she would be content.

Once the wheels were set in motion, things moved apace. Valuers, assessors, auctioneers and photographers came in their hordes. Each concentrated on their own particular aspect of the transaction to the exclusion of everyone else's interests.

Margaret stoically made countless cups of tea and coffee but resented their lack of communication with her about what they were doing. She might already have given up ownership of Willow House for all the respect they accorded her, she thought bitterly.

Still, it was the end result that mattered, she told herself, as with a fixed, glassy smile she handed out mugs of drink, and bit back the countless questions that she longed to have answered.

When the proofs of the catalogue arrived, she read it avidly from cover to cover, making corrections she deemed essential. Charles was impressed.

'You'll see these are carried out, won't you?'

'If you think they're necessary?'

'I wouldn't have made them if I didn't think they were important, now would I?' she snapped.

'All right! I'll see it's attended to, Mother,' he promised.

'Good. And now this is well under way what about the flat I wanted in Windsor? Are you ready to do something about that?'

'I already have!' He looked so pleased with himself that she almost laughed. Charles trying to please her was a novelty in itself. 'We've reserved one for you.'

'We?'

'I had to explain the situation to the bank manager. I told you I would have to do that. He has made the necessary agreement with the estate agent handling the sale of the flats.'

'Good. So when this is sold I won't find myself homeless?'

'Of course not! In fact, he is looking at the possibility of completion of the sale of the flat before Willow House is auctioned because you will have to vacate immediately, or preferably the day before the auction, since it is being offered with vacant possession.'

'Quite! And fully furnished.'

'What are you talking about? There was nothing in the specifications about that?'

'There is now. That was part of the amendments I made.'

'Part? You've changed something else as well?'

'Only the reserve price. I've upped it to seven hundred thousand pounds.'

'Another hundred thousand pounds! What are you thinking about?'

'Myself and my future. I want enough out of this sale to buy a new home and to furnish it and to buy myself a car, remember.'

'Mother! You're talking big money here . . .'

'Which is why it's so important that Willow House reaches a figure high enough to cover all this. A seven hundred thousand pound reserve for a fully furnished house standing in its own grounds and with so many local amenities . . .'

'OK, OK. I get the picture. I think you are pushing it, but if the bank manager and the agent handling the auction will agree to it, then I'll go along with your suggestion.'

'Don't worry about it, Charles. They already have.'

'How do you know that?'

'Because I've already phoned and discussed it all with them. I had a feeling you might shilly-shally over the idea, so I thought it best for it to be a fait accompli when I told you.'

As she walked away from his office, Margaret knew that Charles was bristling with annoyance but it didn't deter her in the least. She had never tried to assert her will over his in the past, because she had always felt that he was so much a replica of Reginald she dare not risk doing so for fear of being ridiculed.

Now that she'd achieved it, however, her feeling of inferiority to his superior intellect was gone forever. He was just a pussycat. She even suspected that secretly he might be scared of her abrasive manner. Well, that was all to the good because there were still a great many battles to be fought, and she intended to win them all.

Thirty-Eight

'Right, Charles. Now with all the details concerning the sale of Willow House taken care of, I'd better start organizing this flat so that I can move in before the date of the auction.'

Charles groaned. 'And what is that going to cost?'

'At the moment I have no idea.'

'And will Jason Parker be designing the interior for you?' he sneered.

'There will be no need. The builders have decorated the flat and carpeted and curtained it throughout. Their choice is somewhat conservative but it is quite pleasant and I can live with it. Now it is simply a matter of buying furniture.'

'And where will you go for that? Harrods?'

'No. I'm planning on buying locally.'

'Until Willow House is sold there is no money to buy anything,' he reminded her.

'Ah, that's something else I meant to tell you. The bank manager has advanced me a loan that will be chargeable to your business account if Willow House should fail to sell. It won't, of course,' she added quickly, as she saw his face blanch and tiny nerves begin to throb at the corner of his mouth.

'Mother! You simply can't go round making arrangements like that!'

'Why ever not? That's what banks are for, aren't they? To lend money, I mean. He knows he's on to a safe thing and of course he will be charging me interest on the overdraft so he's earning money.'

The eight weeks between the details of Willow House being published, circulated and publicized and the date of the auction should have been a period of intense stress for Margaret, but it wasn't.

She handed over her spare set of keys to the estate agent who was working in collaboration with the auctioneer so that he could show prospective buyers around, and filled her days in a much more enjoyable manner.

After an intensive bout of window shopping, during which time she sat in so many armchairs, on so many settees, and laid down on so many different beds that she felt dizzy, she found most of the pieces she had set her heart on. When she totalled up what it would all cost, however, she knew it far outstripped her budget.

Margaret toyed with the idea of going back to the bank manager, and asking him to extend her credit, but she had a niggling feeling that this was not only unprofessional but that it would also be letting herself down. Charles would crow. He'd be quick to point out that this was positive proof that she was not capable of managing her financial affairs.

Instead, she made out a list of her requirements and took this along to one of the furniture stores and told them exactly how much she could afford to spend. With their skilled help, she was able to compromise so that her outlay was within her budget.

She still managed to create a furnishing scheme that satisfied her although it meant that she had to forgo many luxury accessories, such as cushions, side tables, lamps and rugs.

'You can always buy the other items later,' they assured her, as they arranged a date for delivery.

Delighted by her achievement, she wanted to live there right away but Charles persuaded her not to do so. 'Willow House has a better atmosphere if it is occupied,' he pointed out, 'and it's as important to you, as it is for us, that potential buyers are impressed.'

She acquiesced, even though it worried her to stay on at Willow House in case Jason came back. There had been no row when she had told him he must leave because she was selling up. He had stared at her stonily, then gone upstairs and packed up all his belongings from his bedroom and from the room he had been using as a studio.

A van had arrived the next day and he had helped the driver to load everything into it and then driven off without even saying goodbye. He left his keys in a plain white envelope on the kitchen worktop.

Afterwards, she had been so engrossed in acquiring her new flat and furnishing it that she had managed to put Jason out of her mind. Moving to Windsor and her new flat would certainly draw a line under her previous life.

The flat was so different from Willow House. Near the river, not far from the castle, adjacent to a park, close to the Windsor Theatre Royal, and handy for the King Edward Court shopping complex. It was the centre of a hubbub of activity. She loved it. Being able to look out of the window and see the boats on the river, traffic passing, people strolling about, was such a novelty that it intrigued her, made her feel so alive.

She longed to invite Jan, Brenda and Thelma over, and see their reaction, not only to its setting but to the way she had furnished it. It was so completely different from both the original style of Willow House and from Jason's scheme. It was cool, elegant and uncluttered. She was glad now that because she had been restricted by her tight budget she had not been able to buy the countless lamps, and cushions, and side tables that had taken her eye.

There was something infinitely calming about having only the bare essentials. She wasn't even sure if she would go back and buy all these extra bits and pieces even if she could afford them later on.

Margaret and her three children all attended the auction. It was as if they were saying a public farewell to their family home and in many ways it was as poignant as a wake.

Charles, smartly sombre in a dark business suit, white shirt and discreetly striped blue and red tie, looked strained, his mouth a taut thin line. Steven, slightly more casual in grey slacks, and a black blazer, seemed relaxed, almost cheerful. Alison, in a charcoal grey skirt that reached to her ankles, hunched into a black long-line jacket, appeared dejected and irritable.

'Now make sure you don't start scratching your nose or patting your hair, Mother, or you may find you've bought the old place back again,' Steven warned jocularly.

'Would that be such a bad thing?' Alison sniffed. 'I think it's terrible selling the family home, especially at an auction. It's the place where we all grew up, so full of treasured memories, leastways it was until that vandal Jason Parker ruined it.'

'That will do.' Steven squeezed her arm to silence her, hoping his mother hadn't heard her tirade. It was bad enough for her having to sell up her lovely home and move into a modern flat in Windsor, without being made to suffer Alison's recriminations.

The hall filled up surprisingly well. There were a number of local people, though whether they were there out of curiosity to hear how much it fetched, or because they wanted to buy Willow House, Margaret couldn't be sure. Her heart was in her mouth as she waited for the proceedings to begin. She had never attended a house auction before and had no idea what to expect.

Once the bidding started it was surprisingly brisk. It began at £350,000, and she felt waves of panic wash over her in case it didn't reach the reserve price. She gave a swift sideways glance at Charles; his face was a frozen mask and she knew he must be experiencing the same doubts about the reserve price as she was.

The bidding moved swiftly upwards, past the magical £600,000 and still rising. One thing she couldn't fathom was where the last bid came from each time. She whispered to Steven, 'I don't understand what is happening. Every time the auctioneer takes a bid from someone in the room, the man on the telephone says something to him. Is he taking bids over the phone?'

'That's right!'

£600,000 . . . £650,000 . . . £700,000 . . . £750,000 . . . £800,000. It seemed the battle between the bidders in the hall and the anonymous unseen bidder on the phone would go on forever. At £800,000, however, there was a long pause and an expectant hush fell over the room. The prospective buyer in the room, a portly man in his late fifties, was looking triumphant when the man on the telephone intervened. 'An offer of eight hundred thousand and two hundred and fifty pounds,' he announced laconically.

The portly man in the room shook his head. Three times the auctioneer announced the new figure before bringing his gavel down.

'Willow House sold for eight hundred thousand and two hundred and fifty pounds,' he announced with genuine satisfaction.

Charles looked as though he was in shock. Impulsively he grabbed his mother's shoulders and squeezed them. 'Brilliant. Absolutely brilliant!' he exclaimed jubilantly. 'I can't believe my ears; it's incredible!'

'I think this calls for a drink,' enthused Steven. 'Your shout Charles?'

They could talk of nothing else as they sat round a small table in the nearest pub. It was an unbelievable victory.

'So, do I get my car?' Margaret asked.

'I think we should be able to afford a little second-hand runabout for you,' Charles said smiling. 'It's unbelievable,' he repeated, shaking his head. 'I would never have dreamed that Willow House would fetch a figure of this sort. It will put the company back on its feet, pay for your new flat, clear the overdraft, and in addition, once we've dealt with the cost of furnishing the flat, will, with any luck, provide that nice little nest egg for you, Mother.'

'So my idea of putting up the reserve price wasn't so silly after all.'

Charles frowned. 'No, it wasn't. Although at the time I was afraid you'd ruined everything and that at the end of the day we'd still have Willow House on our hands.'

'It is the end of a chapter in all our lives,' Margaret said a trifle sadly.

'Things change all the time,' Charles asserted. 'Mine changed when I left home as I'm sure yours did, Steven. What about you, Alison?'

'I am heartbroken that Willow House has gone, I would sooner have seen it pulled down than to know that other people, perfect strangers, were going to live there,' Alison exclaimed dramatically.

'Quite true, but I'm sure that saying goodbye to Willow House must be worse for Mum than it is for us because she has far more memories,' Steven stated.

'The happiest days there were when you were all small. You used to love playing in the garden so very much,' Margaret smiled.

'Yes, that's true,' replied Steven with a laugh. 'It was the Wild West, the African jungle, a fairground and countless other places. Cowboys and indians, cops and robbers, you name it we played it there.'

'Happy days but all so long ago,' Margaret sighed.

As they stood up to leave, Steven offered to drive Margaret back to Windsor.

'Thank you, dear, I want to say goodbye to Willow House first and I'd like to do it on my own,' she said quickly when Steven seemed to be on the point of offering to drive her there.

'You can't go back there, Mother, its not yours any longer,' Charles cautioned. 'I don't want you arrested for trespassing!'

'I can walk past there, surely?'

'Yes, but you shouldn't go inside the gates.'

'Don't worry. I won't trespass. I want to take one last look, that's all.'

'Promise you won't go in! Perhaps you'd better go with her, Steven.'

'Don't worry, I won't,' she promised.

'I'll come with you, Mum,' Steven told her. 'I wouldn't mind taking a last look at the old place myself.'

Ten minutes later they both stood by the gate looking up the lone gravel drive past the huge willow tree towards the house, silently thinking about the past.

Margaret sighed. 'Woman's curiosity, I suppose, but I would like to know who has bought it.'

'We'll probably never know that. One of the reasons for using a telephone bid is so that the purchaser can remain anonymous.'

'Yes, but surely Charles will know when the cheque comes in from the signature on it?'

'Not necessarily. In all probability payment will be made by bank transfer . . .'

'So we'll never know?'

'Not until the buyer becomes part of the local scene, then perhaps we will.'

Thirty-Nine

A fortnight later Margaret stopped her smart little five-year-old blue Citroën outside the gates of Willow House. She sat there for several minutes staring up the drive at the familiar building that had been home to her and her family for so long. To her surprise she felt nothing.

She had expected to feel overcome by remorse about what she had done as she compared it with the compact modern flat that was now her home in Windsor.

She had anticipated experiencing a feeling of great loss, but she remained completely unmoved.

She wondered if she would feel any different if she actually went inside the gates and walked up the drive. That would be trespassing and something she had promised both Charles and Steven she would not do.

She got out of the car and walked over to the gates and stood there expecting a lump to rise in her throat, or for tears to prick behind her eyelids, but there was nothing. Instead there was a feeling of calm satisfaction. It was like looking at a holiday snapshot and remembering all the good times, but not wishing to go back there again.

She wondered who the new occupiers were, but felt neither envious nor resentful. She loved her new home in Windsor and she had been pleasantly surprised by how impressed Jan, Thelma and Brenda had been the first time they had visited her there.

'I had no idea that retirement flats were so well appointed,' Brenda commented.

'No, it's more like being in a hotel than a . . . a home,' Brenda murmured.

'You were going to say, "Old People's Home", weren't you,' Margaret chided. 'Well don't! Never let me hear you say that. These flats are for people over fifty-five. Many of the residents here are still working. There are one or two really old people who walk with a stick or a stroller because they have had a hip operation or are infirm in some way but there are people like that in most streets.'

Even Jan agreed that since they were all getting older they should admire people like that who still managed to retain their independence.

'Heaven knows what we will all be like in ten or fifteen years' time,' she pointed out gravely.

Although Margaret agreed with her in every way she had still hankered to take one last look at Willow House. She hadn't mentioned that it was her intention to do so to any of her family because she knew they would protest and tell her that it was better not to do so.

She moved closer to the gate and stared up the driveway again. She noticed that there was a car already parked in the drive, and wondered if it belonged to the new owner. Then she looked again and drew in her breath sharply.

The open-top sports car was familiar. They must have already called in Jason Parker. She felt the first stirrings of annoyance. The house was perfect! There were absolutely no changes that needed to be made; it was perfect as it stood. What sort of morons were they to want to change anything at all?

'Well, Margaret, I thought you might find your way back here immediately after the auction. I'm surprised you've managed to stay away so long.'

She gasped. She had been so intent on staring at the car that she hadn't realized Jason was in the garden. He was standing within a few feet of her, half hidden by the willow tree and she wondered how long he had been watching here.

'Do you want to come in?' he invited softly.

She shivered and shook her head. 'No, thank you! It's not mine now and the new owner might think I was trespassing.'

'Oh no, don't worry about that. I am quite certain he wouldn't mind at all,' Jason assured her.

'No,' she said firmly, 'I've moved on now, I don't even want to know what changes you've been asked to make.'

'There are no changes being made, Margaret. Willow House is still exactly as you wanted it and it always will be. Not a single thing will ever be changed. It will always remain the way you planned it, the way I redesigned it for you.'

'What nonsense are you talking now, Jason?' Margaret asked sharply.

'I shall go on living here and keeping your memory alive; in fact every day will be dedicated to your memory.'

'I don't understand what you are on about?'

'You will when you take the time to think about what I've just said,' he told her smugly.

'Surely you are not trying to tell me that you are still living here?' Was he a squatter she wondered in alarm, or had he managed to come back again as a lodger.

'Of course I am living here. I am the new owner. I bought Willow House when you put it up for auction.'

Hatred and resentment welled up inside Margaret. She wished she had never come back. She wondered if Charles had known who the buyer was and that was why he had impressed on her that she must not go back, must not trespass.

It was like wandering into a nightmare; she wished it was one and that she would wake up and find herself safe and snug in her new modern flat.

For the first time since she had resolved to sell Willow House she felt tears welling up in her eyes because she had lost the home that had meant so much to her and to her family. All her clever plans were turning to ashes.

Selling Willow House to complete strangers was one thing but the realization that it would be Jason living there was something else. She had sacrificed Willow House in order to sever all connection between her and Jason. Had she done so in vain? It certainly looked like it if he was the new owner and would be living there, she thought despondently.

'Willow House can be your home again, Margaret, whenever you choose to come back to it – and to me.'

Jason's voice, soft and wheedling, was ringing in her ears as blindly she turned away and walked towards her car.